SAVAGE REBELLION
BOOK III

SAVAGE CROWNS

ALSO AVAILABLE

Savage Legion

Savage Bounty

SAVAGE REBELLION
BOOK III

SAVAGE CROWNS

MATT WALLACE

SAGA PRESS

LONDON SYDNEY NEW YORK TORONTO NEW DELHI

1230 AVENUE OF THE AMERICAS, NEW YORK, NEW YORK 10020

This book is a work of fiction. Any references to historical events, real people, or real places are used fictitiously. Other names, characters, places, and events are products of the author's imagination, and any resemblance to actual events or places or persons, living or dead, is entirely coincidental.

Map by Robert Lazzaretti

First Saga Press trade paperback edition June 2023

Interior design by Kathryn A. Kenney-Peterson

Manufactured in the United States of America

1 3 5 7 9 10 8 6 4 2

Library of Congress Cataloging-in-Publication Data is available.

ISBN 978-1-5344-3926-9
ISBN 978-1-5344-3928-3 (ebook)

For Navah

CRACHE
Sixth City
Ninth City
Tenth City
Fifth City
Crachian
Border
Sicclunan
Front
Eighth City
Seventh City

Rok Island
Fourth City
The Bottoms
Capitol City
Planning
Cadre
Third City
Second City
N
W
E
S

PREVIOUSLY, IN *SAVAGE BOUNTY* . . .

THE SEEMINGLY UTOPIAN NATION OF CRACHE HAS BEEN EXposed as the dark and brutal machine it truly is. Three women and one loyal retainer, all from vastly different walks of life, have each uncovered some of Crache's most deadly secrets. Now they all work to dismantle the system that has ruined so many lives and continues to grind up anyone who does not serve its purposes.

Evie, the Sparrow General, leads a rebel army of former conscripts, refugees, oppressed tribal warriors, and Crache's sworn enemies, the Sicclunans, against the Tenth City, only to find their rebellion has already taken root there, and the people of the city itself have overthrown the bureaucracy and seized control. The city becomes a launching point for the next stage of the rebellion, but forces are at work that could snuff out the light of change before it can reach the rest of the nation.

Dyeawan, the brilliant young woman plucked from the streets of the Capitol, takes over the mysterious Planning Cadre that secretly controls Crache. No one, not even her closest friend Riko, knows that Dyeawan engineered the death of the planners' former leader,

Edger, who was an equally brilliant but genocidal dictator. However, Dyeawan finds competition for his position in Nia, Edger's other protégé. Nia challenges Dyeawan for control of the planners, forcing her to compete in an arcane series of contests that push the mind, body, and spirit to their limits.

In the course of meeting these challenges, Dyeawan learns she is actually Edger's daughter, one of many children he fathered and fostered from a distance. Dyeawan was forced to grow up alone on the streets of the Bottoms as an experiment to determine how an adverse environment would influence her intellect and personality. She also learns Nia is her half sister, another one of Edger's experiments.

This shared revelation bonds the pair and helps them overcome their rivalry. They agree to guide the Planning Cadre together, but the older members of the planners, as well as the shadowy Protectorate Ministry that does the Cadre's bidding, are still very much opposed to the new ideas and leadership of these two young women.

Lexi's husband, Brio, once served as pleader for the Capitol's most vulnerable section of citizens known as the Bottoms. He was then targeted, abducted, and conscripted into the Savage Legion. After his disappearance, Lexi sends Evie to find him, then reluctantly assumes the mantle of pleader and advocate for the Bottoms. Immersing herself in the lives and plight of the people there, she becomes deeply beloved by those Crache keeps in the shadows.

Because of this, Lexi is taken captive by a clandestine group known as the Ignobles, the descendants of the royal class who ruled the land before the rise of Crache and the abolition of monarchies and nobility. The Ignobles have spent centuries infiltrating the Crachian bureaucracy in order to bring it down and restore the rule of noble blood. Their leader, Lady Burr, wishes to use Lexi to unite the abused underclass of Crache in an uprising against the Planning Cadre and the Protectorate Ministry, hoping to cause a civil riot that, coupled with the Sparrow General's ongoing rebellion, will provide the Ignobles with the opportunity they have long awaited to seize power.

However, when giving the speech the Ignobles have planned to rally the people of the Bottoms to their cause, Lexi chooses instead to sacrifice herself by exposing the Ignobles' intention to take over and rule as brutal oppressors. As a result, Burr's chief agent, Kamen Lim, mortally stabs Lexi and tosses her body into the audience.

Meanwhile, Lexi's dedicated retainer, Taru, is taken into custody by Crachian authorities while retrieving proof of the Savage Legion's existence, then conscripted into the Legion themselves. While being ferried to the front with the rest of the Legionnaires to fight the rebels, Taru's ship goes down at sea, and the retainer washes up on the shores of Rok Island, the only nation to ever successfully resist Crachian rule. Reunited with Captain Staz of the *Black Turtle*, the two convince the fiercely independent and idiosyncratic Rok to join the rebellion's fight against Crache.

After witnessing the death of her Savage Legionnaire mentor, Mother Manai, who was captured by the Skrain, Evie leads the rebels in a daring predawn attack against the Crachian army. She aims to use the element of surprise to overcome the Skrain's superior numbers and armaments. While the tactic gives them an early edge in the battle, the Skrain eventually regroup and sacrifice their own massive siege towers to turn the tide against Evie and her rebel army.

With the Skrain bearing down on the rebels' scattered forces, Taru and the Rok Islanders appear to arrive just in time to save the day. However, to Taru's shock and terror, the Rok reveal they have no intention of interceding on behalf of the rebels. They are content to watch the two armies destroy each other so that the Islanders can sweep away whatever is left, eliminating what they perceive as the threat of Crache.

It seems there is nothing that either Taru or Evie can do but watch as the rebellion and its heroic architects are destroyed by the Crachian machine once and for all.

And now, the conclusion . . .

PART ONE

RETHINKING REBELLIONS

JAILBIRD

A BIRDCAGE. THEY HAVE ACTUALLY BUILT A GIANT FUCKING birdcage and locked Evie inside of it.

A long time after waking, curled up at the bottom of the thing, she is still at a loss. Not by her capture or witnessing what may have been the fall of her rebellion, but by her prison. It's entirely out of character for the Skrain. It's out of character for any artifice of the Crachian machine, really. Crache isn't much for flair or imagination. The symbol that adorns every Skrain banner, the sparse, simple shape of an ant, is well chosen. Crache is a nation of utility above all else. The long caravan currently slouching at a glacial rattle over the countryside has more than a few wagons fitted with cages; Evie can see them from her perch, the ants headed back to their colony. Constructing this ornate monstrosity especially for her (at least she surmises that as its purpose) instead of simply chucking her into a regular prison wagon like refuse is decidedly un-ant-like.

Yet here Evie sits, between tall wrought-iron bars wrapped around her to form a perfectly slim cylinder. There are a few flourishes of concentric circles and sculpted ants adorning the spaces between those bars, as well as the square pad on the cage door, from which hangs the largest key lock Evie has ever seen. The Skrain have lined the hard bottom of the cage with stale-smelling hay. She isn't certain whether it's for effect or for when she will inevitably have to piss inside this contraption.

Evie can only guess the whole "Sparrow General" persona must really be shaking up the status quo back in the Capitol, so much so they feel they have to lean into that persona to defeat the newly spun legend.

Not that she thinks of herself as a "legend," of course.

Even if she did, her current status as a source of amusement for the Skrain foot soldiers constantly trudging past her is humbling, to say the least. They revel in treating her like a shaved monkey in a menagerie. She can only imagine what a welcome distraction it is from lugging their full armor kits along with spear and shield on foot through the wretched heat of the day.

If they're not bending over and flipping up their tunic flaps to give her a view of a full moon, they are flashing their poorly groomed genitals at her. The accompanying verbal abuse is just as crude, if less imaginative.

"That's a proper sparrow, that is!" one of the soldiers chuckles. "Bloody proper!"

What accent even is *that?* Evie wonders, digging a fist against her churning guts.

Their attempted humiliation of her isn't as wrenching as Evie is certain they'd hoped. The motion is the worst part. The whole cage is constantly swinging from a hook arched behind the largest horse-drawn wagon in the Skrain caravan. It hasn't stopped swaying and jostling her for hours. She's felt like she's been throwing up for at least half that time, but Evie is always intent on waiting until one or more of the soldiers rides or walks close enough to the cage for her to vomit through the bars onto them.

The only feeling strong enough to divert Evie's attention from her stomach is the searing pain in her left leg. The back of her calf muscle feels as though angry hornets are nesting there. She can't contort herself to see how long or how deep the gash from the battle is, but it definitely feels deep and long enough. They haven't yet given her any water to drink, let alone an excess to clean her wounds. Neither has a surgeon, or even a drunken Skrain field medic, so much as tended to a single scrape. They seem to have simply checked her armor for weapons and then tossed her into her current confines.

Perhaps, if she's really lucky, the infection in her leg will kill her before they reach the Capitol. She knows that's where they're taking her. Her constant audience has made that clear enough. The whole Skrain army is very excited about the prospect of Evie being paraded inside her cage up and down the narrow streets of Crache's greatest city, on display for the whole of the citizenry to see.

Evie doesn't really want to die, of course. But the idea of that spectacle seems a pale alternative at the moment.

Mostly she just wishes she'd seen that lance coming, the one that slashed her calf and pierced her horse on the battlefield. If she'd avoided that single sharp edge, her horse wouldn't have gone down, and even if the outcome of the battle had remained unchanged, her own fate might have been different, perhaps even cage-free. At the very least, she'd be more comfortable right now.

Evie still doesn't quite understand what happened there at the end of the battle, only that more of her people survived and hopefully escaped than she imagined was possible when she saw the Skrain, regrouped, bearing down on them and realized their sudden guests, the Rok Islanders, weren't charging to the rebellion's rescue.

Except they did, finally, or at least enough of the Islander army charged to make a difference.

It didn't make any sense to Evie. If the Rok had indeed come to join the rebellion, why hadn't they charged sooner, and in full force? If the reverse was true, and they were willing to sacrifice the rebels to weaken the Skrain, why hadn't they waited longer? Why hadn't they continued to sit on the horizon until the last of Evie's rebels had fallen, taking as many Skrain soldiers with them as possible?

Evie remembers thinking at the time, as much as she could cogently form thoughts while deflecting blades trying to end her, that the Rok's charge seemed half-hearted and uncoordinated as it barreled towards the fray. Whatever the truth of those events, when the Rok chariots crashed into the wreckage of the Skrain siege towers and practically rode over the clashing armies, Evie knew only that she had to get what was left of her people to safety. It was too late to hope to turn the tide of the battle, and Evie did not trust the Islanders as allies enough to be sure they wouldn't turn their blades and chariot spikes on the rebels.

The last truly vivid memory she has of the battle's end was opening the throat of a Skrain soldier, then turning her head to seek Bam with her gaze. She found him pummeling enemy soldiers not half a dozen yards from where she stood, Sirach cutting Skrain to ribbons not far beyond that. Evie had shouted a simple order at him, to gather everyone he could and retreat. No sooner had the words screeched out than several Rok chariots blasted the ground between them and she lost sight of Bam, Sirach, and the rest.

Immediately after that, her world went to black. She must have been hit from behind, knocked out, because her next conscious memory is of the bottom of her birdcage. She had a headache for a while, but that pain has since faded into the background, replaced by the worsening fire in her leg.

The pounding of shod horse hooves tearing up the ground below breaks Evie from her reveries. She peers through the bars of her birdcage at a mounted Skrain who rears his horse to heel so he can gaze up at her. His helmet is more elaborate than the average ground-pounder, marking him as a captain. His face shows the wear and scars of advancing age, but the expression on it says the man thinks quite a lot of himself.

Skrain soldiers generally all look the same to Evie, regardless of rank or added pomp. She remembers this captain, however. That face is burned into her brain. He was the master of ceremonies who presided over the deathmatch between Sirach and Mother Manai, Evie's mentor and most trusted advisor among the former Savage Legionnaires. Evie watched from concealment in the massive Skrain encampment as her lover was forced to kill her best friend while the soldiers laughed and drank and made merry.

"How is our most honored guest enjoying her accommodations?"

"I could use a drink," Evie, too tired and too cut up to conjure witty banter, admits in a voice that is labored and hoarse. "And a surgeon, to be honest."

The blustery man's expression takes on a look of mock horror. "What inconsiderate hosts you must find us."

The Skrain captain fishes a deflated wineskin from his saddlebags, unstopping it and tipping his head. Evie watches as he squeezes a brief jet of rice wine from the skin.

Licking his lips, he tosses the empty-looking thing through the bars and into Evie's cage.

Evie sighs. Without shame or hesitation, she picks up the skin and tips back her own head, both hands twisting the flattened bladder into a single braid, as if she's attempting to wring the neck of an animal. She manages to force a few remaining droplets of rice wine to fall upon her cracked, blood-scabbed lips, her tongue greedily lapping them up.

She ignores the pleasure Evie knows is plastered all over the captain's face as he is treated to the sight of her demeaning herself.

Evie extends a hand through the bars, offering the captain his wineskin.

"Keep it," he says, sounding more cautious than generous.

Not as stupid as he looks, she thinks.

"Besides, it might be the only thing you have to chew on for a goodly while. Our larders are a bit on the empty side—this rebellion of yours has played hell on food production in every city."

"Might I have the honor of your name, Captain?"

"Silvar," he informs her proudly. "Feng Silvar."

"Thank you. I won't forget it."

"You honor me, Sparrow General. I'll see about that surgeon for you. We can't have you falling out before we've had the chance to formally introduce you to the people of Crache. They've heard so much about you, after all."

"I hope to live up to my reputation."

"Few do," Captain Silvar says, snapping the reins of his mount and galloping away grandly.

When he's gone, Evie drops the wineskin to the dirt below, leaving it to rot under the wheels and hooves of the caravan. It's a useless gesture, but it feels good.

Sinking back against the bars, she tries to ignore the itching and minor agony of her leg, closing her eyes and sending her mind elsewhere far away.

What remains of her life may be brief and unpleasant, but at least Evie has a new goal.

Before the Crachian machine finally crushes her between its jaws, she will see Captain Feng Silvar dead by her hand.

DEFEETED

NO ONE HAS MUCH TO SAY DURING THE LONG WALK BACK TO the Tenth City. It's not a march so much as a shamble, the same way the rebellion is now less an army and more a smattering of beaten and battered survivors just trying to stay on their feet. Ex-Savages, refugees, Sicclunan soldiers, perhaps a third of the field that charged the Skrain at dawn are all that remain of the Sparrow General's motley force. Everyone else is dead or captured or scattered to the winds.

The only real sounds are those made by the wounded, many of whom will surely be upgraded to the dead or dying by nightfall. Their groans and pleas and curses rise and fade like the broken breeze of the afternoon. Those who've lost limbs are being pulled by hand on hasty, makeshift litters. Those who can walk are helped along by as many of their fellow rebels as it takes. Beyond that, no one seems to have any comfort or consolation left to offer them.

Even Sirach, never one at a loss for words, regardless of how macabre the situation, remains all but silent. She carries one slim, half-moon-curved blade in her gloved hand, lifting to examine it occasionally like some lost relic. Sirach lost the weapon's matched partner during the battle, and the blade feels wrong somehow without that other weight in Sirach's opposite hand. She almost wants to toss it into the dead grass at the band's feet and leave the blade to rust.

What good is a weapon designed to be dual-wielded without its mate? she ponders darkly.

Bam lumbers not far from her, a planet of sullen and wounded flesh unto himself. His head is hung low, filthy tendrils of curls an impenetrable curtain hiding his face. The shame and rage are radiating from his every pore with each heavy step he takes. He hasn't slung his impossibly large mallet across his back. Bam still carries the haft with his blood-soaked fists. The smashed entrails clinging to every inch of the mallet's hammerhead gleam brilliantly in the afternoon sun, making them seem like something shiny and ornamental instead of the ghastly human remains they are.

Sirach knows the big man's pain. She knows for Bam it is not losing the battle, not even possibly losing their entire rebellion. Bam is feeling, not just the loss of Evie, but blaming himself for that loss. He styled himself her protector, always at her side, yet he's allowed her to be taken from them.

Sirach knows the source and shape of his pain because she shares it, every bit of it. She blames herself for leaving Evie behind as much as Bam does. That shame, that hurt, they are only compounded by rage. Sirach has spent a lifetime divorced from sentimentality; there is no place for it in the life of a homeless guerrilla fighter, she has always believed. Yet before the battle, Sirach told herself she could accept Evie's and her own death together on the field, but living apart would somehow be worse than that ultimate defeat.

She hates that she allowed herself to become that emotionally tied to anything, let alone another person.

Worse and more enraging to Sirach than that, though, is the knowledge she was right about surviving without Evie beside her.

With all of that welling up inside as she continues to trudge along, Sirach needs to escape it. The fury and the guilt are too much, especially right now.

She picks up her pace until she is beside Bam, practically engulfed by his mountainous shadow.

"You didn't do anything wrong," Sirach assures the colossus. "She's your general. She gave you an order, and you followed it."

That order consisted of the last words Sirach heard her lover speak before the battle took her away. Evie told Bam to rally whoever was left and ferry them to safety, to use the deluge of Rok chariots as cover for a hasty retreat. Then they were separated, and the last either of them saw of Evie was her blood-soaked hair as enemy soldiers carried her away on the Skrain side of the battlefield.

Bam remains silent behind his tangled hair, his chin dropped to his chest like a hanged man swinging from a gallows.

"Listen to me," Sirach says, more sternly. "They won't kill her, not here. She's their prize. They'll try to take her back to the Capitol. And I promise you here and now, they will never make it there with her. We'll see to that."

For the first time, Bam lifts his scarred chin to meet Sirach's eyes. His own, large and dark and sunken, flash with a sliver of hope.

She smiles for him as warmly as she can manage through the maelstrom of emotions and caked blood on her face. It seems to turn that sliver of hope into an honest-to-gods glimmer. Bringing comfort to others is also a thing for which she never made time before joining Evie's rebellion. It feels undeniably good, and she immediately resents that.

Sirach does not stop smiling, however.

The sun at their backs is getting low, and the Tenth City is still little more than a vague shape in the distance ahead.

A tall figure Sirach doesn't recognize partially obscures her view of that shape. From the cut of their hair, Sirach marks them as an Undeclared. Other than Spud-Bar, the armorist, she has yet to meet another Undeclared among the ex-Legionnaires.

There are none labeled thusly among the Sicclunans. Like much of so-called Crachian "civilization," the notion of forcing every intersex citizen to choose one identity over another and branding them if they refuse is utterly barbaric to Sirach's people.

"Do you know them?" she asks Bam.

He shakes his head, eyes sharpening on the lanky figure striding proudly several yards ahead of them.

"I'll be back," Sirach says, patting him reassuringly once more on his shoulder.

Sirach livens her step, marching up to the head of the scattered ghost army where the unfamiliar warrior treks along, as silent and as sullen as the rest of them.

"What's your story, Savage?" she asks.

"Don't call me that."

"It's just a word. I didn't mean it as an insult."

"It is a word Crache chose to apply to those they oppress, to justify that oppression."

"That's very profound. Perhaps if you'll give me the honor of your name, we might advance this conversation to more pressing issues."

"Taru."

"My name is Sirach. When did you join our Sparrow General's rebellion?"

"I came with the Rok Islanders."

Sirach, surprised, stops walking for a moment. She's forced to jog to catch up with Taru, who never breaks stride.

"I see," she says. "They have an odd way of saving the day. Was it their first time?"

"They had no intention of 'saving the day' for any of you. They were going to let you all die in that valley."

Taru sounds entirely bitter about it.

Sirach, on the other hand, feels a shocking lack of offense. The Rok are much like the Sicclunans, driven to the brink of extinction time and again by Crache. They no doubt feel they owe no one but themselves.

"That makes sense. What changed their minds, then?"

Taru sighs heavily. "Nothing. I managed to . . . commandeer their conch."

"You called the charge," Sirach says, more voicing a realization than asking a question. "That also makes sense. They didn't seem altogether organized or committed upon joining our little dust-up."

Taru says nothing.

"We owe you a sizeable debt, then," Sirach tells them.

"I am owed nothing," Taru insists, their emotions rising visibly for the first time. "I am a failure."

"How so?"

"I am retainer to Gen Stalbraid. I allowed my De-Gen to be taken and conscripted into the Savage Legion. I failed to protect his wife when I myself became conscripted. For all I know, they are both dead now. I have failed them."

The name of the Gen is familiar to Sirach. Crachian Gens are hardly her area of expertise, however. It takes her a moment to find some connection to the name in her head.

"Brio," she says a few moments later. "That's his Gen, isn't it?"

It is Taru's turn to stop walking, causing Sirach to follow suit. The towering retainer peers down at Sirach with eyes that have gone abruptly and disarmingly soft.

"You know him?" they all but whisper.

Sirach nods. "He lost half a leg fighting us before Evie started the rebellion, but he survived. He's a smart man. His voice has been helpful during our councils. Not that I'd ever admit that to his pretty little face."

Taru seems at a loss, as if a hard truth they'd been forced to accept has been upended.

"Where is he?"

In answer, Sirach juts her dirt-and-blood-smeared chin ahead of them, indicating the walled city in the distance.

Taru looks to the horizon.

Without another word, the retainer resumes their stride, but it is even longer and more powerful now, filled with renewed purpose.

Sirach watches them go, cocking her head curiously.

"Well then. This should be interesting."

After a time, she takes up the march once more.

The gates of the Tenth City await them.

CONCHBLOCKER

BEFORE THE END OF THE BATTLE . . .

TARU WATCHES THE SKRAIN SCUTTLE OVER THE WRECKAGE of their own siege towers, very much like a swarm of the same ants whose image adorns their armor, preparing to descend on the broken and scattered line of the rebellion. Taru can even see the so-called Sparrow General, unmistakably branded by the bright-red bird painted on her otherwise pitch-black armor. She seems impossibly small from Taru's vantage, but no less fierce as she attempts to rally what's left of her forces to face the overwhelming onslaught of the regrouped Skrain.

This will be the end of them, Taru's heart says to them. *Brio could even be down there. He could be dead already.*

Taru's gauntleted hands dig painfully into the edge of the chariot. They stare down helplessly at Staz, watching the serene, elderly little ship's captain, looking utterly absurd yet no less fierce in her oversized Islander's armor.

She truly is ready to watch them all be slaughtered, Taru marvels.

"You are right," Taru admits, nearly breathless. "You never lied to me. I made assumptions."

"It's in the nature of ants to presume."

"I am *not* one of them," Taru insists. "I never have been."

"You've spent your entire life among them," Staz points out, without judgment. "Impossible not to let some of their bad habits bleed into your soup, if you take my meaning."

"Is there nothing I can do to sway you to action?" Taru all but pleads.

"We will take action," Staz reminds them, for the first time showing signs of irritation in her gravelly old voice. "When the ants are at their weakest."

"This is not the whole of the Skrain army! You will meet larger forces the closer you press to the Capitol. You are wasting good fighters down there you will need later!"

"Island folk and ants don't mix well, present company excluded. Can't imagine we'd fight very well together. Besides, you've seen how salty and difficult the other captains can be. Just getting them to make landfall here was enough of a chore. Trying to convince them to fight alongside ants? Not even my soup is strong enough to bring them around."

"I keep telling you, those are not 'ants'! They're fighting with their lives *against* the ants!"

"And they are doing a fine job. They fight well; they will die well, and for a cause in which they believe. It is a good death. You should take pride in that, if not comfort."

Taru is practically flattened by the hopelessness of it all. There seems to be nothing, not a single significant action they can take. They have come so far, beaten by Aegins, conscripted and branded by the Skrain, having broken that bondage and surviving a shipwreck that killed thousands, then rallying an entire island nation behind their cause and finally crossing the sea with them.

All of that only to see it end here, watching the people Taru swore to save cut down before their very eyes.

Staz has said it herself; Taru is free to charge across the valley on their own and join the fray. But one fighter will make no difference in this outcome. The rebels need the whole of the cavalry to come to their aid if they are to have even the barest chance.

The retainer looks back at the passive, waiting ranks of Islander foot soldiers. They don't even seem focused on what's happening in the valley below. They could just as well be watching a parade to which they'd been dragged against their will.

Taru's frantic gaze falls finally on the spiked shell chariot at the very end of the long row of its fellows. It is outfitted differently than the rest. A tall column that looks more like an immature version of one of Rok's native trees rises from the front of the rig. Affixed to it is a massive, polished conch shell at least half the size of Taru themselves. It has been fashioned into an ominous-looking horn. The cavernous mouth of the conch is angled forward at the top, while a sculpted lip piece winds down to meet a waiting island warrior, who stands next to the driver.

"That horn . . . it calls the chariots to charge."

"Yes," Staz says.

Taru blinks down at the tiny woman in surprise. Taru wasn't even aware they'd spoken the thought aloud.

The retainer's mind stops racing. In fact, it slows to a very deliberate crawl.

"What are the calls?" they ask Staz.

"The long bellow sounds the charge, three short bellows call to retreat," Staz informs them idly, not a hint of suspicion or curiosity in her voice as she continues to watch the battle unfold.

Taru nods, their mind hitting a dead stop of decision.

"I hope," they begin earnestly, "if we meet again, we can remain . . . friends."

Staz looks up at the tall warrior then, confusion in her small, withered eyes.

Without any more words, Taru bounds over the side of the chariot, clearing its jagged exterior spikes and large right wheel.

Taru runs flat-out, as fast as their long and powerful legs can be willed to move. They sprint up half the length of the Rok Islander's line, no one making a move to stop them, most of the fish scale–armored fighters barely taking note of the retainer.

Even in Taru's excited state, they can't help marveling at what a peculiar people the Rok remain, so unlike the rest of the world the retainer knows. The Islanders are a people thoroughly committed to the ideal of tending their own garden, utterly unconcerned with a single vine growing outside it, however twisted or threatening the alien vine might be. Until it intrudes into their personal patch of land, until it is all but choking their own seedlings, it is merely an irrelevant oddity.

Taru ducks between the chariots at the end of the line and leaps up onto the back of the hornblower's rig. One Rok Islander stands at the conch, while a second holds the reins. Both turn to regard them with curiosity more than any kind of surprise or even suspicion.

"I apologize for this," Taru manages breathlessly, before ramming the hardest part of their head into the nose and mouth of the chariot's driver.

As his spine is bent back awkwardly over the front of the rig, teeth and blood flung into the air above the man's face, Taru flattens a hand and stiffens each finger rigidly against one another before driving the edge of their palm into the base of the hornblower's neck. Taru doesn't want to collapse the Islander's windpipe, only stun him enough to stop him from reacting. While the hornblower gasps for the air that is no longer reaching their lungs, Taru grips the driver by his scale armor and flings his limp body from the back of the chariot.

The hornblower has just begun to regain his composure when Taru juts a hard knee into the Islander's groin. As he doubles over, the retainer drops down to a knee and drapes the man's body over their shoulders, hefting him up and dropping him over the side of the rig.

The long bellow sounds the charge.

Taru steps to the slender reed at the end of the horn, licking their lips. They fill their lungs with as much air as they can take in before pressing those lips around the reed and blowing into the conch.

The bellow is impossibly loud and thunderously deep, like the rumbling mating call of some ancient and gargantuan beast. Taru maintains the bellow as long as their lungs will possibly allow, until the final moment when they feel like overfilled wine bladders fit to burst. When Taru lets go, they find themselves doubled over at the front of the chariot, gasping for breath.

When Taru recovers, it is to the sound of shredding earth and bizarre war cries. The retainer straightens to peer above the railing of the rig.

Their drivers, who by now are fully aware of what's happening, hold the chariots nearest to the conch. The drivers' counterparts, weapons drawn, are leaping down from the backs of the converted spiked shells, racing towards the end of the line to deal with Taru.

Beyond those few rigs, however, the majority of chariot drivers have reacted instinctively, responding to the bellow of the ceremonial shell as they've been trained to do. Dozens of spiked war rigs are now rolling full tilt across the valley towards the heart of the battle among the siege tower wreckage.

Heart racing, Taru draws their short sword and proceeds to smash the magnificent conch to pieces with the flat of the blade. It pains them to do it. The act feels at once like a deep betrayal and a heinous sacrilege. The Rok Islanders saved Taru's life, embraced them as one of their own. Who knows how old and sacred and historically significant this conch is to their people? But Taru can't risk the charge being recalled.

The retainer has just finished reducing the horn to shrapnel when growled curses in a language they don't recognize draw their full attention once again to the back of the rig.

In the next moment, an enraged Islander is thrusting a pronged spear at Taru's midsection. Taru parries with their short sword, batting aside the blow and stepping past the head of the spear to close the distance between them and their attacker. The retainer rams the pommel of their sword into the bridge of the Islander's nose, stunning and blinding him at the same time.

They can see several more Rok soldiers climbing up over the

back end of the chariot. With as much force as the retainer can muster with their hips and back, Taru kicks the bloody-nosed Islander square in his chest, sending him flying off his heels and into the others attempting to storm the rig. The Islander's limp, heavy body bowls the rest of them over, clearing the back of the chariot if only for the moment.

That moment is all Taru requires. They turn away as soon as the Islander whose nose they've obliterated has left his feet. Taru takes up the reins of the chariot and snaps them smartly and sharply, urging its mounts to action. Before the boarding party of Rok Islanders can regroup, Taru is rolling away from them and the rest at high speed, digging a trail down the valley after the others.

The retainer realizes halfway to closing the gap that they are ill equipped to fight effectively from the basket of the chariot. They fashioned a poleax on the voyage over from Rok, but Taru left it leaning beside Staz when they fled the sea captain's rig. The retainer resigns themselves to the idea they will have to use the spiked shell of the war rig itself as their weapon.

Taru watches as the bulk of the Rok Islander cavalry begins chewing up the siege tower debris beneath their powerful hooves and wheels. They crash into the sweeping Skrain, the Crachian army's advancing line rolling up like a severed tendon. Armored bodies are trampled and flung in every direction. The bodies of rebels join Skrain carcasses, the fighting too thick for the Rok Islanders to avoid the rebels even if they tried. However, even if the Rok do not consider the rebels allies, they know the Skrain are their true enemy, and they focus their rage and blades on anyone bearing the symbol of the ant.

The chaos of the moment and commanding the chariot does not give Taru much time to feel relief, but at least they know the rebels will have some semblance of a chance to recover now.

Taru does their best to steer the rig whose reins they command into the thickest groups of Skrain they can locate on the battlefield. More than once, Taru is shaken from their feet, having to grip the edge of the chariot to steady themselves as the rig rocks like a ship in a heavy storm. They don't want to rear back on the reins and slow their momentum, but allowing the mounts to run flat-out becomes untenable.

An arrow whizzes close enough to their cheek to draw blood as Taru prepares to bring the chariot's mounts to heel. But they never get the chance. In the next moment, the reins fly free from their gloved hands, the world around them becomes oddly and surreally silent, and Taru realizes they are airborne. One or both of the chariot's wheels must have finally collided with a large enough obstruction to flip the entire rig into the air, and Taru has been thrown clear of the entire spiked contraption.

They have what seems like an immeasurably long time to contemplate their landing as they practically float through the air above the battlefield. The ground is impossibly far away until it is suddenly rushing up at them at an equally impossible speed. At least their path seems to be free of debris and bodies, enemy or otherwise.

It strikes Taru at the last moment that they are no longer certain who counts among their enemies. They have betrayed the Rok, they have risen up against the Skrain, and the rebellion won't know them from a Savage still bound in service to Crache. They will more likely than not be run through by the first sword that crosses their path, regardless of who wields it.

That is their final thought before Taru collides with the ground. It is not nearly as sharp as a blade, but it is just as unforgiving, something that no doubt would occur to Taru if their brain weren't rattled into total darkness in the next moment.

LOOSE THREADS

"I DO NOT UNDERSTAND THE POINT OF THIS, UNLESS IT IS you taking enjoyment in my performing a task poorly."

The two sisters, or half sisters to be more precise, sit together in Dyeawan's humble quarters, the same small room she has occupied since she first came to the Planning Cadre keep as a lowly servant.

Dyeawan's legs lay before her on the floor, her back braced against the side of her straw-mattress bed. Nia, her own legs folded beneath her, sits on the edge of the bed behind Dyeawan. Nia's fingers are awkwardly tangled up in the ends of her sister's—the Planning Cadre co-leader's—hair. Dyeawan now has several rows of wildly knotted, uneven braids against her scalp.

"Thank you for indulging me," Dyeawan says, the same small smile occupying her lips that has resided there since they began the impromptu grooming session.

"So indulging you is the point," Nia persists, clearly frustrated with her work.

"Yes. All those years dragging myself across the alleys of the Bottoms, I tried very hard to keep my dreams in check. Especially my daydreams. But one dream I allowed myself now and then was having a sister. And when I imagined what that would be like, it was always simple things like this. Having someone to braid my hair when the heat was unbearable. I remember I saw two fishmonger's daughters doing it once. The older girl braided her little sister's hair, then showed the younger girl how to do it. It took her several tries to get it even close to right. They laughed the whole time. I watched them from behind some barrels all afternoon. The barrels were filled with chum and stank horribly, but I didn't care. I've thought of them often since."

Nia goes quiet for a while. Her hands stopped working several times during Dyeawan's story.

"I doubt I am living up to the fantasy," she finally says, more softly than before.

"You're doing just fine," Dyeawan assures her.

They stop speaking after that, and Nia's hands begin working much more diligently, if not any more skillfully. Dyeawan can feel the intention and commitment in her sister's fingertips, as if her older sibling sees the purpose of this seemingly simple exercise where before she did not.

The ability of people to learn and grow is our greatest redemption, Dyeawan thinks.

She can still recall a time when she lacked the vocabulary to articulate realizations like this. Not having the words didn't make the thoughts any less potent, but they do help to clarify things for her now. She and Nia both grew through the trials that pitted them against each other, through the machinations of Oisin and the Protectorate Ministry to kill Dyeawan. The ability of the two of them to put their suspicions and animosity aside was Dyeawan's redemption. It quite literally saved her life. And here they sit, on a path to becoming sisters in more than arbitrary blood.

As if in response to her mind's wandering, an excited knocking vibrates her chamber door.

"Enter," Dyeawan bids whoever is on the other side.

The door is pushed open just enough for Riko's lithe form to slip inside.

The younger girl pauses, halting whatever words were about to spill excitedly from her lips. She begins to giggle.

"What is it?" Nia demands.

"You two are *so* cute!"

Dyeawan can feel Nia's entire body tense behind her, either from self-consciousness or outright embarrassment. Dyeawan feels no shame, however. She also appreciates the fact that Riko, easily her closest and most loyal friend in the Planning Cadre, has shown no jealousy or resentment over Dyeawan's new relationship with Nia.

"You look like you have news to share, Riko," she gently urges.

"Oh yeah! The rebellion," she begins, more seriously. "Word has come to the Capitol that it has collapsed. They're supposed to be bringing that Sparrow General woman back. Alive. In a *cage*. Is that what I made that ridiculously big lock for?" Riko seems slightly mortified.

Dyeawan looks back at her sister, whose expression betrays nothing.

"What about the situation in the Bottoms?" Nia asks Riko.

"Acts of resistance and outright violence against Aegins are on the rise this week. So far by all reports, the Aegins are following orders to hold a perimeter around the Bottoms and not retaliate.

But who knows how long they'll keep their daggers in their baldrics, yeah? From the stories Dyeawan has told me, they're a knife-happy bunch."

"She should be brought here," Dyeawan says. "The Sparrow General. We must speak with her."

"That depends upon the Ministry," Nia reminds her. "It has always been the structure of things. The Ministry liaises between the Planning Cadre and the bureaucracy. We ourselves have no direct line of communication with the Skrain."

"That will have to change," Dyeawan says, more to herself than to the other two.

"Be that as it may," her sister continues, "the Protectorate Ministry may have its own agenda concerning this Sparrow General."

"I want to speak with her," Dyeawan repeats with more iron in her tone.

"I understand that, sister."

"There's something else," Riko informs them.

"Good news, certainly," Nia says, the sarcasm sounding unpracticed and unfamiliar coming from her.

"Walls painted in the night, and not just in the Bottoms. The west courtyard wall of the Spectrum got the whole mural treatment the night before last."

"More Sparrow General propaganda?"

Riko shakes her head. "This is new."

"What was painted on the wall, Riko?" Dyeawan asks, knowing her friend needs focusing from time to time.

"Oh, right. 'The Ragged Matron Lives.'"

Nia furrows her brow at the girl.

"Who?"

"Lexi Xia," Dyeawan says without hesitation.

Riko nods. "Has to be, yeah?"

"So she's officially become their martyr," Nia adds dourly. "The people in the Bottoms."

"Martyrs aren't difficult to find in the Bottoms," Dyeawan assures her. "They're created every day. By us."

It is easy for Nia to forget her newfound sister's origins, Dyeawan is aware.

Reports vary concerning the night Lexi Xia was publicly executed, but what was made clear to Dyeawan and the Planning Cadre was that the interim pleader for the Bottoms gave a speech both exposing and denouncing a group called the Ignobles, whom the Protectorate Ministry identified as the descendants of a nobility long dissolved and banished from Crache. They have apparently been infiltrating the bureaucracy that replaced them, and they attempted to use Lexi to rally the residents of the Bottoms against Crachian leadership. Instead, Lexi told the people the Ignobles were not their saviors.

And they killed her for it.

Lexi Xia's body has yet to be recovered, however.

"It's entirely possible they hid the body or disposed of it themselves in order to propagate this new 'Ragged Matron.'"

"Not a very flattering name either, huh?"

Dyeawan shakes her head. "It doesn't matter. It's another story we'll have to deal with."

"But she helped us, didn't she? By stopping the people from rallying to these Ignobles, whoever they are."

"She didn't ally the people to us, either. She was kind to them where we have failed to be, again and again. And she was taken from them. They're angry at everything and everyone that has ignored and brutalized them. And we were responsible for that long before the Ignobles murdered their Ragged Matron."

Nia is unable to mask the frustration in her voice. "Then how do we get them on our side and focus their anger where it belongs?"

"Feeding them would be a start," Dyeawan answers.

Riko is studying Dyeawan's scalp with the same hawk-eyed concentration she aims at the miniature components of the many gadgets and contraptions she creates for the Planning Cadre.

"What is it?" Dyeawan asks.

"The braids in your hair are a little uneven."

Dyeawan does not have to glance over her shoulder at Nia to know the look of no doubt restrained displeasure that is forming on her face.

Riko removes from the leather-encased menagerie of arcane tools perpetually hung at her waist a two-pronged metallic measuring device. She carefully, almost instinctively, fits the prongs between the parallel braids of hair atop Dyeawan's head.

"Is that *really* necessary?" Nia practically fumes.

Snapped out of her clinical trance, Riko looks up from Dyeawan's scalp to blink at Nia in genuine confusion.

Dyeawan reaches up and gently takes hold of Riko's wrist, urging her friend's hand and the measuring implement away from her scalp.

"It's all right, Riko," she assures her friend. "Asymmetry is in fashion right now."

"Oh," Riko says, blinking in surprise. "I guess I'm not much for keeping up with things like that, being penned up here."

There is another knock at Dyeawan's chamber door, more timid than Riko's. A few raps followed by silence, then a final, almost hesitant tap on the old wood.

"I'll get it, yeah?" Riko asks Dyeawan, who nods.

Riko practically skips to the door and pulls it the rest of the way open. She looks back at Dyeawan with a mixture of surprise and confusion.

Matei stands awkwardly in the doorway. He's holding a carved wooden box in his hands. He looks as contrite as a little boy preparing to confess to his mother that he broke her favorite pot.

Matei was one of Dyeawan's first true friends in the Planning Cadre, along with Riko. He helped to put together her tender, the wheeled device that allows her to sail through the winding corridors of the keep. It has been months since they've spoken, however. When Dyeawan began ascending through the Cadre, defeating the trials necessary to join the planners, Matei began to retreat. At first, he would find reasons not to spend time with her and Riko, but before long, he simply began ignoring them altogether.

The young man clears his throat before speaking. "Could I . . . could we speak for a moment? Just, um, the two of us? If that's okay?"

"Soliciting the head of the planners is what council chambers are for," Nia insists. "This visit is inappropriate."

"Nia, please," her sister bids. "Of course we can talk, Matei."

She looks up at Riko, then to Nia. "Give us the room. Please."

Riko nods happily, but Nia doesn't even attempt to hide her disapproval. Still, she rises from behind Dyeawan and slowly joins Riko beside the door.

"We have more to discuss," she reminds Dyeawan.

"And we will. While you finish my hair."

Riko stifles a giggle even before Nia shoots her an icy glare.

The two of them leave through the door, and Riko deftly closes it behind them.

"What is it, Matei?" Dyeawan asks when they're alone.

"I wanted to . . . to apologize," he finally manages to stammer.

"You don't have to apologize to me," Dyeawan says, and she means it. "You never owed me anything, Matei."

The young man is already shaking his head in disagreement.

"I've been ignoring you, for a long time. I've been . . . unkind. Mean, really. I've been cruel to you. And you didn't do anything to deserve it. I was just . . . jealous, I guess. And suspicious, maybe? Like . . . I felt like you lied to me, somehow."

Dyeawan is genuinely confused. "Lied? To you?"

"It's silly!" Matei offers quickly. "You didn't. I know that now. But that's what I told myself, when you started getting so much attention from Edger, and how you passed all their tests. I told myself you must have just been pretending to be some girl from the streets of the Capitol. Like you had this plan all along to come here and fool them. Fool us."

"I only wish I were that clever," Dyeawan assures him.

"I was wrong," Matei admits. "I just . . . wanted to be you. But I should have been proud of you. I should have encouraged you and been there for you, like Riko did. I'm sorry."

"There is nothing to forgive, but I'm glad you are here now. I have always liked you. You did so much for me when I was first brought to this place."

It's easier, even now, for Dyeawan to think of the Planning Cadre as an entity that enveloped her, rather than remember it was Edger, specifically, who adopted her.

"Anyway," Matei says. "Maybe it's dumb, but I brought you this. I made it myself."

He holds out the wooden box to her, and Dyeawan reaches up to take it, immediately surprised by its weight.

"What is it, besides a box? Knowing you, I'm certain there is more to it."

"There is," Matei confirms. "It's a puzzle, a cipher. I don't imagine it will take you long to figure out, but I thought it might, you know, amuse you."

Dyeawan holds the box in her hands, smoothing her palm over its lacquered top. There appear to be no seams in the wood, no way to open it.

"Thank you, Matei," she says warmly. "Not just for the gift, but for coming here, saying those things. I never stopped thinking of you as a friend."

"That means a lot to me. I know there are a lot of things happening now, important things. I just . . . want to help you however I can."

"I need that help, believe me."

"Okay. Good. I'll go now. Maybe we can sit together at lunch again? Like we used to?"

"I'd like that."

He smiles for the first time since entering the room. It's not a large smile, but it pleases Dyeawan to see.

Matei leaves.

When he's gone, and when the door to her chambers is closed once more, Dyeawan feels very alone. It is an unpleasant feeling, almost like a premonition, though of what she can't articulate, even with her newfound vocabulary.

She examines the box again. The whole thing intrigues her. Not the box itself; Matei's apology. Everything he said was absolutely true.

But despite the truth in his words, Matei was lying to her. She knows it. Dyeawan simply isn't sure *what* he is lying about.

THE LAST LEG

TARU WAS RAISED FROM CHILDHOOD TO BE A VENERABLE Gen's retainer, protector of kith-kin, their property, and their business affairs. They were plucked from the lowliest wharf in the Bottoms by Brio's father, taken into the twin towers of Gen Stalbraid, given fine clothes and good food and their first real bed. They were welcomed as a member of the Gen, never held at arm's length, embraced and treated with warmth and kindness. They were trained in combat by some of the most skilled masters in the Crachian Capitol, the makeshift blade Taru once fashioned from a stolen hull hook and used to survive the city's most dangerous streets replaced with an expertly forged and crafted short sword.

The sense of duty Taru feels towards Gen Stalbraid is stronger than iron. Their affection for Brio, at whose side they served since both of them were children, and who always treated Taru as an equal, is boundless.

All this history and these feelings are a maelstrom within Taru as they lay eyes on Brio again for the first time in what feels like ages. Taru is already resolved to remain the steadfast rock upon which Brio has always relied, despite their battle-torn appearance and the markings of the blood coin upon their skin.

What Taru is simply not prepared for is the sight of Brio missing half of his right leg.

The retainer is a statue as Brio warmly and happily embraces them, stunned into silence and immobility. This was not the way they imagined this reunion. It was difficult enough even to envision such a thing would happen, to somehow keep hope that Brio was alive and surviving among the Savage Legion.

"My friend, what's wrong?" Brio askes, taking a step back. "Are you injured?"

Taru shakes their head emphatically.

Brio cannot help noticing the towering retainer's eyes lingering on the space between his severed kneecap and the floor.

"Oh, don't trouble yourself about that," Brio assures them. "I'm learning to get around just fine."

Taru feels the welling in their eyes. Tears do not come easily to the retainer. Their upbringing in the streets of the Bottoms taught them to repress emotion, to never wear it outwardly, lest their peers and predators in those dangerous quarters see it as weakness.

"The Savage Legion armorist who called on Te-Gen, they did not tell us . . . I did not know about your . . . leg."

Brio stares up at Taru oddly.

"My friend, are those tears?"

"No, I . . ."

"I'm sorry, I didn't mean to embarrass you," Brio says quickly. "I'm only . . . surprised. Please, there's no need for you to pity me, and even less to blame yourself for this. It was not your doing."

"I should have been at your side from the start. I never should have let you go alone to the *Black Turtle*—"

"They meant to have me. There was no avoiding it. If you'd been with me, you would have fought bravely, I'm certain. I'm equally certain you would have dispatched many Aegins. But above all, I am absolutely certain you would have been killed, and I'd be exactly where I am now. The only difference is we wouldn't be having this reunion."

Taru manages to nod, accepting this, at least in principle. Still, the retainer either cannot or will not meet Brio's gaze.

Brio reaches up and rests his hands gently against Taru's broad shoulders.

"I cannot tell you how happy I am to see you standing here, alive and well."

For the first time in perhaps their entire life, Taru allows the feelings inside to flow through the retainer's body unchecked. The strong shoulders in Brio's hands begin to quake, and Taru weeps openly. Their large arms slowly encircle Brio, hugging him against the retainer's stained armor.

"I cannot help feeling as though I have failed you, and Te-Gen . . . Lexi."

Taru feels Brio shake his head against their chest. He holds Taru as fiercely as the retainer holds him, for as long as Taru needs.

"How was she when you saw her last?" he asks gently, when the strongest waves of Taru's tears have subsided.

"Well. But I have no idea what has become of her since they took me. She has no one now."

"She has herself. Lexi was always far more capable than our fathers credited her. Than even I credited her."

"You would be so proud. She stepped up to fill your role as pleader. Stood up to the Franchise Council. Helped the people of the Bottoms as you would have. I only hope she . . ."

"You found me," Brio reminds Taru. "Together, we will find her. I refuse to believe otherwise. All right?"

Taru bows their head in assent, sucking back what remains of their tears and sorrow.

"Terribly sorry to interrupt."

Sirach is watching them from the doorway, arms folded across her leather-armored chest.

"They're here," she informs Brio. "It's time. You two should come with me now."

Taru is surprised. "Both of us? To your war council?"

"I wasn't so badly brained on the field that I can't count."

"I'm surprised you're soliciting either of us," Brio says. "I wasn't sure you'd be interested in anything I have to say now, to be honest."

"Evie trusted you," Sirach says, though her tone implies she doesn't feel one way or another about that fact. "Loved you, in fact. She spoke highly of your counsel. I know she would want you to speak to her point of view as we decide what to do next."

"You don't think she would want command to fall to you?"

"I speak for my fellow Sicclunans. Evie wasn't one of us."

"This would seem a prime opportunity to take command," Taru points out. "Regardless of what Evie might want."

Sirach nods thoughtfully.

"The more impulsive side of me agrees with you. But the more pragmatic side knows we can't lose what's left of the Savages if we want to salvage this rebellion Evie has started. They still worship her. They need to know she's being represented. And they aren't going to take orders from someone who was trained to kill them."

"That is a fairly well-reasoned view," Taru admits.

Sirach shrugs. "It's where we find ourselves. Besides, I'm not ready to betray her like that yet. Not until I know for sure she's dead."

Neither Brio nor Taru seem ready or willing to speak on that particular point. Use of the word "dead" clearly disturbs them.

"If we've settled the issue of command, will you join me so we can figure out the rest? Time isn't exactly on our side."

"Of course," Brio says.

"You are certain my attendance is acceptable?" Taru asks.

"It's fine by me." Sirach appraises Taru from head to toe. "Besides, I know talent when I see it."

Together the trio leaves Brio's spare room, descending the narrow staircase to the main floor of the same tavern on the edge of the Shade where Evie first met the architects of the Tenth City's liberation.

Kellan, the hearty and temperate blacksmith, and Talma, the fiercely plump butcher and midwife, are both downstairs awaiting them. Chimot, Sirach's lieutenant, and Bam, the last of the Savage Legion's Elder Company, join them.

It is not the war council it once was, but every member wears an expression of determination rather than defeat.

"Where is Yacatek?" Brio asks. "Did none of the B'ors survive?"

"I wouldn't be surprised if all of them did," Sirach said. "Survival is what they excel at, more so than even my people. But none of them have returned to the city."

"What does that mean?" Brio asks.

"We have to consider that their participation in our joint effort, or what's left of it, has ended."

Despite how calmly Sirach presents this scenario, Brio is visibly shaken.

Talma is the first one to speak in the wake of the revelation about the B'ors.

"Our people here in the Tenth City are afraid the Skrain are coming for them now that they've . . . after the battle didn't entirely go your way."

Sirach grins wryly. "Well, if things continue to not go entirely our way, they'll have every reason to worry. For now, though, they're safe enough. The Skrain were sent into retreat by the Islanders, who now stand firmly between the Crachian army and all of us here."

"What's to stop the Islander army from swarming over our walls like a nest of scorpions someone waved a lit candle at?" Kellan asks.

"Utter and wanton disinterest?" Sirach offers.

"What my daring commander means," Chimot chimes in quickly, "is that the people of Rok have not crossed the sea for the first time in their history to sack an already sacked city. They came here to fight the Skrain, to fight Crache."

"Whom they see as 'Crache' may not be as simple as that," Taru says. "But I do agree, they will have no interest in turning around and coming here. They will press on towards the Capitol, meeting the Skrain as soon as they can."

Kellan nods his shaven head. "Then so long as word of what happened out there doesn't reach the rest of the Skrain and the Gens holed up in their Circus, things should stay calm within the city walls."

Sirach's smile turns a touch venomous. "So sorry we let you down."

"No one 'ere said such," Talma shoots back at the Sicclunan warrior. "Ain't gonna pretend we're 'appy about the outcome, but we all made our beds."

"You have to meet with the Rok Islanders," Taru insists, taking most of them by surprise. "You have to convince them combining forces is the only thing that makes sense for all of us."

Sirach raises a delicate brow. "You do remember the part where they watched my colleagues and me being slaughtered, yes?"

"I understand how it appears," Taru relents. "However, you need to understand the Rok mind. They are not like the rest of us. It was not . . . personal."

Sirach actually laughs. "It felt pretty personal to me."

"Sirach—" Brio begins to interject.

"Why don't we ask Evie how she feels?" she persists. "Oh, but we can't, can we?"

"Sirach!" Brio thunders, echoing throughout the battered rafters of the tavern. The uncharacteristic outburst is enough to get her attention.

"I would think you might have learned to be somewhat more open to new alliances by now," he reminds her. "You fought beside Savages you were sworn to kill. How is this any different?"

Sirach has no answer for that, at least not right away.

"Even if we're open to it," Chimot says when she sees her commander isn't going to reply, "it doesn't seem like the island folk particularly want our help."

"They don't know they need it yet," Taru explains. "They haven't met the full force of Crache on Crachian ground. They still think they can defeat them as they did when the Skrain tried to take their island. They are a hardheaded people, but a fair and righteous one. We need to convince them."

"Our first order of business should be to get Evie back," Sirach tells them all, as if she hasn't heard a word Taru has said.

"Sirach, I want to see her returned to us safely too," Brio says. "But we can't make that a priority right now."

"As far as I'm concerned, it's our *only* priority. If we want to rally what forces we have left, if we want to convince new bodies from the rest of the Crachian cities to rally to our cause, we *need* Evie. The people believe in the Sparrow General. She is the person they flocked to before, and to whom they will again. Conversely, if the Skrain march her through the streets of the Capitol, chained and broken, if they execute her and preside over a nationwide tour of her head only, we are finished. *No one else* will join us, and the Savages and Crachian refugees we have left will slink away."

"Even if she were here, it still wouldn't be enough," Taru insists. "Not without the Rok army. We *have* to fight together. That is how this war will be won. Separate us, and the Crachian machine will do what it does best, consume us piece by piece."

"How will you convince them?" Sirach asks. "You're the one

who ruined their plan. You got a lot of them killed who might otherwise have lived. You think they've forgotten that?"

Taru stares back at her with hardened eyes. "If they need my life to make this peace, that is what I will give to see this thing done. But this alliance must be forged if we have any hope of overcoming Crache."

Even Sirach seems sobered by the measures Taru is prepared to take.

"All right," Sirach relents. "You and Brio play peacemakers. It's not a role I'm good at, anyway. But if they'll fight with us, the Sicclunans will fight with them. Fair enough?"

Taru looks to Brio, who nods wearily.

"I think they'll use your skulls to serve soup, though," Sirach adds.

"They are talented soup makers," Taru says quietly, almost to themselves.

"Good then." Sirach slaps her hands against her hips. "While you attend to matters of diplomacy, Chimot and I will retrieve our Sparrow General."

Brio is caught entirely off guard. "Wait, what? You can't be serious!"

"I'm quite serious. I like to stay busy. And as I said, peacemaking is not my line."

"It is likely a suicide mission," Taru warns. "You would have to circumvent the Rok just to catch up with the Skrain, then somehow penetrate their highest security. Even if you managed it, how would you possibly escape and make it all the way back to us?"

"Well, if you manage to woo the Islanders, we'll only have to make it back to them, yes? Besides, we're a stealthy lot. Right?" Sirach shoots a glance at Chimot, who nods, albeit reluctantly.

"Right," her lieutenant says without enthusiasm.

"I go with you," Bam's deep, thrumming voice says to the Sicclunans.

That takes everyone aback. None of them have ever heard the giant speak before.

A grin slowly spreads across Sirach's lips. "You'd be welcome, big man," she says.

Brio hangs his head, issuing a rough sigh.

"Evie wouldn't want you to do this," he says, though he already sounds defeated.

"I don't care what she wants," Sirach informs him. "This is my decision. We both have ideas about what this rebellion needs to live. Fine. I give you leave to do yours, and I'll thank you to bless mine."

Brio raises his face and manufactures an entirely insincere smile.

"Consider yourself blessed, then," he says. "I truly hope you don't get yourselves, and her, killed."

"If we do, at least we'll have ruined their plans. You have to learn to treasure the small victories, Brio. It's the Sicclunan way. Right, Chimot?"

"Right," Chimot says, with even less enthusiasm than before.

FRAYING AT THE EDGES

"THIS IS THE THIRD TIME THEY HAVE CANCELED OR WITHdrawn from meeting with us. With *me*."

Dyeawan considers how the words sound as soon as they pass her lips. More than that, she considers what they signify about how she sees herself and her position at the top of the planners, and thus at the top of Crache itself.

It strikes her as very much an attitude Edger would have taken.

Dyeawan's tender is positioned alongside the head of the table she had fashioned to replace the absurdly winding contraption that dominated the meeting space of the planners in Edger's time. The concentric circular design of the old table was patterned after the symbol of the planners themselves and meant to represent a confluence of minds rather than a hierarchy of leadership, or some such nonsense, but mostly it meant no one seated at that "table" could see each other without craning their neck.

Riko sits atop the table with her legs folded beneath her. Despite wearing the same gray tunic and concentric circles pendant of a planner that Dyeawan wears, Riko refuses to give up her overencumbered tool belt, bulging at the hips with her handmade gadgets and instruments.

She's currently busying herself with putting the finishing touches on a new toy she has designed, a miniature horse with intricately jointed legs that an arrangement of wind-up gears within its body animate and allow it to trot like the real thing.

"Right now they're just late, yeah? You don't know that they're not coming."

Mister Quan, as tall as a shadow in the early morning, sweeps silently into the confines of the planners' inner sanctum. Nia is following at his heels, her entire body radiating with tense, nervous energy.

"They are not coming," Nia informs the pair already sitting at the table.

Dyeawan can't help flashing a knowing glance at Riko, who responds by shrugging.

"What's the excuse this time?" Riko asks.

"The unrest in the Bottoms."

"Ministry agents are openly policing the streets now?" Dyeawan asks.

Riko snorts. "Ministry agents would get lost trying to find the streets of the Bottoms."

"While I might not have phrased it the same way," Nia says, "I agree with the sentiment. They are balking. I cannot remember a time when the Ministry outright refused to work alongside the Planning Cadre like this."

"They are not refusing," Dyeawan points out. "Yet. They are still making excuses."

"How important a distinction do you feel that is, really?" Nia asks.

"One is a direct act of conflict. The other signifies they have not yet decided to initiate such conflict. I feel as though that is a very important distinction to us right now."

Despite the tension of the moment, Riko is grinning as she looks from Dyeawan to Nia and back at Dyeawan again.

"I love watching you two natter at each other. It's like you've been doing it your whole lives."

That brings a smile to Dyeawan's lips. She glances fondly up at her sister.

Nia is not amused.

"Riko, may I speak with our venerable leader alone for a moment?"

"Family stuff, yeah? I got it. No worries."

Riko pushes herself up with her deceptively strong arms, unfolding her legs and leaping deftly from the tabletop. She places her newly crafted toy on the chamber floor and winds its gears, causing the mechanical stead to convincingly gallop away. Riko follows it out of the room, mimicking its gait with her own and laughing all the while.

Rather than being entertained, Dyeawan frowns. Keeping the secrets Nia and Dyeawan share between the two of them, and Mister Quan, is a protective measure. She knows that. However, being dishonest with Riko, even by omission, feels wrong to her.

"What is the true reason the Protectorate Ministry suddenly refuses to sit with us here?" she asks Nia once they are alone with Mister Quan.

"Do you really need an answer to that question?"

"I assumed you asked Riko to leave so we could discuss this openly."

"Perhaps they don't want to assign a new liaison to the Planning Cadre because they know the last one died here. Unnaturally."

"They know, or they suspect?"

"With the Protectorate Ministry the line between those two things is so thin as to be irrelevant. You've been among them long enough to know that."

"Are you angry with me?"

"No," Nia answers, perhaps too quickly to be convincing.

"Do you regret what we did? What you did? To save my life."

"I regret it had to be done."

Dyeawan believes that.

"I feel some resentment, yes."

Dyeawan believes that, too.

"Resentment that we're sharing leadership of the Planning Cadre?"

"Not over that—not anymore. But I have spent my entire life here. This place, the structure of it . . . has always been an immutable force that powered my whole universe. Now everything feels uncertain. Chaotic. I feel as though my center is gone. I have never endured this before. I know it is not your fault."

"But it is difficult for you not to blame me."

Nia nods.

"I understand," Dyeawan assures her. "I do. It was never my wish to harm you, or anyone here. I believe all of my actions have been necessary. That does not mitigate the damage they have done, collateral or otherwise."

"None of this is important right now," Nia insists.

"It is important to me."

"We have more pressing matters to deal with. The responsibility to stabilize the Capitol, along with the rest of Crache, falls to us, whether the Ministry wants to acknowledge us or not. The situation in the Bottoms is escalating."

"But we also have to consider that the Protectorate Ministry itself is now a problem to be solved."

"As a threat to us? You faced them down before, when you took that seat."

"I faced down Oisin. And it settled nothing. He continued to scheme and plot in secret until he felt the time was right to strike."

"And you think that's what the rest of the Ministry is doing now?"

"Hopefully they are still hesitant, but at the very least, they are considering their options. Oisin moved against me because he thought you would be all too happy to see me dead and take my place. If the other Ministry agents are refusing to meet with both of us, they know they can no longer rely on you to step in and lead the planners."

"There's still Trowel and the others." The older planners.

Dyeawan shakes her head. "They might conspire with them against us, but the Ministry knows they cannot trust the future of Crache to those relics. Edger told them as much when he was alive. That's why Oisin took his orders."

"Then what are their options at this point?"

"As I see it, either they will, however reluctantly, come to terms with us and mend this divide . . ."

"Or?"

"The Protectorate Ministry will decide they want to test their hands at running Crache themselves. Without any planners instructing them."

Nia can scarcely seem to comprehend that.

"You really think . . . but what would that mean . . . truly, that we—they would force us to submit to their will?"

"Edger believed in liquidating anyone he couldn't control. I imagine the Ministry feels very much the same way."

"So what will we do to defend ourselves? You cannot crush the entire Ministry under the wheels of your tender."

Dyeawan glowers at her.

Nia, curt though she can be, immediately and visibly regrets her choice of words.

"I didn't mean—I simply meant that violence is not our strength."

"I don't really know how we defend ourselves, sister. I expect we will do the same thing we did in that vision chamber when Oisin set upon us: whatever we can."

"You seem very calm, considering you're talking about our potential murders."

Dyeawan regards her calmly.

"In truth? I never expected to live this long."

This does not seem to bring Nia any comfort at all.

IN THE SOUP

TARU IS NOT EASILY AMUSED. HUMOR, LIKE EMOTION, IS A thing the retainer learned to do without during their largely joyless upbringing in the Bottoms. However, watching Brio bounce about in his saddle for hours like a toddler trying to stay abreast on their jogging parent's shoulders has come near to breaking the retainer. They've worn a steady smirk for the better part of an hour now, and Brio's red-faced, twisted-lip expression of frustration and sheer awkward effort have caused them to stifle more than a few outright bursts of laughter.

"I can feel you judging me, you know," he mostly grunts through clenched teeth.

"Not at all," Taru assures him.

"It pleases me you seem to have moved past your guilt over my missing appendage, anyway."

"How so?"

"In that you seem to have no qualms about the fact you clearly find amusement in a one-legged man struggling to stay in his saddle."

"Your stump has nothing to do with it," Taru states plainly. "I strapped it to your saddle myself. The truth is, you have always been helpless on horseback. In fact, it was worse when you had both legs and no straps to secure you, as I recall."

"There was no need to master horsecraft in the Capitol," Brio protests. "We rode sky carriages everywhere."

"You never wanted to learn," Taru reminds him. "You have always abhorred being out-of-doors. You only ever came camping with your father and me because he made you. In fact, I recall several trips once you reached manhood when you outright refused to accompany us."

"I refuse to feel shame for enjoying four walls, a roof, a hearth, and an inside privy with a well-maintained sewer. It always struck me the point of conquering the elements was to not return to being at their mercy."

Taru ceases to argue with him, merely shaking their head.

Brio falls silent for a time, a look of contemplation breaking through the straining of his face as he continues to wrestle with the saddle.

"I do regret not coming along for those last few trips with you and my father," he admits a while later. "I remember telling him it wasn't good for his health to be out there, sleeping rough. I could see how he was fading. But I suppose I didn't want to believe the old man only had so many outings left in him. I told myself there would always be time to humor him."

"He never took it personally. 'I raised him to be a pleader, not a woodsman,' he would say to me. 'What else should I have expected?' He never judged you for it." Taru barely withholds a smile. "The truth is he wasn't much of a woodsman, either. If I hadn't been there, I doubt he could have found his way back home."

Brio laughs at that, loudly and warmly and genuinely. It pleases Taru to see and hear.

After a while, Brio stops laughing, and his tone turns serious.

"Is this folly?" he asks. "The two of us, alone, petitioning the Rok?"

Taru shrugs their armored shoulders. "What good would coming to them in force accomplish? We are not seeking a fight. If we cannot sway them on our own, then we cannot sway them."

"The part you're not saying is if they decide to kill us, at least we won't have sacrificed any of our soldiers."

"That is why this mission cannot be accomplished without you, De-Gen. Your unfailing insight."

Brio regards Taru with an odd smile. "I don't recall you being quite so . . . jocular."

"Lexi's influence, I expect."

Brio nods, his thoughts straying to his wife. At first, the memories and thoughts are happy, and they keep the smile on his lips.

But it doesn't last. Picturing her quickly turns from smile inducing to heart aching.

Taru can see where his mind is taking him.

"Besides," they say, trying to distract him, "the Rok might kill me, but Staz adores you. You are the key to this whole negotiation, I suspect."

"No one adores me that much," Brio insists.

"I know firsthand that is far from true, De-Gen."

The smile returns briefly to Brio. It's faint, but it makes Taru happy.

It is hours on horseback before they ride upon fresh tracks

left by the Rok Islanders' war caravan. It is another hour following those tracks before a heady, appetizing aroma greets the pair. They haven't even spotted the outskirts of the Rok Islanders' camp yet.

"What *is* that?" Brio asks, his palate clearly intrigued.

"Soup," Taru says without hesitation.

"How do you know?"

"They like soup."

"Fair enough. Who doesn't like soup?"

"No," Taru states flatly. "They *really* like soup. It may be the cornerstone of their entire society."

Brio doesn't even attempt to mask his utter confusion.

"Soup?"

The retainer nods definitively.

"Soup."

He processes the information quietly for a moment, and then, "All right then."

They can see fires burning in the distance now. Taru's sharp eyes spy a perimeter barricade around the camp composed of thorny obstructions. They soon realize the barricade is made of the spiked shell baskets of Rok chariots, freed from their mounts and upturned on the ground.

Taru hears an unnatural rustling in the short grass around the hooves of their horses. They catch flashes of metal in the waning sunlight.

In the next moment, the razor prongs of tridents are poised at Taru's and Brio's throats. The Islanders holding the hafts of the tridents are draped down their backs in woven sheets of grass plucked from the valley floor. They were invisible as the pair rode up to the camp.

Taru knows better than to so much as allow their hand to stray near their weapon.

Brio, for his part, appears thoroughly unperturbed by the piercing tips tickling the veins in his neck.

"Good evening, friends," he greets the Islander sentries. "My name is Brio, this is my retainer, Taru. We are friends of Captain Staz of the *Black Turtle*, here under her continence."

The sentries exchange looks that are amused as much as they are confused.

"Never heard Ol' Staz talked about as having 'continence' before," one of them says, drawing laughter from their fellows.

Brio smiles cordially down at them. "I'm sure she'd like to hear it herself once before she gives up the wheel. Can you take us to her, please?"

The sentries seem to consider the proposition.

"No weapons," the one from before says.

"Of course!" Brio acquiesces immediately. "I am unarmed, and my retainer will be happy to relinquish their blades."

"They will?" Taru asks with raised brow.

"They *will*," Brio assures them sternly.

The pair are relieved of their horses, Taru their sword and hook-end, and escorted past the blockade perimeter of the camp. Brio uses his crutch to make the trek, and Taru is careful to slow their pace to match his.

Taru wasn't sure precisely what they expected, but the sights and sounds that greet them are far from whatever preconceived notions they may have harbored. This camp of war is playing out much more like some kind of annual festival or celebration. There is singing and dancing and blaring instruments made of shell and string and hide. Brio is very nearly set on fire by an Islander expertly twirling a long branch that is ablaze at both ends. Games of skill are contested between Islanders out to prove who has the best aim with trident and knife, both being winged through the air in every direction at targets both stationary and moving.

Everywhere there is laughter. Everywhere there is bickering that invariably leads to more laughter.

Taru feels a pang in their chest, knowing they could have had a place among these people whom the retainer admires and respects, and who accepted them in a way Crache never would.

The price was simply too high, they remind themselves, and they do not regret their choices.

Taru recognizes the assemblage of Rok sea captains from the meeting in the longhouse back on their island, during which Staz and her fish stew convinced the entire nation to go to war. There are a dozen of them gathered around a great bonfire, the flames taller than Taru. Each captain occupies a Rok-style grass-woven mat, sitting cross-legged and maintaining their own smaller, individual fire over which they are all simmering their own pots of soups and stews.

Brio and Taru, the retainer in front, are led through the ranks of the salty old sea hands tending their sacred family recipes.

Captain Staz is stirring her concoction with a long-handled spoon, her pace and motions so slow and mechanical they appear almost hypnotic. She does not look up at the towering retainer, even as their shadow cast by the bonfire light engulfs her.

"Conch rolled in crushed ditfa root?" Taru asks, recalling the secret Staz shared to her rich, red stew.

The captain of the *Black Turtle* shakes her small head, continuing to slowly stir the pot.

"The fish in your bays are trash," Staz informs Taru. "I wouldn't feed Crachian fish to our mounts. I did bring dried ditfa from home, but the meat is venison. Your game isn't much better than your fish, though. An insult to my grandmother's stew recipe, really."

"Your grandmother was an insult to her stew recipe!" another haggard voice shouts at her.

Taru recognizes Captain Florcha of the *Razor Fin*, whose voice was the loudest and most opposed to the idea of the Rok crossing the sea to fight the Skrain.

Taru can smell the woman's brine soup from across the fire, as sour as death. Taru recalls another captain mocking its weakness, and the retainer wonders idly if the woman has changed her recipe to make it stronger, or if it is what is considered "weak" among the Islanders.

"Does your sister still use tort seed instead of ditfa?" Taru asks the captain.

"Is this reminiscing you are doing with me supposed to make me forget you attacked us, or that you threatened the very success of our first assault on the ants?"

Taru has no answer for that.

Perhaps sensing as much, Brio hobbles forward, interjecting himself between the retainer and the Rok captain.

Upon seeing his face in the bonfire light for the first time, Staz finally stops stirring her pot. Her tiny, withered face becomes alight with joy in a way Taru had not previously witnessed.

"Brio, my handsome boy! You come here to your auntie Staz right now!"

Brio inches forward, gripping his crutch so that he may lean down and embrace the small woman through her impossibly puffy deck coat.

"You've lost weight," Staz remarks, staring openly at the stump of Brio's leg.

"I was in an honest-to-goodness battle," Brio announces grandly.

"You? No, you weren't made for fighting! You're a sweet boy, a smart boy."

"I wasn't given much choice."

"I can see that," Staz says, eyeing the blue runes still staining his skin.

"In any case, it pleases me to see you here, taking the fight to Crache on their own ground."

"It wasn't a decision we arrived at lightly," Staz assures him, then, looking at Taru, "and though we've started off on a bit of a shaky foot, we've already got them running."

Taru can't help averting their own gaze under the Rok captain's scrutiny.

"Well now," Brio begins heavily, "I do not claim to be any kind of military strategist, but I do know there is a marked difference between running and regrouping. I also know the Crachian machine well enough to know the Skrain are currently doing the latter."

The joy that lit Captain Staz's face fades somewhat, replaced by a quizzical look.

"Have you come here as a pleader, Little Brio? Are you petitioning me now?"

"I am no one's pleader anymore, Auntie," Brio tells her solemnly. "I . . . I don't know what I am anymore, to be honest. I am neither Savage Legionnaire nor rebel soldier. As you said, I was not made for fighting. But all I've ever done, really, is try to solve the problems of the people Crache has written off. I suppose I am still doing that, and it has brought me here."

Brio locks eyes intently with the diminutive captain, raising his voice for the rest of them to hear.

"I've come here because this is where I knew I'd find one of my father's oldest friends, someone I consider family. I've come here because we share a problem, an enemy, and I believe we can only solve that problem and defeat that enemy together."

"We do not need to fight with ants to defeat ants!" Captain Florcha protests.

"I am speaking to my boy here!" Staz fires back at her. "Tend to your soup. It smells like the wrong end of a rotted-out horse!"

"Your stew looks like that horse's blood!"

Staz waves a hand at her dismissively.

"Your words have a familiar ring to them," she tells Brio, again looking to Taru.

Brio follows her gaze, his eyes warm and admiring upon his retainer.

"My friend here speaks highly of the people of Rok. They say they owe you their life."

"They have a finicky way of expressing gratitude. They commandeered our chariot fleet. They spilled Rok blood. They smashed a two-centuries-old conch horn to splinters. *Those* are the acts of an enemy."

"I am not your enemy," Taru insists. "I did what I felt I had to do to save my friends, my family. For all I knew, Brio was down on that battlefield."

Staz cocks her head and says nothing. It's clear to Taru the Rok captain had not considered this before.

"You did what you felt was right for Rok," the retainer presses. "The rebels understand that. It's the situation in which we all found ourselves. They do not bear you any ill will. They are willing to fight beside you even now. Because that is what makes the most sense. They are willing to do the smartest thing for the situation as it stands now. They are trying to think as the Rok do."

Staz smiles up at the retainer. She nods approvingly.

"It is good to see you understand now, at least."

"The rebels cannot be an effective shield for you anymore," Brio adds. "They are of the most use to you fighting beside you, thickening your ranks and giving you the added strength you will need to face the full force of the Skrain. Even now, they are drawing every available soldier from every unoccupied city. You won't have waves and rocks and your sailing fleet as your greatest weapons when you face them. This is their style of battle, on their terrain."

Staz nods again. "That is all well and good, but it does not square things with your friend here. The retainer and the Rok are at odds. Offenses were committed; hospitality was betrayed."

Taru draws a deep breath. "If my life is the only thing that will pave the way to a true alliance between the Rok and the rebels, then you may have it."

Staz frowns. The many lines around her almost-imperceptible mouth deepen.

"The great tree here thinks we are as bloodthirsty as the ants!" Captain Florcha hollers.

The rest of the captains murmur and jeer in agreement.

"You know what your problem is, my friend?" Staz asks Taru. "You have it in your head that the answer to everything is some bold, life-sacrificing gesture. The world does not have to be so dramatic as all that."

Taru is truly confused, and looking to Brio provides no hint that he is any less so.

"If you do not want my life, then how can I make amends to you for my actions?" Taru asks.

Before Staz can answer, laughter, hoarse and raucous and belonging to Florcha, fills the ranks surrounding the bonfire.

"Karay-Karay!" she cries out.

The other captains repeat the word, and suddenly they are all chanting it in unison, over and over.

The rest of the camp slowly takes up the call, and in moments the repetition of "Karay-Karay!" is deafening.

Taru leans close to Brio.

"What is 'Karay-Karay'?" they ask.

Brio considers his words carefully before answering.

"Something that apparently will *not* kill you," he says. "Although I get the sense you may wish it did. But I could be wrong."

SONGBIRD

IT TOOK THE SKRAIN A FULL DAY AFTER EVIE REGAINED consciousness in her cage to finally dispatch a surgeon to attend to her. In that time, Evie developed a comforting series of mostly fevered dreams about using whatever instruments that surgeon would bring for her to stab them in the throat with and escape her captivity. She fostered grand visions of taking the surgeon hostage, using them as a human shield to wade through the Skrain, and then, only after escaping with her prey on horseback, happily and merrily opening their neck.

When the surgeon finally arrives, Evie harbors every intention of following through with her feverish fantasies.

A simple, immutable, wholly unexpected problem puts a massive dent in her plans, however.

The surgeon is just too damn nice.

It's late into the evening, and the caravan has set up camp for the night. They've lowered Evie's cage from a wrist-thick pulley chain so that it sits upon the ground. Captain Feng Silvar accompanies the hunched-over doctor, and it is then that Evie learns the captain is the keeper of the keys to her cage.

And it is *keys*, as in more than one. There appear to be half a dozen, in fact. Evie has felt too ill to examine the massive lock upon the cage door, but it apparently contains six different locks within, each of which the captain has to spring with a different key before he can remove the thing and open the door.

To begin with, the surgeon appears impossibly old and frail. Worsening matters, he looks like a turtle, an adorable little wrinkled one outside of its shell. He has a bald, bulbous head that sits atop a long neck, and a nose that is somehow both wide and pointed at the same time. One of his eyes, the right one, clearly went bad at some point, and he wears a large, thick lens strapped around his pulpy little head to help magnify the one eye's failing vision.

"My name is Murrow," he introduces himself, his voice raspy and syrupy, soothing despite its roughness. "The boys and girls call me Cutter, for obvious reasons. Don't fret, though, I only cut into folks who really need it, and only as a last resort."

"Are you a soldier?" she asks. "Or were you, rather?"

He shakes his head. "Oh no. I have no stomach or aptitude for fighting. No, I was a Gen surgeon for many years, but I grew weary attending to the every minor ache and pain of the privileged. I decided to spend what time is left to me helping those who at the very least truly need my help."

Murrow, with concerted effort, kneels in the doorway of her open cage. He wears a many-pouched vest over his otherwise plain gray tunic. Those pouches are filled with well-cleaned metallic implements, as well as wads of silken bandages and various bottles and vials filled with liquids, powders, and even clipped roots. He removes a pair of thin yet razor-sharp-looking shears from his vest's kit and begins carefully slicing away the thick leather of Evie's already-torn pants around her spear injury.

The old surgeon frowns disapprovingly as he gets his first look at her festered wound.

"They should have called me to you sooner," he mutters, almost more to himself than Evie. "This is a terrible way to treat people."

That is when Evie decides she simply cannot kill the old half-blind turtle, the first person among the Skrain to offer her any real kindness.

"Still, it could be worse, I suppose," he continues. "Did someone attempt to burn this?"

"I did," Evie informs him.

"Where did you get fire?" Captain Silvar, looming behind the surgeon, demands.

"I made it. Found a twig mixed in with all this hay here. Made a pile and managed to stoke a small flame by rubbing the twig between my hands."

"Very clever," Murrow commends her.

"I tried to burn the wagon carrying my cage too," she tells Silvar brightly. "But the fire wasn't big enough."

The Skrain captain only grunts in reply.

"You did a fair job, considering," Murrow remarks. "There's still a good amount of infection here, but it would certainly be worse if you hadn't taken measures. The fever might even have killed you by now."

"I am nothing if not resourceful," Evie says without pride.

"Not resourceful enough, it seems," Silvar adds.

"The best of us have bad days," Evie fires back.

"You only get one of those on the battlefield."

"Leave it be, child," Murrow urges her quietly.

He removes a long, hollow needle attached to a miniature bellows from one of his pouches.

"This is going to sting, although probably less than the blade that cut you."

"What is it?" Evie asks.

"It will kill the infection from the wound that is already spreading through your blood. It should cure your fever and other ailments as well. I make it from what grows on the rotten food the Skrain discard and the cooks use for compost to help their herbs grow."

"Sounds delicious."

Murrow chuckles. "It's not meant to please the senses, only cleanse the blood. You may want to take a deep breath."

Evie complies, inhaling deeply.

He lances her thigh with the needle as she exhales, its tip finding a pulsing vein. The surgeon squeezes the bellows and injects its contents into Evie's bloodstream.

The potion from the bellows hurts far worse than the needle piercing her flesh. It burns at the point of injection, spreading from there with an oppressive weighty feeling, as if someone mixed clay with mud and poured it into her veins.

"Try to relax," Murrow bids her, gently stroking her calf below the wound. "The pain and heaviness will subside, I promise."

"I believe you," Evie says, realizing it's the truth, that she trusts this man despite the circumstances.

The elderly surgeon begins tending to the wound itself, first cleaning it with both water from a skin and a bruise-colored solution from a small stopper bottle. The solution burns worse than the festering gash, but Evie knows it is another cleansing fire. She bears it silently, trying to breathe in through her nose and out through her mouth in a slow, steady rhythm.

Once the wound has been thoroughly cleaned, Murrow removes a coil of thread and a much thinner needle from his kit.

First, he offers her a small red pod.

"Chew lightly on this chili," he instructs Evie. "Don't break through the pod, and *definitely* do not swallow. It will help with the pain."

Evie nods silently, plucking the chili from his hand and popping it inside her mouth.

He begins sewing up the open wound, delicately and expertly feeding the needle through the jagged ends of her flesh and deftly weaving them back together. Old and withered though he appears, Murrow's hands remain strong and steady, and his skill is obvious.

Evie chews as gently as she can on the bright red pod. It releases just enough of its juices to coat her tongue. She isn't sure what type of chili it is, but the heat is intense. She feels her brow sweating anew, and the sensations created by the pepper do indeed distract from what is happening to her gashed leg.

All the while, Evie stares beyond Murrow at Captain Silvar, whose eyes never stop surveying the scene. A dozen scenarios in which Evie ends up in possession of the Skrain captain's keys flash through her mind, none of them remotely plausible under the present circumstances and in her condition.

"There we are," Murrow announces when he has finished. "This leg should heal just fine. There will be no cutting today, at the very least."

"Good," Silvar says. "We want you to be able to stand tall and proud in your cage when we bring you through the streets of the Capitol."

"When will the company tailor be by to fit me for new pants?" Evie asks politely.

The Skrain captain actually laughs at that.

"Why, I think you look perfectly suitable as you are. A little ragged and a little bloody will play well for the crowds."

Murrow quickly bandages the freshly stitched section of her leg.

"That is all I can do for you, my dear, I'm afraid," he laments as he begins the slow and arduous process of standing back up.

"Thank you for your kindness and attention," Evie says, and she means it. "I won't forget it."

"All in service," he says with a gentle smile.

Waving goodbye to her, Murrow steps aside to allow Captain Silvar to slam the cage door shut. He strains as he hefts the giant padlock to snap it back into place.

"Can I give you my dinner order now?" Evie asks.

"A surgeon, dinner," Silvar complains. "Next you'll want my best jug of wine and silk sheets for your cage."

"I am a terrible houseguest, it's true," Evie admits. "You should just ask me to leave."

The captain laughs again. "You just hold on to that sense of humor of yours. It may be all you'll have left. Take her back up, boys!"

He leaves Evie to be hauled back up into the air by the chain attached to the top of her cage.

Evie has to grip the bars to steady herself. She grits her teeth, cursing through them at the mother who birthed the captain. Her leg still feels heavy from where Murrow injected her, and her mouth is still aflame from the pepper he gave her, but there is undeniable relief around the area of her spear wound.

She stares out through the bars of her cage at all the tiny fires of the massive Skrain camp.

"You're all going to regret letting me live," she promises them, speaking the words into the night sky.

Evie thinks she might believe the sentiment more if she weren't so damn hungry.

EMPTY NEST

GREENFIRE ACTUALLY PREFERS STALE BREAD, DYEAWAN HAS found. The many times she has fed the plump little fowl freshly steamed bread from the kitchen, soft and smooth and pillowy, Greenfire has pecked at it with his beak for long, contemplative moments before finally consuming it with an almost offended reluctance. When she has day-old bread, however, and tears it into small brittle pieces for him, her pet duck snaps it right up, eagerly and hungrily.

She never tires of studying the duck's behavior, identifying the unique little quirks of his personality. He is the first pet Dyeawan has ever had, ever cared for with her own hands. She has come to love him as much as she does her other friends at the Planning Cadre.

She keeps Greenfire in a spacious, iron-barred cage hung from a crooked stand beside her bed, where she can easily remove and stroke his feathers when she is seated on her mattress. Dyeawan has placed a large shallow pot at the bottom and fills it with fresh water every day. She watches him float contentedly atop the makeshift pond every morning and every night. She finds it helps her think, helps her sort out the many problems she faces as the head of the planners.

Dyeawan is sitting up in bed, watching as Greenfire gobbles up his final bit of bread for the night. The duck haughtily tucks its long neck into the recesses of its feathery body, settling in to slumber. He looks utterly peaceful, unaware of any of the horrors of the world. Dyeawan is envious.

After he's asleep, she reaches for the small, lacquered puzzle box Matei gifted her as part of his apology. Dyeawan hasn't had much time for it since he visited her, dealing with everything happening in the Capitol as well as the unsettling issues with the Protectorate Ministry.

She feels awake, despite the waning hour of the evening, so she decides it might be a worthy distraction.

Dyeawan recalls thinking there were no seams to the box when she first examined it. Now, holding it up to the lamplight of her small room, she can see there are indeed seams; they are just incredibly fine. The box is tightly constructed, as she would expect of anything designed and built by Matei. Still, there are no visible latches or grooves by which to open the thing.

She begins pressing the flat of her palms against each side of the box to test whether or not they will slide. At first, it appears a futile gesture, but then one end of the box abruptly shifts forward, the small panel of wood slipping beyond the edge of the box's back. That allows Dyeawan to then slide the front panel of the box into the space created by the side panel. It's impressive, elegant even. There are no hinges or screws or nails. The shifting panels that compose the box are simply wood fixtures sliding through other wood fixtures.

With a few more reconfigurations, Dyeawan realizes she has freed the top of the box. She easily lifts the lid away, peering inside for the first time. She half expected it to be empty, assuming solving the puzzle is the reward, but neither assumption proves to be true.

At first glance, the thing within appears to be a dead, preserved insect. It is laid perfectly atop the bottom of the box, its six legs delicately folded into a perching position. It is larger than any spider she has ever seen, if it is a spider. Dyeawan has never seen coloring like what adorns its bulbous body, covered in what she notes are hundreds of fine little hairs that appear surprisingly soft. The color is a mixture of deep purple and bright red, the shades melding into one another in wild, seemingly random patterns.

Dyeawan isn't frightened when the creature begins to move within the box. Her curiosity is piqued, certainly, and she extends a fingertip to reach inside and gently stroke the fine hairs on its bulbous body.

Her finger is hovering less than an inch from those tiny blue threads when the creature launches itself from the bottom of the box with its powerful legs, spinning around in midair before landing against the side of Dyeawan's exposed neck. The thing moves so fast she doesn't even have time to wince or shrink away. She can only gasp, the muscles of her torso tensing as its two sets of legs dig against her flesh.

Dyeawan never sees its stinger, but she feels the small, thorny appendage pierce her neck. It doesn't hurt, not really. There is only a little pressure, followed by the slight discomfort of a foreign object penetrating her skin.

When the warmth begins spreading through her veins, quickly

turning to a cold rush, Dyeawan begins to panic. It is too late to act, however. She opens her mouth to call for help, but no words are issued. It is then Dyeawan realizes her arms have fallen to her sides and she cannot lift them. When she attempts to look down, she finds her head is locked in place and she cannot command it to move.

She begins blinking rapidly, partially from excitement and partially because her eyelids seem to be the only part of her body she can still move. That doesn't last, either. One moment her eyelids are fluttering, and in the next they have locked, snapped wide open so she is staring wide-eyed straight ahead.

That is when the top half of her body, now completely frozen, falls against the bed, perfectly placing the back of her head into her pillow. She might be a princess in some fairy tale, so pristine is the pose she imagines herself in at that moment.

The rest of her body is now as inert and beyond the control of her mind as her legs have been since she can remember. Dyeawan finds she can't even move her eyes. Her gaze is fixed at the ceiling.

Even in the vision chamber, when she was drugged and nearly killed, she never experienced a total helplessness like this.

Her senses are still very much alive, however. She can feel the insect at her neck withdraw its barb, its many legs scuttling across her throat and up her face, pausing against her cheek. She is terrified the next thing she will feel is its stinger piercing her eyeball.

Finally, the venomous creature skitters away, leaving her face entirely as it crawls across her bedsheets. Dyeawan tracks it with the corner of one eye until it disappears over the side of her bed.

You're still breathing, she reminds herself. *Your lungs are still working. If you're still breathing, then that thing's venom isn't meant to kill you, only paralyze you.*

It is a small comfort, but a comfort nonetheless.

Dyeawan cannot know how much time has passed when she hears the door to her bedchamber creak open a while later, just enough to allow the passage of a body into her room. The light from the sconces in the corridor beyond is soft and brief and appears as a sliver on the wall before the closing of the door snuffs it out.

Dyeawan can't make out the figure that has entered her room at first. They are merely a large shadow moving towards the corner of her gaze, just outside the light of the candle she keeps burning on her night table. The figure carefully moves her tender from where it always rests at her bedside. She can hear the conveyance's wheels spinning and the whisper of the straps and gears that control them.

Dyeawan is almost as enraged by this as by the state of her body; she hates when people move her tender without her permission.

A heavy weight settles down against the scantest edge of her mattress, leaving an abundance of space between the figure and her immobile form.

"I was starting to think you didn't like my present."

It's Matei.

Even if she didn't recognize his voice immediately, his cherubic face leans over hers a moment later.

He appears calm, if more than a bit curious.

"I didn't know what would happen if you opened it right away," he admits. "I tried to make the design difficult enough that you'd at least have to set it aside for a while. But you . . . you're so smart. It did occur to me you might pop it open right then, as soon as I gave it to you. I really didn't know what I'd do if that happened. Even though Nia and Riko had left the room, there's no way they'd believe it wasn't my fault. It was . . . exciting, actually. Taking that risk."

It was exciting.

He's lost his mind, Dyeawan thinks. *This isn't the Matei I know.*

"I've been watching you through your window every night since I gave you the box," he explains, looking out that same window at the faint light of the moon. "I almost couldn't stand it anymore, the waiting. You can't believe how fast my heart was beating when you finally picked up the box."

Dyeawan attempts to move *something*, any part of her body. She summons every ounce of will within her, but she can't even wiggle one of her fingertips. Her vocal cords appear to be completely paralyzed. She can't even wheeze.

"I meant everything I said to you," he prattles on, staring at her in the candlelight. "I want you to know that. I really was sorry, and I really did figure out I was wrong about you, and that I was acting like a child."

Dyeawan remembers believing his apology, but also knowing he was holding something back. There was a dishonesty she couldn't identify or articulate, but she never could have conceived of how deeply it ran or how dangerous and unhinged its intentions truly were.

"I also figured out one of the reasons I was so mad at you was because I want to *be* you. I wanted the planners to think I was clever, even brilliant, and make me one of them. I wanted to be like Edger one day. But I knew that would never happen, even with you in charge. I'm just a competent pair of hands, you know? Just a builder. I'm not a planner. Except I guess I kind of am, huh? I came up with this plan, and it's working."

Matei reaches his hand towards her face. Dyeawan's mind screams silently in frustration, her whole being wishing to pull away from him.

His fingertips stop just short of touching her cheek.

"The Protectorate Ministry doesn't like you very much," he tells her, practically whispering now. "I think they really wanted to kill you themselves, but I guess they don't want to cross that line with the planners—the young and the old. They know that if the rest are aware the Ministry killed one planner, they'll all worry they could be next. But if you die while the Ministry isn't even on the island . . ."

But what's your reward, Matei? Dyeawan wonders, although the answer seems obvious. *They won't let you lead, but they'll give you a gray tunic, I'm sure. You will get to sit at the planners' table.*

"I could have put something lethal in that box. We have a menagerie of things like that here in the keep. But I wanted to face you. I told myself that you deserved to know the truth. And that if I was going to do this, I had to do it myself. I had to look you in the eyes. Killing you with poison would be cowardly. This is what I told myself, but now . . . the truth is, I think I needed you to know it was me who did this to you. I wanted you to know I was better than you, smarter than you."

He pauses, and then leans close to her again so he can look into her wide, motionless eyes.

"Does that make me evil, Dyeawan? Am I an evil person now?"

Despite everything, Dyeawan truly is not certain.

This must have always been there, she thinks, perhaps because contemplating Matei's nature distracts her from what is happening, or about to happen.

He's still very close to her when he says, "You know, when you first came here and we kind of took you in, Riko and me, I thought . . . maybe you and I . . . Riko never looked at me that way, but I thought you might. I thought we could . . . you know, that we could be . . . together."

She feels his hand slide across the exposed flesh of her stomach, and the sensation churns and knots her guts.

As quickly as it found its way there, Matei abruptly jerks his hand back. He leans away from her, turning to face away from her on the edge of the bed.

"I wouldn't do that to you," he says bitterly, without looking at her. "You know I wouldn't do that to you, right?"

The sudden display of shame and feigned righteousness confuses Dyeawan, but she is thankful for it all the same.

Matei still refuses to look back at her as his arm slides across the bed. She feels his fingers curling against and gripping her pillow, and then he is gently wriggling it free from under her. Dyeawan's head flops gently against the flat of the mattress as Matei pulls the pillow to him.

"I'm going to put this over your face and press down hard," he tells her, as though he is also reinforcing the plan for himself. "You'll go to sleep. That's all. It will be like you're drifting off to sleep, and you'll just stay asleep after that. It won't hurt. Okay?"

Dyeawan has read enough to know suffocating to death is decidedly *not* like going to sleep, though she is in no condition to argue the point.

She can't help wondering if she deserves this. She murdered Edger, after all. Dyeawan has always thought of the act as "necessary," but it certainly wasn't necessary by way of self-defense. He was no threat to her life, however many others he sentenced to death simply for the abilities they lacked. She doubts Edger ever would have harmed her. Yet she killed him. Her own father.

Dyeawan waits for the pillow to descend over her face, blotting out the light and casting her into darkness.

But Matei hesitates. She hears the wheels of her tender rolling back and forth, as if he is idly pushing and pulling it.

A cough erupts from deep within her throat, and with it she can feel her lips and tongue twitch, just a little. Her breath quickens, her chest rising and falling rapidly, and Dyeawan realizes her mind is beginning to regain control of her breathing.

"I was so proud when I finished this for you," Matei is saying, talking about her tender. "Especially when I saw how happy it made you."

Stop. Touching. My. Tender.

Without even meaning to, Dyeawan swallows. It's the first motion she's been able to execute since the thing in the box stung her.

She tries to scream, but it feels like attempting to push a boulder up a steep hill. Things that feel like they could become words can't quite rise all the way up through her throat.

"What's this lever here?" Matei asks, indicating the one in front of the litter. "I didn't put that there."

New lever.

If it's possible, Dyeawan's eyes suddenly widen even more.

I take it back, her mind screams. *Pull it. Pull that lever. Pull it now!*

Matei sounds as though he has completely forgotten he came here to murder Dyeawan.

"Is it . . . is this a new brake control? It's not connected to—"

Dyeawan hears what definitely sounds like a mechanical lever being pulled.

What follows is a loud *click* followed by a sharp hiss of air.

Across the room, a ceramic water pitcher on Dyeawan's small dressing table shatters, spilling its contents over the table's edge and onto the floor.

Dyeawan begins to blink. She finds she is once again able to shift her gaze. First, her eyes dart to the broken ceramic pitcher. There is a slender steel bolt protruding from the wall directly behind it. Dyeawan thinks she can make out a small dribble of viscous red running down the wall from where the bolt is embedded.

Her eyes dart back to Matei just in time to watch him slip from the edge of the bed down onto his knees.

He attempts to turn towards her, his shoulder slumping against the side of the bed. As he does, Dyeawan spies him clutching his stomach with both hands where the bolt pierced it. The entire front of his tunic is stained with blood, which is beginning to drip audibly onto the floor.

The bolt must have punctured the large portal vein in his midsection.

Matei stares up at her helplessly, his mouth agape. More blood is dribbling over his lower lip.

"What . . . what . . ."

"I . . . made . . ." Dyeawan softly croaks, surprised to have found her voice. "I . . . made . . . some . . . modifications."

In truth, Riko actually made the modifications to her tender, after Dyeawan's last conversation with Nia about their safety. Riko is also the one who honed the bolt's point to an impossibly fine degree. She'd bragged to Dyeawan it would go through three Protectorate Ministry agents if they all stood in a straight line.

It had certainly gone straight through Matei.

The boy who'd been her friend and just attempted to be her murderer finally flops forward onto her bedchamber floor. Blood continues to spread out from beneath his body. His hesitation was his first fatal mistake, but his curiosity was actually what killed him.

Although Riko's engineering skills helped.

Dyeawan still can't move anything below her neck, but she is confident those abilities will return to her. Her mouth feels impossibly dry. She keeps swallowing and licking her lips in an attempt to remedy this.

She's surprised to feel sudden moisture against her cheek and realizes she is crying. Dyeawan isn't sure whether she's weeping for the Matei she thought she knew, or because she finds herself surrounded by blood and death far too often in this place.

In either case, she lets the tears flow.

Sometime later, when her eyes have dried and Dyeawan is beginning to regain control over her fingers, she looks over at Greenfire, slumbering peacefully in his cage. Her little duck slept through the entire ugly scene.

Once more she finds herself envying the creature, and Dyeawan wonders if she will ever know that kind of peace again.

HEART-SHAPED LOCKS

DESPITE SAVING HER LEG FROM A GANGRENOUS FATE, IT IS another two nights before they feed Evie any kind of proper meal. The rice is at least a day old, no doubt left over from whatever they gave the infantry for the previous evening's supper, but Evie quickly devours it in clumps with her fingertips despite the fact it feels like steel pellets in her mouth. The water she washes it down with is so murky she thinks it is tea at first, but it doesn't taste tainted, at least.

If they were going to give her day-old rice, Evie wishes more than anything, more than actual freedom at that moment, they'd given her even a spoonful of oil and a pan in which to fry it. There are few things better than fried rice in the darkest hours of the night, and the best is always made from yesterday's cooked grains.

In her days as a retainer, Evie would often make fried rice in the kitchen of the Gen she served—all before accepting Lexi's mission to infiltrate the Savage Legion and find Brio. The children she guarded would sneak out of bed in the late hours and join her. It was their little secret, something they kept from their parents and other Gen members. The little ones always said her fried rice was the *best*. It still gave Evie a warm comfort.

She hasn't thought much about them since leaving the Capitol, but they float to the top of her mind now. The boy, Yensin, was ten when she left. He wanted more than anything to be a puller when he grew to manhood, one of the great hulks who turned the mighty cranks that operated the Capitol's sky carriages day in and day out. No matter how sternly or how often his parents explained being a puller was hard labor for empty-headed brutes, or that he was far too small and frail to ever become one of them anyway, Yensin would not be swayed. To him, pullers were larger-than-life figures, greater and more powerful than any Skrain soldier or Gen retainer.

The girl, Reese, was two years younger, and all she ever wanted was for Evie to teach her how to fight. Her parents forbade it, but during their late-night snacking sessions, or as they waited for the sky carriage to take the children to school—while her brother obsessively watched the pullers at the station—Evie would show Reese simple maneuvers like palm heel strikes and eye gouges. The girl was fond of shredding the flowing wrap skirts her parents made her wear, and Evie had been morbidly looking forward to the chaos and grief she would cause them when she reached her teenage years.

She wishes she'd appreciated them more when they were in her charge. Evie, known back then as Ashana, always viewed it merely as a job, one for which she'd been fortunate enough to be uniquely suited. Retainers, particularly hulking armored warriors, were steadily falling out of favor with the Crachian bureaucracy and out of fashion among the Gens. But worrisome absentee parents still wanted guardians trained in combat to escort their children around the city, and unassuming women who could pass for nannies became the vogue.

Evie resented it more than a little. She was still so bitter at being put out of Gen Stalbraid, cut off from Brio, who she'd loved. Perhaps that's why she always kept the children at a distance. It is only now that Evie, alone in this brutal world, realizes it was a gift, being able to touch their young lives, to shape them in some small way. It was a gift just to be able to watch them grow and become more themselves every day. It was certainly better than guarding some pompous, corrupt Gen leader.

She does not regret becoming the Sparrow General, but being a glorified bodyguard was a better life than she credited it.

"This is the strangest zoo I've ever heard of."

Evie nearly chokes on her final clump of stale rice, jerking back against the bars in surprise.

The voice, so familiar, somehow came from above. Evie looks up, through the top of her cage, staring at the crook of the metal arm that holds her prison off the end of the caravan's largest wagon.

The stalk of that arm has gained weight.

She has to squint into the dark of night, allowing her vision to adjust before she can fully make out the new shapes that have been added to the cage's mount. There are two figures, draped from head to toe in pitch black, hoods covering everything but the barest slits over their eyes. Short swords, their long handles wrapped in rawhide dyed the same dark color as their garb. They are both clinging to the highest reaches of the metal arm like howler monkeys hanging from the sturdiest branch of the tree.

"Sirach?" Evie whispers, feeling as if she has somehow woken up in a dream.

"Evening, lover. Sorry. *General.*"

Evie can't see Sirach's grin, but she can feel it and hear it in her words.

"How are you here?" she asks.

"Oh, you know," Sirach begins casually, "Chimot and I were out for our usual constitutional, and we both realized we hadn't seen your new place yet. It's nice. A little cramped, but if cozy is your taste, I suppose."

Evie squints tightly against the darkness. She can see the stormy colors of Sirach's eyes. The small bits of flesh visible around them through her hood are stained red.

"You've got blood on you," she says.

"It's not mine."

Evie grins. "It rarely is. I hope you don't expect me to climb up there once you've freed me."

"Oh no. We've prepared a soft landing for you. Look down."

Evie turns and peers through the bars, past the bottom of her cage. A giant covered in black cloth is standing, silent and still, on the ground directly below. They look like a shadow cast by a mountain.

The mountain's shadow waves at her like a child bidding goodbye to their mother on the first day of school.

That can only be Bam.

Evie smiles. It is her first smile in days. She waves back at him gratefully.

Turning away from Bam, she stands and grips the bars, staring up at Sirach and Chimot.

"How are you going to get this cage open?" Evie asks them. "The bars are solid, and you've never seen a lock like this before."

"There is very little we haven't seen, General," Sirach assures her.

She contorts her body to nod at Chimot.

Sirach's lieutenant dangles her body gracefully from the metal crook by her arms. Pressing her legs together, she begins swinging to and fro, building momentum. Once she has turned herself into a slender pendulum, Chimot launches herself at the side of Evie's cage.

Evie tenses noticeably, panicked the resulting clatter will bring the Skrain.

There is no clatter, however. So graceful and expert is Chimot that she lands on the cage and secures hand- and footholds on the bars without so much as causing the cage to sway, let alone creating any noise.

Evie watches as Chimot deftly works her way around the body of the cage to the door. Sirach's lieutenant removes several small metallic picks concealed beneath the right wrist of her black garb. Even the metal instruments have been coated in black powder so as not to draw or reflect any light and blend into the darkness. She begins digging one of the picks into the face of the cage's monstrous padlock.

Evie waits, not the least bit optimistic upon seeing the simple tools the woman is employing.

"I've never seen a lock like this before," Chimot whispers a moment later.

Evie sighs.

"I told you. It takes six different keys just to open the damn thing."

Sirach doesn't risk flinging herself through the air like Chimot. Instead, she shimmies up the rest of the metal arm's length and descends from the top of the cage, climbing down the bars to position herself beside her lieutenant. She actually jostles the iron construction a fair bit more than Chimot did, but Sirach is almost as silent in her movements.

Evie watches as the two confer over the lock. At one point she begins darting her eyes past them, anxiously looking for any stray Skrain that might happen by at the exact wrong moment.

"Who keeps the key around here?" Sirach finally asks Evie.

"Captain Feng Silvar. The Skrain who forced you to fight Mother Manai."

Sirach's eyes darken within the hood.

"Well, that will be a bonus, then."

"He's not here anymore," Chimot tells them.

Sirach's head snaps towards her angrily.

"What? What are you talking about?"

"The infantry. We watched them pull out before dusk."

Sirach begins cursing an entire arcane litany under her breath as the moment of recall hits her.

"Pulled out?" Evie asks. "Where are they going?"

"This caravan is taking you back to the Capitol," Sirach explains bitterly. "The bulk of the Skrain are leaving to mass with the rest of the forces Crache is pulling together to meet the Rok Islanders. We heard the sentries talking about it."

Sirach turns back to Chimot. "The good captain may be gone, but the keys are still here."

"We have no idea who has them now," Chimot hisses.

"Then we'll search every swaggering ass in this camp!" Sirach insists.

Evie thinks she feels her soul leaving her body, she is so deflated in this moment.

"There's no time," she laments. "There's no way to open this cage and there is no time for you to find those keys."

"Listen to me," Sirach says with an almost manic determination. "We will drive this whole damn wagon out of here with your cage attached if that's what it takes."

Evie laces her hands through the bars and rests them gently against Sirach's clenched fists, stroking her white knuckles.

"You know that would be suicide. We would never make it in this lumbering thing. We couldn't clear the camp, let alone drive it all the way back to the Tenth City."

"What are you saying, then? Are you asking me to just leave you here?"

"I'm telling you that you have to. There is no other choice."

"I am *not* leaving you here."

She can see the wetness forming at the bottom of Sirach's eyes.

Evie has never seen the hard-as-nails Sicclunan warrior and assassin like this before.

She leans forward and kisses Sirach's fists, one and then the other. After, Evie reaches through the bars and cups her hood-covered cheeks, holding her lover's tormented eyes with her own.

"You are the finest person I have ever known, despite how hard you work to hide it. But your dying here will *not* help me. Please go back. They need you more right now."

Her words echo the final words of Mother Manai, who sacrificed herself on Sirach's own blade when the Skrain decreed only one of the two would be set free.

The memory has clearly not faded for Sirach, as Evie watches those words sober her.

"Oy!" a drunken voice hollers up at them. "Sparrow General! You want a drink?"

Two Skrain soldiers, both waving jugs of wine in their hands, have wandered between the wagons. The soldiers are so drunk they don't even notice Bam standing there until the one who yelled at Evie bumps right into him.

"What in blazes is this now?" he murmurs, reaching out and feeling Bam's massive form as if he were searching a bale of hay for something.

They all watch from above as Bam reaches out, as easily and undisturbed as one might reach for a pitcher of milk, and breaks the soldier's neck with one quick, terrifyingly powerful jerk.

Before the soldier's fellow can react or raise any alarm, he is stung at the neck by a tiny, feathered nettle. His free hand slaps it as if he is trying to swat an insect. His mouth opens, but nothing issues from it. In the next moment he drops to his knees, keeling over onto his side, motionless.

Evie turns her head to see the end of a blow tube perched against Chimot's lips.

When she looks back down, Bam is already dragging the fresh bodies beneath the prison wagon to conceal them.

"You have to go now," Evie instructs Sirach. "*Now*. There's no more time."

Sirach reaches through the bars and clinches the back of Evie's head by her hair, jamming their lips together desperately.

"This isn't over," she swears to Evie when they've parted. "I will get you out."

"I know you will," Evie says.

Sirach and Chimot begin scaling the bars. As quickly as they appeared, they shimmy back down the crooked metal arm supporting the cage.

"I know you will," Evie repeats to herself, eyes shut tight and forehead resting against the bars, too broken to watch them go.

PART TWO

VICTORY & RUIN

READY TO ROK

TARU HAS SLOWLY COME TO UNDERSTAND THAT THE LOOSE translation of "Karay-Karay," for which there are apparently no literal Crachian words, is "we don't want to kill you, we just want to laugh at you until you wish you were dead."

It quickly became clear that to repair their relationship with the Rok and smooth the way for an alliance between the Islanders and the rebels, Taru was going to be forced to complete a series of trials, or challenges, all of which they would have to conquer in order to be declared victorious. Staz referred to them as "provings," assuring Taru that each event was more of a ceremonial rite every fighting Rok Islander endures before they are allowed to join a ship as part of a real crew.

Taru remained dubious. They assumed the point was for their mettle to be tested as a Rok warrior's would. If Taru is successful, by Rok standards the Islanders would have to accept the retainer as one of their own and they would forgive Taru's transgressions against them.

It is round about the time the Rok strip Taru to their doe-skinned underclothes and begin slathering the retainer in sesame oil that Taru starts to suspect that all they are meant to prove to the Rok is their humility and willingness to take a joke.

It makes a bizarre form of sense, Taru supposes. Contrition and redemption through willing acts of public embarrassment is a tradition that certainly would prevail in a culture shaped largely by salty old bickering aunties.

It began innocuously enough, like a competition Taru thought they could win. The first "proving" would pit the retainer against one of the Rok's chosen in a trident throw, each attempting to achieve a farther distance than the other with their three-pronged mariner's staffs. The trident was one of the Rok's oldest and most favored native weapons, so it only made sense.

The retainer should have known something was amiss when the Rok brought out their competition. The boy, for man he certainly was not, stood less than half as tall as Taru, with arms that looked as thin and fragile as cornstalks in the hottest months of the year. There was any number of fully-grown warriors among the Rok army with muscles that rippled, and who looked like they could throw the boy as far as a trident.

"You've trained on the spear, yes?" Brio had asked the retainer. "This is the same thing, I would expect."

"I was trained to gut a boar, or an opponent if entirely necessary. The Skrain are schooled in javelin and spear throwing. There was never much call for it as a retainer. Someone running away from you is hardly a threat to your personal security, are they?"

"Point taken," Brio said.

Taru and the boy were both given identical tridents and positioned side by side behind a line of rocks arranged upon the ground.

"You have the honors, my friend," Staz informed the retainer. "You go first."

The rest of the captains were gathered around the tiny woman, all of them standing behind Taru, watching expectantly.

It seemed the height of absurdity to Taru. The entire fate of three nations, the lives of a million people, the future of the world as they knew it, all of it resting on the retainer's ability to throw a stick farther than an underdeveloped teenager.

Taru gathered the idea was to "push" the trident rather than hurl it. At least that is what their basic spear training preached. They also gleaned the best results for distance would be garnered by treating it like an arrow and aiming more up rather than straight ahead.

They took a few trial runs at the throwing line, practicing the form they would use to launch the trident. With each simulated throw, Taru could hear and even *feel* the amusement and mocking of the Rok Islanders spectating. The retainer did their best to ignore the cacophony.

When they felt comfortable with the movements, Taru backed away from the line of stones, several feet, and inhaled a deep breath. On their exhale, the retainer strode forward, building to a brief run, and when their feet reached the throwing line they let their trident fly.

Its arc was long and high. Taru is a powerful individual, and that was reflected when the trident fell to the earth at least fifty feet across the Rok encampment.

Brio was quick to applaud the effort.

He was the only one.

Taru did their best to show no emotion, but in truth they were pleased and even proud of the throw, silly as they still found this entire idea.

After Taru's throw, the boy smiled up at the retainer, his teeth filed flat in the Rok style.

The retainer knew that was a bad omen.

He hefted his Rok weapon easily and casually, almost resting it on his shoulder. The boy did not take any practice runs or feign any throws to get his form down. He simply took one easy step towards the line of stones, lifted the haft from his slight shoulder, and released it.

His trident did not fly through the air. His trident absolutely disappeared. One moment the boy was holding it, his noodle of an arm cocked back, and in the next moment the trident was gone. His speed and power were as blinding as they were sudden. Taru could not even track his throw.

The retainer narrowed their eyes into the distance, hawk-like, searching for where their opponent's trident had finally landed. Taru saw their own trident clear enough, still protruding from the ground a respectable few dozen yards ahead.

The boy's trident was nowhere to be seen.

For all Taru knew it still hadn't landed yet.

"I think we can safely assume you have been out-thrown, my friend," Staz remarks. "Although you are free to go look for the other trident, if you like."

The rest of the captains snicker, a few laughing outright.

The rest of the Rok Islanders watching, which pretty much comprises the entire camp, don't hold back. Their laughter is loud and raucous and seems to last forever.

Beside them, the boy pats Taru on the back soothingly.

"You throw good," he offers, still smiling.

Despite everything, or perhaps because of it, Taru can't help but smile back.

"Does this mean Taru has failed?" Brio asked Staz.

"The Karay-Karay has little to do with failing or succeeding," the captain explained. "As I said, it is a proving."

The next event was a race to open one of the burry tree's large-shelled fruits without the use of blade or mallet. Taru's competition this time was not a frail-looking boy, but the oldest Rok Islander woman the retainer had yet seen. She looked like a raisin dried in the sun and wasn't much bigger than one. Her head appeared permanently hunched against her chest. She was forced to look at the world with an upturned gaze.

Taru was even more confused than during the trident throw, but the task itself was clear enough.

For a full minute, Taru based the burry tree fruit against the ground, smashing it against every rock in sight. The retainer tried stomping on its shell, but only succeeded in unbalancing themselves and falling on their ass, much to the delight of the Islander audience.

All the while the ancient woman merely cradled her burry tree fruit, watching the retainer with a small and delicate smile on her face.

Sweating, panting and out of breath, Taru finally found themselves on their knees, staring down at the undisturbed shell of the mottled brown fruit they'd been unable to penetrate.

They looked up at the old woman, who held up a single, withered digit as if bidding Taru to watch her closely.

As the retainer did, the woman began gently tapping the burry tree fruit shell. There didn't seem to be any order or pattern or reason to it. She simply rapped a knuckle against the shell here and there, occasionally lifting it to her ear and shaking it gently.

Finally, the woman lowered the burry tree fruit against her stomach, staring down at it intently. Holding it with one hand, the fingers of her other hand curled and her thumb extended. She pressed the tip of that thumb against a spot near one end of the fruit's shell.

Taru marveled as, with one deft motion, the decrepit old woman easily pressed her thumb through the shell and inside the burry tree fruit.

Once she'd fashioned a hole, the ancient one raised the shell above her head, having to rotate her face against her chest in order to position her lips and tongue to lap at the juices that poured from the shell.

Everyone cheered wildly.

Taru just wanted to lie down on the ground and pass out.

The final proving requires Taru to be oiled down, and they have almost passed the point of even asking why.

"You will have to climb the length of one of our burry nut trees without the aid of rope or spike. The most skilled of our fighters can do this within five snaps of a finger."

"It would seem to me . . . won't all this oil hinder my efforts rather than help them?"

"Yes," Staz answers simply.

Taru only nods. It makes as much sense as anything else thus far, they suppose.

"We don't have trees like yours," Taru points out, recalling the impossibly tall, slender, smooth island trees with their large bladed fan leaves.

"We brought a few trunks with us," Staz says. "They make good battering rams. It won't have the top, but you can pretend."

Taru watches as, indeed, half a dozen Rok Islanders ferry the cut-down trunk of an entire island tree, sans leaves, into the open space of the camp. They raise what must be its thirty-foot length and plant it in a hole they've dug deeper than Taru is tall, packing the soil in around the tree to stabilize it.

"Who am I competing against this time?" Taru asks Staz.

"Only the tree," the *Black Turtle*'s captain says.

Taru never climbed trees as a child, at least not recreationally. They have scaled a few to hang food safely out of the reach of bears, but that's about it.

Taru takes a running start and leaps at the tree, attempting to gain as much height as possible straightaway by jumping up its length rather than climbing. The retainer's legs are powerful, and they do indeed find themselves a good five or six feet off the ground before they even set upon the tree, wrapping their arms and legs around it.

Unfortunately, Taru's oiled body immediately slides right back down the trunk until they are actually sitting on the ground at its base.

The fighters of Rok are, once again, much amused.

Standing back up, Taru examines the tree once again. There are no real handholds to speak of. Only the pressure of their grip will keep them adhered to the trunk. They will have to hug with their legs and use their arms to move them up, and then reverse the procedure, repeating the process until they've slithered up to the top like a slug.

Girding their loins, Taru hops back up onto the trunk, squeezing as hard as they can with their powerful thighs to hold them in place, then reaching up with their arms and hugging the trunk tightly before pulling, inching their body upwards.

It's working, but it is excruciatingly slow and unbelievably punishing on Taru's body. Ten feet feels like a hundred miles, and every time the retainer glances down at the ground below them, they feel their body peel dangerously away from the trunk. The Rok Islanders have now begun chanting in unison, although what they are chanting is anyone's guess. It certainly isn't Taru's name, and they doubt the chant is one of encouragement and support.

Every muscle in Taru's body feels ready to burst from the strain, but the top of the tree is finally within reach. Feeling secure in the hold their legs and single arm have on the greased trunk, they begin extending their free arm towards that pinnacle. The distance proves just a bit farther than Taru anticipates, as their fingertips can't quite extend past where the top of the trunk has been severed clean.

Remembering not to look down this time, Taru begins readjusting their grip to inch just a sliver more up the length of the tree trunk.

That readjustment proves to be one too many.

As soon as their fingertips slip from the surface of the trunk Taru knows they're done. Their hand follows, and then their entire arm glides right off the tree. At the same time, Taru's thighs give out, relenting just enough for the oiled space between them and the trunk to work its magic, sliding them into a virtual free fall.

Halfway down the length of the tree Taru finally lets go. The air rushes up around the retainer, ringing in their ears a moment before the cold, hard ground embraces them, that "embrace" being far more of a full-body punch that makes them feel as though their spine is going to burst forth through their chest and stomach. Their vision goes completely black, and the oxygen that rushes out of their mouth and nose is in no hurry to refill their lungs.

When the world comes back into focus, Taru finds they are staring up at the faces of several Rok sea captains, most of them red from laughter.

Staz is no exception.

"I am fine," Taru assures them in a voice that sounds like it has been squeezed between the jaws of a vice. "I just need . . . a moment. I can . . . make it."

"We have decided that was close enough, my friend," Staz informs them, reaching down to none-too-gently pinch Taru's cheek.

"Close enough?" Taru asks, taken aback, even in their current state.

"Yes. Our soups are ready, and it is time to eat. Besides, we have run out of ideas."

It takes a moment for this last word to truly resonate for Taru.

"Ideas?" they repeat. "What do you . . . mean, you are out of . . . ideas?"

The Rok captains begin giggling anew.

"This is . . . not a real thing, is it? This 'Karay-Karay'? You . . . made it all up simply to . . . toy with me."

Staz shrugs. "Karay-Karay merely means the evening's entertainment. Island nights are long. We get bored."

With effort, which feels in this moment as if it exceeds anything they have thus far been required to do in their entire life, Taru props their body up on their elbows—they might be casually reclined to an unknowing observer. The retainer continues to stare up at the deeply lined faces above them.

With a heavy sigh that causes them great physical pain, Taru asks, "Does this *at least* mean that—"

"Yes, yes," Staz interrupts, waving her childlike hand impatiently. "We will all fight the ants together. Us, you, Little Brio, and all your rebel friends. Now, come eat. You look thin."

ACCUSATIONS

IT STILL FEELS AS THOUGH SHE HAS COME BACK FROM THE dead. Dyeawan has fully recovered from the paralytic venom Matei's puzzle box creature injected into her body, but regaining the use of most of her muscles and limbs hasn't extinguished the feeling she has grappled with since that night, the gnawing suspicion she left some piece of herself behind in her bedchamber with Matei's blood-brained corpse. She simply feels *different*. Dyeawan cannot articulate what that difference is, but some ineffable thing she had before is no longer present.

The story has spread through the whole of the keep. There was no hiding what happened, and Dyeawan, along with Nia and Riko, decided that was the wrong thing to do. Mister Quan found her the next morning, only barely able to finally sit up of her own accord. She'd spent all night struggling with Matei's body next to her bed.

Her sister and best friend were horrified when she told them the story, but in typical fashion, Riko couldn't help but ask, "But my bolt launcher worked, though?"

Indeed, it had saved Dyeawan's life, as she'd designed it to do. They simply couldn't have foreseen the circumstance.

The whole of the planners are convened around the table Dyeawan quite literally built herself. As has become the custom, the younger members of the group, the "next generation," as they are often and pejoratively referred to by the others, fills one side of the table. The "old guard," as Edger thought of them, the senior planners, stodgy and ancient and set in their ways, none of which leave room for new or bold innovation, occupies the other side.

Though it pains her physically and emotionally, Dyeawan tells the whole tale again, this time for the rest of the planners to hear. She tells them exactly what Matei did, what he admitted to doing, and, most importantly, she repeats everything he said to her about the Protectorate Ministry's involvement.

When she is finished, expected silence follows. The young men and women to Dyeawan's left and right universally look disturbed and outraged. There are eyes on her filled with sympathy, and not only belonging to Nia and Riko. On the other side of the table, however, the expressions of the faces staring back at Dyeawan could more accurately be categorized as annoyed, or perhaps deeply inconvenienced.

Trowel, the most vocal of the old guard, is predictably the first to speak.

"What was done to you . . . what could have been done to you still . . . is a terrible thing," he admits. "A terrible act committed by a disturbed young man. It is clear he was so disturbed, in fact, that I do not see how we can trust a word he said."

Dyeawan's side of the table becomes a choir of irate voices expressing their disapproval.

She is quick to raise her hands to gently gesture for quiet.

"While I for one in no way doubt your recounting of these events, or what Matei said," Trowel offers, quite diplomatically, "I plainly do not see how we can base such a serious accusation solely on the word of a delusional boy. He was clearly obsessed with you, and that obsession drove him to madness. How can we possibly know if what he told you was true or a fantasy of his own creation?"

"Matei would never have attempted something this bold without support!" Nia insists. "He knew this was an assassination. He wasn't delusional enough to think he could get away with this without the backing of the Ministry."

"Again, we cannot possibly know the truth of that. All we have is his word."

Dyeawan is not surprised, but it still feels like a betrayal, even after everything they've done to undermine her.

"You are right," she admits. "All we have are his words."

"If you are not even slightly interested in listening to reason," Nia all but fumes at the old man, "then *why* are we even convened here?"

"We *have* listened," Trowel protests. "But you are correct in presuming this is not the only matter to be discussed today."

Nia looks to Dyeawan, as if to ask if she knows what the frustrating old man means, but Dyeawan only shakes her head.

"We wish to speak reason of our own," he explains. "To you, Nia, specifically, who Edger groomed so long as his protégé and true successor."

Nia blinks in surprise, clearly caught off guard by the statement.

Before any of them can question Trowel further, the clacking of many boots precedes three Protectorate Ministry agents. All of them are draped in the black tunic and cape of the order, the eyes plucked from eagles that adorn their pendants gleaming in the light as if they are still alive and perceiving everything around them. They enter the meeting space of the planners grandly, almost preening, it seems, at least to Dyeawan.

She has never seen the agent in front before, but the woman certainly stands out, even in the intentionally nondescript garb of the Ministry. Her skin contains no pigment, and her eyes are tinted with just enough translucent blue to stand against the white.

"My name is Strinnix," the ghostly agent informs them all, but her eyes are focused on Dyeawan. "I would like to offer the Protectorate Ministry's respect and gratitude to this body for your tireless service to and wise guidance of Crache."

"I smell an ambush," Riko whispers to Dyeawan, and rather than her usual jovial self, the girl sounds genuinely alarmed.

"Thank you, Agent Strinnix," Trowel replies. "The Protectorate Ministry remains an integral element of that process."

"Why have you finally decided to join us?" Nia asks the agent impatiently, ignoring Trowel's reproachful gaze.

"You convened this venerable enclave to speak of murder and of truth, yes?"

"Yes," Nia answers.

"Then I have come to the right place, for I have truth to share about two murders."

Something sinks within Dyeawan, and she grips the arms of her tender all the more tightly, hoping that is the end of her visible reaction to the agent's words.

"What murders are you talking about?" Nia demands.

Strinnix extends a slender, gloved finger and points directly at Dyeawan.

"This girl . . . she callously murdered Edger in order to take his seat. My colleague Oisin, your longtime liaison to the Protectorate Ministry, knew this. And so she killed him, too."

Dyeawan hears the clamor she would expect from the planners on her side of the table. Shock, disbelief, resentment, and counter accusations. What interests her more in that moment is the complete lack of reaction from the old guard across the table.

They all clearly knew this was coming, and none seem more pleased about it than Trowel.

Dyeawan looks to Nia, finding Nia's jaw clenched tight, a stony expression on her face.

Dyeawan isn't certain what her sister is feeling.

"The Protectorate Ministry deals in misinformation and outright lies," Nia reminds them all.

To Strinnix, she says, "*We* taught you how. Edger taught you how. You cannot possibly expect us to believe you based on your word alone, when your motivations may very well be to destabilize the planners."

In response, Strinnix digs beneath her half cape and produces an object in one black leather–gloved hand.

It is a hollow needle, bellows attached.

The sinking within Dyeawan continues.

"This was found near Edger's body, in the shallow rocks of the God Rung. It contains blood. It is the blood of a wind dragon. You all remember Ku, Edger's most treasured companion and the creature who allowed him to speak where his . . . condition . . . did not. It was assumed upon the discovery of Edger's body that Ku entered the wind dragon's mating cycle early and in the fervor of heat that Ku ripped out Edger's throat. I submit to you that the creature's frenzy was triggered by an injection, and that bellows was the instrument."

Dyeawan attempts to appear as calm as possible on the surface. But inwardly, her heart is pounding and her mind is racing. Ordinarily, her memory is an exact portrait of every sight she has ever seen, every moment she has ever experienced, practically from the time she was born.

In *this* moment, however, she cannot for the life of her actually recall tossing that bellows into the sea. She remembers that was her intention, but Dyeawan cannot summon the memory of actually doing it.

"You never denied being the last one to see Edger alive."

It is not a question, but Dyeawan shakes her head anyway.

"I was with him at the end," she confirms.

Nia's gaze is boring into her, intense and demanding in its expectation.

"How do you know it's wind dragon's blood?" Riko fires back at the agent.

Strinnix shrugs, unconcerned by the question. "The color, the smell. Your own experts here at the keep are welcome to examine it for themselves."

"That doesn't mean—"

"Riko, stop," Dyeawan interrupts her.

Everyone falls silent, and Dyeawan can feel all eyes on her.

She closes her own for a moment and allows herself a deep, cleansing breath.

"Edger took me out to the God Rung," Dyeawan begins. "He gave me lenses so I could see clearly under the water. I suspect several of you, if not all of you, know what I saw. Edger had what he would call a 'weakness' for people he considered to be . . . like him. Afflicted. Less able than others. 'Defective,' by Crache's standards. That's why he took me into the Planning Cadre. But he felt he could only 'keep' a few of us. The rest—anyone culled from the cities who all of you determined could not contribute enough to our society—they ended up at the bottom of the bay. Edger oversaw the deaths of *thousands*. He took me out there that day to try to teach me that it was necessary. It only convinced me of what I'd suspected for a long time: that Edger was a monster. I could not abide that. I could not abide him. And I could not abide what he had done, what he would continue to do. So I killed him."

At some point during Dyeawan's confession, Nia stopped boring a hole into her with her gaze. Dyeawan's sister is now staring into the middle distance, locked inside her own thoughts.

The rest of the younger planners say nothing. Dyeawan scans their faces quickly, expecting to see expressions of anger or betrayal. Most of them simply look confused, however.

This revelation about Edger's ongoing program to liquidate Crache's disabled citizens is not something any of them can skip past. It must be sitting as heavy as Dyeawan's admission.

"And Oisin?" Strinnix presses her.

"Oisin was trying to kill *me*," Dyeawan says, her eyes narrowed at the agent. "I was defending myself."

"And me," Nia adds, though her voice sounds very empty.

"Indeed," Strinnix says, her tone one of unmasked disbelief.

"You keep your own counsel, as you always have," Strinnix tells them. "It is not the Protectorate Ministry's place or intention to decide how to proceed. But in light of this confession, I do not see that you have much recourse. We will leave you to deliberate."

Sweeping her half cape aside, the black-clad agent turns and leads her two silent cronies from the chambers.

Trowel waits until they are gone to speak.

"As I see it, we must vote, as one body, to expel Dyeawan from the planners. If she is so expelled, she must then be judged as any other murderer caught by Crachian authorities."

"Agreed," the fossil to his right seconds.

Before his death, Edger revealed he'd elevated Dyeawan to the planners in part to give him a majority vote against the old guard. Dyeawan in turn elevating Riko to the planners has maintained that majority, assuming the younger planners still vote with her.

Trowel can't possibly be counting on swaying the next generation that despises him and his ilk. He and the Protectorate Ministry know Nia is their only hope of breaking that majority control in this instance.

Nia is still staring straight ahead, refusing to even look at Dyeawan.

"I'm not going to ask you for forgiveness," Dyeawan whispers for her ear alone. "Not now, not ever. I did not do this to harm you. You know who our father was, the good and the bad. All I will say to you now is that they are not doing this to give you some sort of justice, or even revenge. They are using this to divide us, to finish what Matei began. They are trying to use you."

Nia finally turns her head to meet Dyeawan's eyes. Her own have reddened around the edges; she is clearly holding back tears.

"And you're not?" Nia asks.

"No," Dyeawan says firmly. "I am not."

"I formally call for a vote of no confidence in Planner Dyeawan," Trowel announces to the table. "I, for one, believe she must be removed from our ranks immediately and I vote thusly. All in favor of such action, indicate with a show of hands."

He raises his own, as if the planners require a demonstration.

His side of the table quickly mimics the gesture, all of them voting to remove her.

"I vote 'no'!" Riko proclaims, leaning forward and practically spitting the word at Trowel.

Dyeawan looks at her friend, almost in disbelief.

"Edger was an asshole," Riko says. "You all *heard* what he did. What he wanted Dyeawan to become. And you all have the gall to call *her* a murderer?"

There isn't enough gratitude in Dyeawan's heart for Riko, though she has no way to express it here among the others.

One by one, the younger planners begin shaking their heads. Not a single one of them raises their hand.

It all falls to Nia.

Dyeawan finds she does not want to look at her sister in that moment.

They all wait. For an agonizing amount of time, which has seemed to slow down immensely, Nia neither speaks nor moves. She continues to stare pensively at nothing.

I've lost her, Dyeawan thinks frantically. *I've lost my sister as quickly as I found her.*

Finally, heaving a deep and troubled sigh, Nia shakes her head no.

"Very well, then," Trowel manages, though it is clear his frustration and rage are barely contained. "The motion to remove Dyeawan from the planners does not pass."

With that, the old man stands from his chair and practically storms out of the meeting chambers.

The rest of the old guard follow suit.

No one says anything. There is no celebrating among the planners who remain. They all look to Dyeawan, all but Nia. They seem to be waiting for some cue or instruction from the leader they have supported.

"There is nothing I can add that will make what you've heard here today easier to take," she tells them. "You chose me over them, and I promise you, it was the right choice. But I want you all to sit with what you've heard. You need to decide if I am still the one among us you want to lead, or if Nia should take over alone."

Most of them seem to let that sink in before they react, and when they do it is to silently relinquish their seats and walk off in their own direction, until only Dyeawan, Riko, and Nia remain.

"Thank you," Dyeawan says to Riko.

"I wish you'd told me yourself, yeah?" Riko says, not quite frowning, but with a troubled, crinkled brow. "I get why you didn't, and you've dealt with enough today, so I won't give you any more grief. But I do wish you'd told me."

"I understand. It is the only secret I've ever kept from you, and it is the last. I promise."

Riko smiles weakly.

"I believe you," she says.

Looking over at Nia, it seems to dawn on Riko the sisters have their own issues to discuss.

Rising from her seat, she leans over and briefly hugs Dyeawan around the shoulders.

Dyeawan is truly grateful for the gesture, taking a surprising amount of comfort from it.

When she and Nia are alone together, Dyeawan isn't sure what to say.

Nia solves that problem for her.

"Riko was right," she says. "Edger was a monster. But I knew that already. It was just . . . ugly to hear it spoken aloud like that."

"I worry I am no better than him," Dyeawan admits.

Nia looks up at her with an intense expression.

"You are better than him," she says. "I am just not certain how much better."

Dyeawan nods, accepting this without rancor.

"I suppose we will find out," she says. "Since I'm not going anywhere just yet."

"Neither is the Protectorate Ministry," Nia reminds her darkly.

EVERYONE LOVES A PARADE

IT CERTAINLY IS NOT THE WAY EVIE IMAGINED MAKING HER return to the Capitol.

Has it been one year now? two? since Evie thought of herself as Ashana, the name she identified with during the whole of her life in the Capitol. Her fellow retainer, Taru, summoned her back to the Xia Towers of Gen Stalbraid, where Evie had spent her childhood before being cast out over her budding romance with Brio, on whose shoulders the Gen's future rested. Evie sat with Lexi in the very same room in which she had played with Lexi and Brio as children. Lexi told her Brio had been conscripted into the Savage Legion, and she needed Lexi's help to find him. It was dangerous, perhaps even futile, but Lexi was asking Evie because she knew Evie was the only woman who loved Brio as much as she did.

Upon accepting the mission, Evie imagined that when she returned to the Capitol, certainly no more than a few months from the day she left, it would be after successfully completing her assignment. She would ride back in on a stolen horse, a safe and liberated Brio's hands secure on her hips. She would present him triumphantly to his Gen, asking no reward. It would be enough to prove to them the little girl they cast out was good enough, perhaps even better than they were.

There may have even been a wild fantasy or two about how Brio would lovingly and politely deny Lexi in favor of a romantic reunion with Evie.

That last part seems the most absurd now, though all of it has become so patently ridiculous to her. Evie can scarcely remember being the woman who was that sickeningly in love with the idea of her childhood sweetheart, and who harbored those broken feelings of abandonment and inadequacy that needed to be satiated.

They have placed her cage in the bed of a much slimmer wagon, one designed to navigate the narrow streets and alleys of the Capitol. A single stallion pulls it, while one Skrain soldier holds its reins and another rides guard, spear resting between their knees as they sip liberally from a wine jug. The Skrain have exercised the good sense to position the backs of their heads out of reach of Evie in her cage, regardless of how hard she strains her arms through the bars.

And she's tried. Several times. Mostly out of boredom.

It is not much a procession otherwise. There are a few soldiers astride mounts behind the wagon, and one out front bearing the standard of the Crachian ant. Perhaps a dozen Aegins are accompanying them on foot, six flanking each side of the paltry collection of pomp. That's it. The rest of the caravan they arrived with is camped outside the city, where Evie saw the Capitol's reserve troops gathering, no doubt to go join the war effort against the nation's new threat, the Rok Islanders.

Crache is not given to grand celebrations, particularly spectacles centering on the military. They train and outfit the Skrain to be enforcers of the system, not to be celebrated by the people—quite the opposite, in fact. Crache has always seen a great danger in mythologizing even its own soldiers. The nation wants no heroes, state-sanctioned or otherwise. They want no faces, period. That would give those individuals power, and a group of such individuals far too much power. Crache wants its citizens to mythologize only the machine that runs their society, and their place as cogs within it.

When they first ride through the city gates, no one really takes notice. It is a while before anyone recognizes her, in fact. None of them has ever laid eyes on her, of course, but her armor, the red sparrow splattered on her chest, tells the story clearly enough. Even after they notice her, however, there isn't a single raised voice that Evie hears. Her presence in the Capitol of the nation she swore to bring to its knees is met with almost total silence.

Evie isn't sure *what* she expected, exactly, but she definitely envisioned more booing. At the very least she imagined they would throw rotten fruit and vegetables and perhaps the odd pile of horse droppings at her.

They do gather as the procession makes its slow trek through the heart of the city. The people line the streets, and those lines begin extending farther and farther ahead of them as they go. She watches them whisper to one another, but the chorus of shrieking denouncement never comes. Not a single angrily tossed object flies her way. They all simply stare at her like an ape in a traveling menagerie, and not even a particularly fascinating ape in many cases.

Reading their expressions is more difficult than she thought it would be, as well. There are, of course, those of pure Crache-

ingrained disapproval and disgust at the sight of a figure whom they have been conditioned to believe is a traitor to their vast and perfect paradise of a nation. There are plenty of those.

What surprises Evie is how many of them stare up at her cage with looks of sadness and disappointment, and not at her, she thinks. There is something sympathetic in many of the faces. And these are not the desperate and starving people of the Bottoms. These are shop owners and Gen attendants and even Gen members themselves. Many of those in whom she feels and sees the most sympathy are the young, Crache's rising generation who will inherit the nation.

She should speak to them, she thinks. She should speak to anyone who will listen. This is the last platform she will have, after all. Surely past this, death awaits her.

They haven't gagged her. Perhaps they want her to be able to shout at the onlookers. Perhaps they think she will create a backlash of fervor herself.

Evie doesn't know what to do, what to say. She looks up through the top of her cage, watching a sky carriage filled with the afternoon trade being pulled by colossal chain links towards the Spectrum. She wonders idly if the people aboard the carriage can see her out of its windows, or if the view is too narrow.

The wagon shimmies to an abrupt halt, drawing her attention away from the world that exists in the tops of the Capitol buildings.

Evie stares out from her cage at the slender passage ahead of the procession.

Their way is being blocked, not by an unexpected obstruction like cross-traffic or another wagon with a broken wheel, but by several columns of robed and hooded figures clustered stoically in the middle of the street.

There must be several dozen of them at least, standing in four straight lines with military uniformity and poise. The robes they wear aren't any manner of uniform, though; they are all ragged and torn patchwork affairs without a matching stitch among them. *These* are the people of the Bottoms who are usually absent from the rest of the city. While they would appear as fixtures of the downtrodden and poorly kept streets beside the docks, they look entirely, even disturbingly out of place in these clean paved roads without a single crack in them, among these gleaming, freshly painted buildings and all the well-appointed, well-fed people lining the sidewalks.

Evie watches as the Skrain and their escorts from the city peacekeepers slowly come back to life. The guard in the buckboard in front of her lethargically removes the spear from between his knees, shifting the butt end of its haft against his armored hip. Alongside the military processional, many of the Aegins' hands move to the hilt of the daggers sheathed in baldrics across their torsos.

One of the bizarre street druids stands apart from the columns, Evie notices, out in front between the rest of the battalion in tatters and the sorry procession of Skrain and Aegins.

As Evie looks on, a rough, scarred hand appears from the depths of the man's sleeve. It slowly peels back the hood of his frayed robe. Beneath, he is a surprisingly young man with a gaunt face that is scarred worse than his hand. Each cheek is marked by a bizarre blossom of waxy flesh, as if something once burst forth from inside his mouth. His hair is stringy and dark, covering most of his forehead. His deep-set eyes are calm and passive as they stare up at the Skrain.

There isn't a drop of fear in him that Evie can detect.

She hears the clatter of shod hooves as the soldiers on horseback riding behind her trot forth around each side of the wagon, urging their mounts forward to position themselves between Evie and the filthy horde barring their path.

To make matters worse for her captors, the halting of the procession and the gathering of street people is attracting even more attention from the citizenry than the sight of Evie in her birdcage. They are pouring in from every corner, filling the previously empty space on the sidewalk and around the wagon.

"Oy! You people go on about your business!" one of the Skrain on horseback shouts at the everyday spectators beginning to congregate throughout the scene.

Some listen, but most do not.

Finally, the ranking Skrain soldier addresses the columns of ragged druids still occupying the middle of the street like macabre sentinels.

"You lot need to disperse immediately!" he instructs them. "I'll give you just a few ticks to break this up and get back to the Bottoms, or I swear we'll ride you down just where you stand! You hear?"

Those tattered robes might be stuffed with hay and feathers rather than bodies, such is their complete lack of response and absence of movement.

The Skrain officer urges his mount forward by its reins, his other hand drawing his sword from its ant-adorned scabbard. His horse clops up to the one with the petal blossom scars on his cheeks, and the Skrain turns the mount so its flank is facing the young man.

"If you're the appointed leader of this rabble," the officer addresses him, jabbing the point of his short sword harmlessly against the breast of his robes, "you'd best speak reason to them now. Encourage these people to disperse and crawl back into whatever slop hole it is keeps you warm at night. You hear me, boy?"

The shadowy hollows of those eyes peer up at the Skrain officer fearlessly, but the man does not answer.

The officer digs the tip of his blade into the uncovered one's chest, piercing his robes.

Evie thinks she sees the kid wince, but if he does it is scarcely a phantom of an expression.

"I understand," he tells the Skrain officer, and it is clear he is intentionally speaking loud enough to be heard by as many people watching as possible.

With the sword's tip still dug into his chest, the boy with the petal blossom scars reaches up and grasps the middle of the soldier's blade with his bare hand. He does not simply hold it; even from inside her cage, Evie can see blood flow freely over his knuckles and the back of his hand down his wrist as he clenches his grip against the sword's sharpened edge.

The Skrain officer is so taken by surprise he actually attempts to pull the weapon back, but he is unable to wrest it from the young man's grasp, or even move it. The boy appears impossibly strong for his slight frame.

A sudden look of fury and fiery hate overtakes the young leader's scarred face.

"Long live the Ragged Matron!" he screams into the ether of the cityscape.

Behind him, dozens of equally enraged voices shriek the mantra in unison.

"Long live the Ragged Matron!"

Once their rallying cry has been issued, every column of robed figures breaks their stoic stillness and sprints forward, rushing at a full run around their apparent leader and the Skrain officer whose sword he is still holding captive. They charge the rest of the soldiers on horseback as one wave of soiled patchwork cloth, crude weapons and bludgeons appearing in their hands from beneath their cavernous sleeves.

Through the sea of bodies, Evie can see their speaker pull the Skrain officer from his saddle by his sword, no heed given to its blade still slicing into his flesh. The officer disappears from her sight, and Evie can only imagine the fate he is meeting on the street below.

Meanwhile, the Skrain soldiers still astride their horses are hacking and slashing at the robed men and women swarming them like angry insects. Their Aegin escorts are attempting to join the fray, but the street all around the wagon is now a teeming mass of bodies pressed against one another, with citizens not involved in the fighting mixed among the robed rioters, dagger-wielding Aegins, and frantic Skrain.

More mounted soldiers are pulled from their saddles by angry hands, and in the next moment, Evie watches several of the robed figures climbing up onto the wagon's buckboard. They immediately pull the driver from his seat and toss him to the sea of bodies.

Evie's guard manages to skewer one of the grubby attackers clean through their midsection with his spear, the robed figure's arms raised and poised to strike with a makeshift club in their hand.

Unfortunately, the soldier can't free his spear before he is seized from behind, robed arms encircling his body and neck and pulling him, screaming, from the buckboard.

Evie spies several more empty Skrain saddles than there were a moment ago as well. The crowd, all of them now embroiled in a full-scale riot, have overtaken their former occupants. Every inch of this street that was silent as death only moments ago is now chaos and violence. The street druids are battling Aegins, Skrain, and the boldest members of the citizenry. Other citizens appear, miraculously, to be attempting to restrain or even fight the authorities on behalf of the contingent from the Bottoms. There is no way to distinguish which citizens are on which side, except by whom they are attacking at that moment.

It is madness. Evie can scarcely believe it.

She peers through the bars, down past the right side of the wagon. If all that weren't enough, a large ox has appeared in the crowd, seemingly from nowhere. It must have come from an unseen side alley, or perhaps even out of one of the buildings, Evie thinks. In either case, it is being ridden and steered by another one of the robed rioters, who guides the beast through the thick of the crowd towards the back of the wagon. She notices a thick coil of chain is wrapped around the rider's body.

She is still puzzling over the sight, somehow even more surreal than everything she has already witnessed, when Evie hears a loud, angry, wet snarling behind her and turns around to see a matching ox with another hooded rioter on the other side. Again, the rider has a length of heavy chain wrapped around them.

Seconds after the beasts have both disappeared into the crowd behind the wagon, two of the rioters bound over the back of the flatbed where Evie's cage rests. Each of them is holding a hook larger than Evie's two fists put together, and attached to the end of both hooks is the same thick chain worn by the ox riders, their lengths extending back out over the edge of the flatbed.

Without a word or revealing their faces, the street druids quickly attach their hooks to opposing corners of her ornate prison.

"What are you—" she begins to shout.

A violent crash accompanied by an ear-splitting clatter shakes her cage. Evie shrinks to her knees instinctively, turning to see the leader of the riot, the gaunt boy with the petal blossom scars on his cheek, clinging to the front of her cage with hands and feet. Blood that surely is not his is splashed across his forehead. Blood that most assuredly is his still streams from his slashed-open hand.

His hard face stares at her through the bars almost curiously, his head slightly cocked to one side.

"Hold on," he instructs her.

Hold on.

What is about to happen strikes Evie's brain like a fist.

"Oh shit," she whispers to herself.

Evie grips the bars in front of her tightly, pressing closer to the strange young man without a thought for her safety or the violent acts she has already witnessed him commit.

She looks back over her shoulder just in time to watch the chains attached to those hooks pull taut, as the unseen oxen are no doubt whipped into an angry charge. Evie turns her head back towards the bars and presses her chin into her chest, closing her eyes and white-knuckling her grip. The next sensation she feels is the gut-flipping light-headedness of her world being literally turned upside down as the cage forcefully topples over onto one side and is pulled from the back of the wagon in one continuous, chaotic motion.

Evie feels and hears the bars below her back colliding with the street. The sound of sparks being thrown grates her ears as the entire prison is dragged across the paved stone. She hopes with everything in her that no bodies were crushed beneath it when it tumbled from the edge of the flatbed, although many were certainly bowled over at the very least.

Eventually the cage stops moving, and Evie opens her eyes to see the rioters' leader still there, staring back at her from only an inch away.

"Let go and move away from the door," he instructs her in the same monotonous tone as before.

Nodding, her mind beginning to catch up to what is clearly happening, Evie releases her deathly grip on the bars and scurries up the overturned cage. Frantic legs continue to race around every side of her prison, and the screams and cries of the crowd are deafening from where she crawls.

Evie watches from the other end of the cage as what she has accepted as her rescuer removes a bulging leather pouch from beneath his robes. Untying it, the scarred one begins pouring what looks and sounds like impossibly tiny black pebbles into each of the keyholes in the large face of the padlock securing the door. When he's done, he tosses the pouch away and stands up on the bars, whistling sharply and holding out his hand.

From seemingly out of nowhere, a slender torch lands in his palm. The fire at the end is scarcely larger than a candle flame.

Evie is entranced. As she looks on, he drops the lit end of the skinny torch over the lock, leaping from atop the cage as he does.

Whatever she is expecting, the lock exploding in flame in the next moment defies all of it. Evie reflexively curls into a ball as the sound of combusting metal assaults her ears.

When she looks back, the lock has been reduced to several smoldering individual pieces.

Before she knows what's happening, the heavy door of the cage is pushed open by several robed arms, which then reach inside to pull her forth.

Once Evie is finally free of the cage, a cloak stitched together from the same tattered patchwork as the robes of her rescuers is flung over her head and body. She quickly finds it also smells like the rags they wear. She feels half a dozen people press around her, and then there is the leader, her liberator, taking her hand and leading her forward. The group of them moves with her, concealing her from view as they guide her from the crowded, riotous street and down the nearest side alley.

As they whisk her away, Evie does her best to plug her nose against their collective stench as one thought races through her mind over and over again.

Who the *fuck* is the Ragged Matron?

EVERY OLD PLAN IS NEW AGAIN

BRIO HAS REPEATEDLY ASSURED TARU THAT THE REBELLION was built on strange and hostile alliances. Sicclunans and former Savage Legionnaires, once the mortal bane of each other's existence, have fought alongside one another and even become friends and lovers. Members of B'ors tribes who consider every citizen of Crache a party of their centuries of oppression and subjugation were a key factor in the rebellion's largest victories. They have enlisted defectors from the Skrain and refugees from the largest cities in the nation, all of whom have been able to work together to bring the ant closer to toppling than any force in its history.

Taru, for their part, has in turn repeatedly reminded Brio that he has never lived among the Rok Islanders.

Staz and the other captains refused to meet within the walls of the Tenth City, which did not surprise Brio or Taru. The retainer even suspects it has less to do with not trusting the rebellion and more to do with a strange sense of being pent up, which on its face should not apply to a people who are isolated on an island their entire lives. But the Rok Islanders seem to view the ocean as an endless extension of the small patch of land upon which their ancestors settled. Being so far from the water seems to disturb them on its own, let alone being enclosed behind the walls of a landlocked city.

It wouldn't have been such a sticking point if the Sicclunans had not further refused to meet in the Rok Islander's encampment. That was entirely an issue of trust, and the Sicclunans said as much outright.

After much ferrying of messages back and forth, a task that fell solely to Taru, the mere sight of whom now causes every Rok Islander to laugh uproariously, the Rok and the rebels mutually agreed upon a spot between the gates of the Tenth City and the Islanders' temporary base camp. Kellan and the blacksmith's people scavenged a large serving tent from the city's abandoned Gen market, which the revolting people had long-since picked clean.

Brio, thinking like a Capitol pleader, put forth that they should transport a meeting table out there as well. Taru quickly threw cool water on the idea, explaining that the Rok weren't a formal folk when it came to congregating to make big plans. In truth, Taru was simply tired of riding back and forth and was in no mood to salvage and mule a giant table out into the wilderness.

Still, they dressed the space warmly and comfortably, with rugs and chairs from the city's abandoned administration building, as well as digging a large firepit for cooking and warmth. Talma supplied a small larder of freshly butchered meat from her shop. The Sicclunans, still the most resistant to the whole proceeding, even supplied a Sparrow General flag, a large black standard painted with the bloodred bird. It gave the space a more ceremonial feel, Taru thought.

The retainer is relieved Sirach, her lieutenant, and the gargantuan ex-Savage, Bam, have returned alive from their mission, though disappointed by its failure. She may be rash, sarcastic, and temperamental, but Sirach is also by all accounts one of the rebellion's best and most respected warriors, as well as one of its most capable strategists. Without her, the Sicclunan forces would surely retreat back across the border, abandoning direct, open action against Crache in favor of the defensive posture and guerrilla tactics that have helped them survive extinction for so long.

Taru does, however, regret that it couldn't have taken a day or two longer for Sirach to reach them, so that the summit between the rebellion and the Rok would have already been concluded.

As such, the retainer is concerned that the coming together of the two armies may end with Sirach jamming a knife through one of the Islanders' ribs. She's still obviously in pain from failing to rescue Evie, and Taru is half convinced she only agreed so readily to Brio and the retainer petitioning the Rok in the first place because Sirach was eager to launch her doomed mission and wanted the talking among the rebels to end.

Taru spent the night before at the meeting site to make sure everything remained as they set it up and no animals or wandering passersby got inside the tent. It was the first night they'd spent alone without duties in as long as they could remember. For the past several months, they'd been sleeping among Savage Legionnaires or Rok Islanders or displaced rebels. Even before that, in service of Lexi, after Te-Gen retired for the evening, Taru would spend most of the night patrolling the Gen Stalbraid towers, a habit they'd developed after the assassination attempt on Lexi in her home.

Rather than enjoying the freedom and solitude, however,

Taru found that evening quite miserable. They didn't like sitting alone with their thoughts. They needed tasks to perform, people to protect.

The simple truth, Taru realizes, is that they are only good in service. That is what they have made of their life, and they prefer it that way.

Sirach joked before Taru rode out from the Tenth City for the final time that the retainer should take someone to keep them warm for the night, that Taru had no shortage of admirers among their new comrades, being as tall and powerfully built as they are. Taru has never had any interest in physical relations, however. The whole process is thoroughly unappealing. They know that is not a common trait among the Undeclared, many of whom are happy to fornicate with whoever strikes their fancy, but Taru has always felt this way.

They derive pleasure and satisfaction from protecting, from serving others they deem worthy. Whether as a retainer or a rebel fighter, it is all they care to know.

The representatives from the rebellion arrive first. Brio, Sirach, Chimot, and Bam all gallop up on horseback, Brio looking no more comfortable or graceful than he ever does astride a mount. Taru is also highly amused by Bam's stead, which has to be twice the size of any other horse in the small cavalry just to carry him without collapsing. The beast's hindquarters alone could feed the Tenth City for a week, the retainer thinks.

"You've prepared everything well," Brio compliments Taru after his retainer helps him dismount and he is secure on his crutch. "We're fortunate to have you, my friend."

Taru bows their head. "I am here for you, as always, De-Gen."

"The pair of you are churning my stomach," Sirach complains.

"Excuse her," Chimot bids them. "I took her wine jug away this morning and she is still pouting."

Bam, gathering their horses to tend to them after the lengthy ride, grunts what sounds like his agreement.

Sirach glares at her lieutenant.

"I am your *commander*, need I remind you?"

"Apparently you do, yes," Chimot answers her, clearly fed up with her comrade's attitude, rank or no.

"We definitely seem ready to save a rebellion to me!" Brio announces brightly.

They all settle into their seats under the tent and, with the morning chill coming on, Taru begins stoking the great fire. Once it's burning, they gather fresh water for everyone from a nearby stream, one of the reasons they chose the site.

The Rok captains arrive an hour later, each of them being pulled to the tent by chariot. Each of the spiked shell baskets is driven by the first mate from their respective ships. They don't seem to have brought along any additional warriors or security, which Taru sees as a good sign, or at least hopes it signifies some semblance for trust on which they can build.

"You're going to locate your cordial side, yes?" Brio asks Sirach nervously, as the captains and their first mates enter the tent.

"Perhaps you'd like me to lick the barnacles from the hulls of their entire fleet while I'm at it," Sirach fires back in answer.

"I meant no offense. I am simply trying to start things off on the right foot."

"I can kill fourteen different ways with my right foot," Sirach informs him.

The brief exchange causes Taru to anxiously eye the many weapons sheathed throughout Sirach's leather-armored body.

"She'll be fine," Chimot reassures them all. "She's just posturing."

"You are truly beginning to grate my final nerve," Sirach warns her.

"I am, or the truth is?"

"Will the two of you *stop*?" Taru finally snaps at the pair.

Thankfully, gratefully, fortunately, the Rok captains and their coterie brought soup.

Several absolutely giant still-steaming pots are borne between the first mates as the Islanders meet them inside the tent. When the aroma from the tops of each tantalizingly molten cauldron hits the nostrils of the rebels, everyone manages to finally shut their mouths. The scent of herbs and freshly cooked meat and spicy broth is heady.

"I believe your people would call this a 'peace offering,'" Staz greets them, motioning for the first mates to place the pots on the ground near the fire. "On Rok, we call it 'after dark.'"

The Islanders have brought bamboo bowls and spoons with them as well. The first mates begin ladling the different soups and passing out hot bowls of broth, first serving their own before dishing out the steamy concoction to the rebels. This seems to visibly pacify the Sicclunans, whose distrust was apparent the moment the soup was brought in.

"This is . . . *outstanding*," Sirach admits, reluctantly yet dreamily.

"This is the greatest soup I have ever tasted. When it is in my mouth, I actually cease to care that you all sat on a hilltop, ready to watch me and my cohorts be massacred without lifting a finger to help."

Staz is thoroughly unruffled by the accusation, merely smiling at the compliment and bowing her head.

"That recipe is mine." She beams.

They all enjoy their soup in relative silence for a time. Even Sirach seems truly pacified.

"We did not expect you to feed us," Taru tells Staz.

"Then you don't remember your time among us very well, my friend."

Taru can't help but smile. "I brought meat to roast in the firepit."

Staz nods. "No worry. It will make a fine second course."

Taru carefully sets their bowl upon the ground between their feet.

"Perhaps we should begin, truly begin, by sharing whatever information our forces have gathered separately about what is coming, what we are to face if and when we press on towards the Capitol."

"We are pressing *on*," Captain Florcha insists, her irritation completely unmasked. "I did not even want to come to this dry wasteland with its depressing stone buildings, but now that we are here, I am *not* leaving until I dance on the bones of the ants in their own house."

"Pardon my choice of words," Brio offers diplomatically. "To that aim, let us share what intelligence we have, so we may best prepare to . . . dance . . . on the bones. As you've said."

Taru finds they have to suppress a burst of laughter rising through their throat.

Captain Staz has no such qualms about chuckling openly at Brio and Florcha.

"Tell us what you know of the ants, then," she says.

He looks to Sirach, gesturing as if he is passing some invisible baton to her.

She only stares back at him blankly.

"As a show of good faith," Brio says, speaking to the Rok captains but looking pointedly at her, "I am sure we have no problem offering what intelligence we have."

The belligerent warrior offers him nothing.

"Sirach? Can you share? The intelligence? With our new friends?"

For long moments the Sicclunan leader continues to say not a word, and Taru thinks they can actually see Brio begin to sweat.

"Of course," Sirach finally offers.

Brio breathes an audible sigh of relief.

"While Chimot, Bam, and I attempted to . . . while we were away, I dispatched the rest of my best scouts to track the movements of the ants, as you call them. The Skrain who broke off from the caravan that you people," she juts her fine, scarred chin at Staz and the other captains, "sent into retreat have fallen back to the Fifth City. That appears to be where their force is massing, which makes sense. It's directly in our path to the Capitol. By all reports, the Fifth City is still completely under Crachian control. Butting up against the largest woodlands in the nation, it's dominated by Gens that control the lumber trade. It's made them unspeakably wealthy and influential, and they owe all that to the bureaucracy."

"The Fifth City is a natural staging point," Taru agrees. "And will be essential to unseating the bureaucracy's control of Crache, for all the reasons you have stated."

"So happy you agree," Sirach dryly remarks.

"That tracks with what our own scouts tell us," Staz says. "There is more, however."

"We still have many friends among the ports of your cities, even now," Florcha informs them. "They tell us the ants have been not only culling every dungeon, they are now clearing their streets of *anyone* not claimed by a Gen or operating a business that serves the Gens."

"Conscripts," Taru says.

Staz nods tightly.

Brio, like the rest of them, is livid. "They are refilling the ranks of the Savage Legion. They're not even trying to hide it anymore."

"Do we have any idea of the numbers this will give them?" Taru asks.

Staz shrugs. "What I know I have told you. My people were unable to get a head count. A lot, would be my best guess."

"But these are untrained, unskilled fighters for the most part, are they not?" Florcha points out impatiently. "What difference can they make?"

"A lot, would be my best guess," Sirach says, darkly echoing the captain of the *Black Turtle*.

"The main force of the Skrain is enough to contend with," Taru points out, speaking directly and soberly to Florcha. "With these swelled-up ranks of Savage Legionnaires, they can create a meat grinder the likes of which you have never witnessed. The Skrain will do exactly what you attempted to do. Sit back and let the chaos consume their foes. You did it because it was a good plan, the easiest path to victory. It is no less a good plan for the Skrain."

"Point taken," Staz relents, shooting a warning look at Florcha as the woman prepares to continue her protest.

Taru looks to Brio. "How can we possibly mitigate a Savage Legion force that size and still hope to contend with the Skrain?"

He does not answer, seeming lost in thought.

"When in doubt, we fight," Staz says. "We take five of theirs for every one of ours."

"And if they have ten for every one of ours?" Sirach asks.

"Then we lose," Staz states flatly. "That is war."

"You do not have to explain war to me. My people have been surviving the Skrain as long as yours."

"But never defeating them," Florcha points out haughtily.

"Your soup is not *that* good, old woman," Sirach warns.

As they bicker on, Taru notices Brio is staring at them oddly. After a moment, the retainer realizes he is examining the fading runes on Taru's face, specifically.

Brio turns to Sirach.

"Ashana . . . Evie . . . the General. She told me a story about how the two of you first met."

One of Sirach's sharp brows rises slightly.

"Yes?"

"She said you infiltrated the Savage Legion's revel the night before a battle and tried to poison their wine supply."

Sirach grins. "I did poison their wine supply. Our good General . . ."

Her voice tightens noticeably as she speaks of Evie, and Sirach is forced to swallow hard before she can continue.

"The General caught me. She . . . convinced me to reconsider my plan."

"You people do like to reminisce, don't you?" Staz observes, watching the exchange quizzically.

Brio turns to her. "It's not reminiscing. It may be a plan. It may, in fact, be our best option."

"You want to poison this new Savage Legion?" Sirach asks, clearly surprised Brio could harbor such a brutal thought, let alone suggest it as a plan. "You want to poison all those innocent people compelled into service?"

Taru is also taken aback by the suggestion.

"Not *lethally*," he clarifies.

Brio points at Taru's face before waving a hand over his own.

"I've been working with Spud-Bar, our best armorer, on a tonic to harmlessly force out the blood coin they shove down every conscript's throat so that these damn runes will fade."

"*Harmlessly?*" Taru asks, eyes wide and offended.

"That is precisely the point," Brio says excitedly. "It is *far* from harmless."

His eyes find Sirach's. Brio grins at her pointedly.

A wide, almost feline smile begins spreading across Sirach's lips.

"You know," she begins, "I could not for the life of me deduce what Evie ever saw in you until this moment."

Brio's own smile falters a bit, but he nods. "Well, that is . . . insulting and gratifying all at once, thank you."

"I am not following," Captain Florcha interjects.

"That's because your brain is as brined as your mother's soup," Staz informs her.

The captain of the *Black Turtle* cocks her small head and regards Brio with something almost like amusement.

"It is a good plan," she concludes. "Now, let's stop talking for a time and eat. We will roast this meat of yours. You all look thin."

PRELUDES

HALFWAY THROUGH AN OTHERWISE UNREMARKABLE breakfast, Dyeawan realizes there is going to be a coup within the Planning Cadre that very day.

Observing people, any and all, is among Dyeawan's favorite pastimes. It always has been, from the time she spent most of her days hiding in the shadows of doorways or among piles of refuse or quite literally inside empty barrels for safety. She has a natural ability to read people, making it virtually impossible to lie successfully to her, but much of that ability has been honed by practice.

Coming to the Planning Cadre has not changed that, and it is an utterly fascinating place to study behavior, she has found. Meals in the dining hall in particular are a silent war of different factions. All of the departments within the Cadre, from the builders to the drafters to the potion makers, keep strictly to their own at meals, the borders between tables clearly delineated by their differently colored tunics. No one ever crosses the makeshift color border, not in the entire time Dyeawan has been in the keep. A group might welcome an unclaimed menial worker, as Riko and Matei did with Dyeawan, but once a tunic is wrapped around your body, your place is chosen.

The planners, the most senior members of the entire Cadre—and the architects and guiding hands and minds of Crache—are quite possibly the worst and pettiest of any group occupying the keep. They are split into even smaller factions, with the younger members having their own table and the senior, largely elderly members occupying a separate table across the dining hall.

Breakfast this morning is a delicious porridge of turtle meat (small water turtles utterly infest the island's bay, making them a common menu item across daily meals), rice, steamed buns, and bananas with a bit of sugar that have been scorched by flame to give them a delicious glaze and delectable molten texture. Makai, the keep's venerable old cook, another so-called damaged stray taken in by Edger because he lost an arm as a child, never disappoints.

Dyeawan sits with Riko. Nia has skipped the meal to oversee a meeting with the builders about repairing the damage done to the Capitol during the riot that resulted in the Sparrow General's escape. The event has caused no end of grief to the planners or whispered gossip within the keep. Dyeawan has found the whole thing deeply troubling and disappointing. She'd hoped to reason with the Sparrow General and find some peaceful resolution to the current conflict, hopefully with the General as an emissary between what remained of the rebellion and the new Rok Islander threat.

Dyeawan tears idly at her steamed bun, pushing small airy pieces past her lips. Riko is already on her second bowls of soup and rice. Dyeawan is watching the old guard's table, first out of habit, and then because the behavior of one diner in particular interests her.

Trowel is a creature almost entirely composed of rigid routines. Every morning for breakfast, Dyeawan observes him consume precisely one full cup of steaming hot tea as soon as it is poured, and then a half refilled into that cup. He accompanies it with a single steamed bun, which he softens in the half portion of tea for easier chewing, being long in the tooth as he is.

This is the first morning in memory Dyeawan has observed him not touch his initial cup of tea. It has gone stone cold in front of him. Further, she's watched him tear off a single piece of steamed bun and try to consume it without softening it in the liquid first. It seemed to be a thoughtless action, as he immediately spit it out upon realizing it was too tough for his withered teeth and sore gums.

At first, she thinks the old man must be experiencing some sort of physical malady, a sour stomach or the like. But his body language, his expressions, they do not speak of distress of the body.

Trowel is nervous, she realizes. Far beyond that, he appears vastly more anxious than Dyeawan has ever witnessed him.

His gaze also keeps straying to her table, if not to her directly. They are brief glances, surely innocuous, but there is something to them that disturbs Dyeawan immediately. Some intuition she can't readily articulate tells her there is a deeper meaning to the old man's small behaviors this morning. There could be a thousand explanations for Trowel's unusual quirks, the deviation in his diet, and his odd glances. Dyeawan knows that, rationally.

Still, a creeping sense of alarm and even dread begins welling within her.

"Are you all right?" Riko asks her. "I know you have a lot on your mind. I mean, you always have a lot on your mind, yeah?

You're like, a super genius. But you seem even more distracted than usual."

"I'm sorry," Dyeawan says without taking her eyes off Trowel. "How is that new toy you were working on coming along?"

Riko's eyes light up. "Oh! Well, I was thinking about the intelligence reports on the army from Rok Islander and how they have those chariots with all the spikes, yeah? And it gave me an idea for a ball that's spring-loaded, so spikes pop out of it in every direction."

"That sounds incredibly dangerous," Dyeawan remarks absently, her attention still far from their conversation.

"Oh no! The spikes are made of bamboo chutes blunted all over with silk, and that's insulated with feather stuffing, so they're totally soft, see."

Dyeawan nods. "And . . . what do you do with them?"

Riko blinks at her.

"You throw them at each other," she says, as if the answer is obvious.

Dyeawan finally breaks from her trance-like surveillance of Trowel to regard her friend.

"You throw—why?"

Riko shrugs with a bright smile.

"Because it's fun! They're for kids. The soft spikes pop out of the ball, and that's fun, and then you throw them at each other, and that's fun. It's a toy."

"I see. Okay then. We can test them out later, if you like."

Riko claps her hands together excitedly, and then returns to her meal.

Dyeawan, meanwhile, resumes her studying of Trowel.

There is a massive sundial erected atop the face of a sculpted boulder in the middle of the dining hall. It looks positively ancient to Dyeawan, like most things in the centuries-old keep. Its face is cast in bronze, and Dyeawan could lie atop it and spread out her arms and legs without touching the edges. A special window has been built into the dining hall, impossibly high up on the wall, just below the ceiling. It is shaped to cast sunlight perfectly against the dial, tracking the hours of the day.

After a time, Dyeawan notices Trowel's eyes cease darting to her table every few seconds and begin obsessively staring at the sundial.

Dyeawan notices something else, without even realizing what it is at first. She narrows her eyes, focusing her gaze openly and directly at Trowel without concern for how he might perceive it.

She has to squint tightly to make it out, but there upon his temple, slowly trickling down his cheek, is a bulbous bead of sweat.

It is a delightfully brisk and cool morning on the island.

That is when her mind finally provides a reason for the sinking feeling in the pit of her stomach.

"We have to go," Dyeawan informs Riko quietly. "We have to go and find Mister Quan. Now."

Riko has a mouth full of mashed bananas and is currently in the process of jamming even more in.

"Wha'?" she mumbles, confused. "Wha's 'appen-eng?"

Dyeawan pointedly pushes her teacup in front of Riko.

"Wash that down, and then stand up slowly and follow me out of the dining hall. We are not going to rush. We are not going to show any sign of alarm. I'll explain in the corridor. All right?"

Riko nods energetically, taking up the teacup and draining its contents. She swallows her dense mouthful and wipes her mouth on her sleeve before rising from the table.

At the same time, Dyeawan paddles her tender in reverse, swinging a wide arc away from the table so that she can steer it out of the hall. As she instructed Riko, she tries not to hurry. She tries to pretend it is any other morning, that she is spiriting away to attend to her daily duties.

Once they are in the corridor, out of sight of the people still eating happily and oblivious in the dining hall, Dyeawan turns her body towards Riko urgently.

"Climb onto my tender. We need to fly."

Riko nods again, eagerly leaping up onto the litter of the conveyance behind Dyeawan, encircling her arms around her securely.

Dyeawan begins working the armrest paddles of the tender with all the strength in her arms, sending the wheels in their tracts spinning rapidly. Soon they are winging their way through the winding circular corridors and descending levels of the keep.

"The Protectorate Ministry and the planners loyal to Trowel are about to move against us," Dyeawan explains. "Now. Today. For all I know, it is happening in the next moment."

Behind her, Riko's eyes widen.

"*How* do you know?"

"I don't," Dyeawan admits. "And I don't know what they'll do to us, either. I only suspect. But I'm asking you to trust my suspicion with your life right now."

"I trust you," Riko says without hesitation. "But what do we do?"

"We have to find Mister Quan. He'll make preparations for us to quietly leave the island, hopefully unnoticed. We can't stay here anymore."

"Leave the island?" Riko whispers.

Dyeawan nods, aware Riko has spent most of her life in this small self-contained world.

"I know it is frightening, but if we stay, we may be killed. It is possible they would only expel you from the planners, but we can't take that risk."

"All right," Riko says, as if processing things. "All right. Where is Mister Quan?"

"He usually tidies up my bedchamber while I am at breakfast, as not to disturb me. He should be there now."

"What about the rest of the planners who voted to keep you?" Riko asks, clearly concerned for their lives as well.

"I do not believe the Ministry will harm them, and Trowel knows he needs their minds at his disposal. He does not want to be rid of them. He merely wants control. He can do that once we are gone."

"And what about Nia?"

Dyeawan doesn't answer her right away.

"We'll give her the choice. Trowel and the Ministry wanted to persuade her to their side. She was raised to be one of them, and that is how they see her. If we're gone, I believe they will allow her to remain on the planners and assist them with whatever they want to do moving forward. But we'll give her the choice to stay or come with us."

They reach Dyeawan's room in record time, and so fast are the wheels of the tender rolling that when Dyeawan applies her brake, the tracts that control them screech over the polished floor of the corridor, sliding the pair several yards past Dyeawan's door.

Riko springs from the back of the tender even before it has completely halted. She sprints to the door and pushes it open.

Dyeawan backs up her tender and turns it towards the open doorway.

"Mister Quan?" she calls to her loyal attendant as Riko enters ahead of her.

There is no answer, which is not unusual. Mister Quan is not much for declarative statements, or statements of any kind, really.

"Dyeawan . . ." Riko begins uncertainly, the concern thick in her voice.

She steps aside so her friend can guide her tender into the room.

Dyeawan slams her brakes as soon as she sees Mister Quan.

He is lying peacefully on his side in Dyeawan's bed, his back to the two of them. Mister Quan is so tall that his skinny legs and slipper-covered feet are hanging far over the edge. There is no one else in the room.

"Mister Quan?" Dyeawan calls softly to him. "Mister Quan? Are you all right?"

Riko eventually pads forward, hands clasped at her chest in front of her pensively, and approaches the bed.

Dyeawan watches as her friend slowly leans over Mister Quan, reaching out with tentative fingers and very gently, almost hesitantly taking hold of his sun-colored tunic.

"Oh no," she hears Riko breathe almost inaudibly.

Dyeawan's hand flies over her mouth and her eyes go wide

with horror as Riko turns the front of Mister Quan's body towards them.

His lifeless eyes are open, staring at them vacantly. There is a dagger still protruding from his chest, rammed in to the hilt.

Dyeawan recognizes the weapon by the eagle engraved on its pommel. It is the dagger issued to and carried by Protectorate Ministry agents.

"Why?" Riko asks, tears in her eyes. "Why would they do this? Why would anyone hurt him?"

Dyeawan's thoughts shift from the grief and sorrow and anger welling up within her to her mind's perpetually analytical side. She begins positing and examining every scenario. Did they come here looking for Mister Quan specifically? Was he their first target, as her most loyal attendant and the one who helped her cover up so many bloody acts? Did they come here looking for her and find him instead? Why would they leave their dagger behind? Is it a warning to her? Or, not finding her in her bedchamber, were they in a hurry to locate Dyeawan elsewhere in the keep? Are they hunting her even now?

In the end, she decides the answers don't matter right now. Whatever their reason for killing Mister Quan, the assault has begun. The coup has officially commenced.

Dyeawan paddles herself backwards a few feet so that she can reach behind her tender and throw the door to her bedchamber closed.

"You are a good climber, aren't you, Riko?" she asks her friend.

Riko looks at her, confused. Her eyes immediately begin trailing back to the macabre and tragic sight of Mister Quan's body.

"Riko!" Dyeawan snaps at her.

Riko shakes her head as if to clear it.

"I'm sorry! What? Climbing? Yes. Why?"

"The corridors are not safe," Dyeawan explains. "I need you to go out that window, scale down the side of the keep, make your way to the dock, and prepare a boat for us."

"I can't just leave you alone here!" Riko immediately protests.

"You have to," Dyeawan insists. "Assuming I can even make it out of the keep, once we are in the open, we will need to depart right away. You have to get everything prepared. Besides, the two of us in the corridors together will only attract more attention."

"What if the Ministry is watching the dock?" Riko asks.

Dyeawan sighs. "I am hoping they'll assume they've caught us completely by surprise, and with my tender it will be impossible for me to escape the keep."

"Won't it? The path to the docks is rocky."

"I will manage," Dyeawan assures her. "But you be careful, all the same. If there *are* agents at the dock, meet me at the God Rung. We'll find another way. You're every bit as clever as me, Riko. I believe in you. You'll be fine. Now go, please."

Riko relents, though Dyeawan can see she is still filled with doubt and reluctance.

Dyeawan sits upon her tender calmly as Riko deftly and gracefully climbs out of her bedchamber window. They both do their best to ignore the agonizing sight of Mister Quan's murdered form upon the sparse, blood-soaked mattress.

Before Riko disappears below the outside of the window, she looks back at Dyeawan.

Riko kisses her fingertips and waves at her friend hopefully.

Dyeawan nods to her, not trusting herself to speak in that moment.

After Riko has disappeared from sight, Dyeawan paddles closer to the bed and extends a shaking hand towards Mister Quan's body.

First, she urges his eyes closed with her fingers.

After that, she curls those same fingers around the hilt of the dagger embedded in his chest, gripping it tightly.

Closing her eyes, her jaw clenched, Dyeawan pulls the dagger free of Mister Quan's body.

When she opens her eyelids she feels the wet, salty sting of tears spilling forth.

Wiping them away with the sleeve of her tunic, Dyeawan quickly cleans the blade on the edge of her mattress and tucks the weapon under her thigh, keeping it close and easily accessible.

She turns her tender around and paddles to the door. With each foot of floor she covers, she feels her heart skip a beat, the fear so palpable she can taste it on her tongue, like copper and acid.

You have to get to Nia, she tells herself firmly. *Together you can make it out of this place.*

The Ministry could be anywhere. They could be waiting on the other side of her door right now. They could intercept her at any point between here and where she believes Nia is obliviously tending to her duties. If Dyeawan is *very* lucky, the agents who killed Mister Quan are waiting for her in the planners' private meeting space, where she would usually go after a meal. It's the logical place to ambush her, but when people are involved there is never a guarantee of logic, Dyeawan knows.

She takes a deep breath, letting it out slowly and clenching her fists to steady her hands.

Pulling the door open just a crack, Dyeawan listens for any sounds in the corridor beyond.

She doesn't hear anything. There are no footsteps, no rustling of cloth or shuffling of feet. There is no one breathing, not even quietly. She trusts the keenness of her senses that much, at least.

Dyeawan relaxes, if only a little.

Just the same, she checks that the bolt shooter built into the front of her tender is loaded, and the lever that releases it is cocked and ready.

If she runs across any Protectorate Ministry agents, she just hopes they'll all be standing in a line in front of her.

LEGENDS IN THEIR OWN TIME

HIS NAME IS KRAY, EVIE EVENTUALLY LEARNS. HE GOT THE scars on his cheeks when he was just a boy of eleven years. Kray was one of the countless ragged children running wild and foraging for survival around the docks near the Bottoms. He was caught "stealing" by Aegins from the chum barrel of a fishmonger. Rather than simply deal him a beating and cast him into a darkened dungeon for a few days, as was their usual custom, the Aegins decided to really have fun with the boy. They dug fishhooks into his cheeks and hung him off the dock, just to see how long he would dangle before the hooks finally ripped themselves free and he was plunged into the murky waters of the bay.

Kray tells her that he can no longer remember their faces, but he still hears their laughter in his sleep every night.

She still doesn't know why they have saved her, but he shares that story easily enough as Evie and her new "friends" make their way clandestinely back to the Bottoms. Kray tells her there are Aegins guarding every clear entrance and exit between the forgotten part of the city and the rest of the gleaming metropolis that is the Capitol. The ragged group is forced to use the sewers to reach the cordoned-off section, descending below the street near the final sky carriage station where service stops before the Bottoms. Fortunately, it's a relatively short trudge through a thick stream of human waste before reemergence in the cracked and neglected alleys of the Bottoms.

Evie comforts herself with the thought that at least the surface of the gray water didn't rise high enough to further infect her leg. And it can't have made them smell any worse than they already did.

She was not born in the Bottoms. She began life in an orphanage near the Spectrum, which was in truth just a grooming house for parentless children to be adopted by Gens and trained to serve them in some capacity. Because of that, they were fed regularly and well taken care of, the way one might fatten a calf for sale. It just so happens Gen Stalbraid were the ones to take her in, specifically Brio's father, and begin training her as a retainer.

The most time she ever spent in the Bottoms was the few weeks she posed as a drunken reprobate, brawling in taverns and alleyways, hoping to be arrested by Aegins and conscripted into the Savage Legion. That was when she took the name Evie, a name that has come to feel more like hers than the one she was given at birth.

The Bottoms are indeed a desperate and craven place, but Evie also remembers their streets as utterly teeming with life. That life may have been hardscrabble, oppressed and impossibly difficult to eke out, but there were scores of people everywhere attempting to survive in a million different ways. It had its own color and culture and rhythm, not all of it a depressing slog. No matter where you put people, or what you did to them, they always seemed to find a path to joy and their own identity.

Evie recalls buskers playing makeshift instruments, sometimes entire orchestras of them, banging on empty ash cans or strumming strings stretched across box tops and finding real music in the crude objects. She remembers gangs of children constantly skittering around in droves, yelling and laughing and playing all manner of games, begging for food from anyone who looked like they had more than the children did, which was pretty much everyone. There were hawkers of all manner of wares: stolen, homemade, and everything in between.

Washers ferrying baskets of clothes from the docks, day laborers returning from toils, sailors and sex workers exchanging goods and services.

All of that has changed.

It hasn't just changed, in fact. It has disappeared. The Bottoms to which she returns with her mysterious rescuers is a graveyard with abandoned buildings in place of tombstones.

There is no one on the streets. Evie doesn't spy a single person occupying a doorway or a corner, or hustling up and down the sidewalk. She sees people through storefront windows, the odd lonely shopkeeper overseeing the inside of an otherwise empty shop, but all of the life Evie recalls has been drained from the Bottoms. It doesn't make any sense. Are they all hiding indoors? It doesn't seem possible. Most of the people in the Bottoms never had an indoors to which to retreat.

"What has happened here?" Evie asks Kray.

"They swept through the streets like the plague they are," he explains, the plague to which he refers being Aegins. "They had prison wagons, a whole fleet of 'em. They took anyone and everyone in sight. Anyone in the street, anyone around the docks; if they weren't a shopkeeper or a shopkeeper's child, they ended up behind iron. If they fought, they were beaten. If they ran, they were chased down or killed. I've spent my whole life here and I never saw the like of it before."

"Did they say why?" Evie asks him.

Kray grins bitterly. "Aegins have never been ones to give you reasons. Their taskmasters weren't saying much, either."

"Taskmasters?"

"Ministry agents," Kray says, speaking the name with venom. "All clad in black with their eagle eyes on their chests. They were runnin' the whole show. Them you *never* see in the Bottoms."

"The Protectorate Ministry ordered mass arrests," Evie says, more to clarify the idea for herself.

"They've been worried about us for a while. But for weeks after the Ragged Matron's sacrifice, they just kept us pent up here, with that Aegin blockage we slipped past. Something must've happened, something that made them scared enough to clear the streets."

"Maybe they were killing two birds with one stone," Evie reasons.

"What do you mean?"

"It's a fair bet the people they took will be conscripted into the Savage Legion. With the new threat of the Rok Islanders, the Skrain will need every body they can hurl at them. The Ministry probably saw this as the way to bolster Crache's defenses and eliminate the threat the people of the Bottoms present to them all at once. It was a drastic measure, but that's what we've come to, I suppose."

That's what we've come to.

It's what I've brought us to, Evie can't help but think.

She caused this. The Sparrow General and her great rebellion caused this mass death and forced sacrifice of the least privileged. Evie's gut churns and bubbles painfully as this knowledge sinks into her brain. No matter how she rationalizes it, no matter how her own people would no doubt reassure and disagree with her, the fact remains that the people who will suffer and die, every child separated from their parents, all of it is a direct result of what she began.

Evie doesn't speak any of this aloud to Kray, though not doing so only compounds her guilt and shame.

Kray and two of his street druids guide her through a maze of cramped back alleys in the heart of the Bottoms. More than once, she thinks she spies a pair of frightened or suspicious eyes gazing at them from the darkness of a cellar window or some hole knocked in a wall. There remains not a soul out in the open, however. That eerie silence never relents. There is only the shuffling of their dirty robes, the padding of their feet, and a thin layer of fog blown in from the docks swelling about their knees.

After a dizzying number of twists and turns, they come to the splintered wooden doors of what looks like an old fruit or wine cellar. There is the smashed remnant of a barrel sitting atop them, probably to discourage casual passersby from tampering with the entrance. Kray quickly moves the broken barrel aside and pulls the doors open easily, beckoning Evie inside.

She discovers darkness and the top of a creaking staircase waiting for her, descending the steps without hesitation. Fear seems a silly thing to harbor at this point; if these people wanted to harm her, they surely would have done it already.

What Evie finds at the bottom of the stairs is a surprisingly clean if cramped and musty-smelling space outfitted with several tidy straw mattresses. Rickety-looking rectangular tables line the walls, a mismatched collection of plates and cups and bowls and pitchers spread across the tops of them. Several large, intact barrels, perhaps larders or containing water or wine, fill each corner of the room. There is one door no doubt leading up to whatever building is above them, and no windows.

"You are as safe here as anyone can be in the Bottoms," Kray assures Evie, descending the staircase behind her.

They bring her water to drink and water with which to wash. It isn't much; a cupful to gulp down and a small bowl for the washing, but Evie knows how scarce fresh water can be in the Bottoms, and she is grateful for both, especially after what she has been through since her capture by the Skrain. Kray also provides her with fresh wraps for her leg. They are far from silk, but they're thick and clean.

Evie begins the arduous process of removing her armor. She has been wearing it for what feels like weeks, and its weight passed the realm of unbearable long ago. Finally shirking her sparrow-emblazoned breastplate feels like being reborn. Evie is able to stand straighter, move freer, and she feels like she has shed fifty pounds of weight from her body.

She strips the rest of her battle-torn armor pieces and clothing away without hesitation or shame. Although she is glad there are no mirrors down here. She doesn't need to see what prolonged captivity in a birdcage has done to her appearance. Evie feels like an entity composed almost entirely of crust, grime, and stubble at this point. She hardly remembers life as a being of exposed flesh.

She attends to her leg first. The clean bandage Murrow applied to her wound on the Skrain caravan's journey to bring her back to the Capitol has since turned almost black. She strips it away and dribbles enough water to clean her stitches, which by some miracle seem to have avoided further infection. Evie carefully rewraps them with the new compress.

She finally, gratefully splashes water on her face, scrubbing it as free of grit and dried blood as possible. It feels better than any lover's kiss.

Evie glances around the room, finding Kray and his people have removed their tatters and are also washing themselves with meager bowls of water. They seem every bit as devoid of self-consciousness as her.

Kray is indeed malnourished, thin through the ribs and slight in his chest to match the gauntness of his face, but his arms and shoulders are knotted with muscle that looks as hard as coiled steel. He has clearly spent time performing the kind of brutal labor that builds such muscles. His torso continues the pattern of scarred flesh on his face and hands. He has been stabbed and slashed half a dozen times, it is clear.

Evie finds herself studying his body a little too long and quickly returns to cleansing herself.

"Forgive our stench," he says when he notices her idly watching them. "It's a tactic. Horse manure, mostly. It deters most city folk from getting too close. Even Aegins think twice about approaching us. And you'd be surprised how well it works in battle. Nothin' breaks a Skrain's concentration and spirit like figuring out they're tussling with someone smeared in dung."

"I hadn't noticed," Evie lies.

Kray says nothing, but from the corner of her eye, she thinks she detects a smile.

It would be his first since they met.

She uses up the water she has been given to scrub as much of the rest of her body as she can. It is hardly bathing in a deep stream with soap, but it is certainly an improvement. She gathers her filthy hair up and ties it into a knot at the back to keep it off her neck.

The leather pants that she wears with her armor have been torn to shreds by spear and surgeon's shears, and they smell like death besides. Thankfully Kray's people are able to offer her a pair of brown wool pants and a clean tunic to replace her soiled one.

Once she's dressed, Evie turns and leans back against the little table, her hands reaching behind her to grip its edges.

"I haven't thanked you yet," she says to Kray. "I apologize for that. Everything happened so fast."

Kray is shaking his head even before she has finished speaking. He pulls a pitch-black jersey down over himself, straightening it out around his thin frame before answering.

"What we do is not for gratitude," he says firmly.

"Still," Evie persists. "Thank you."

He merely dips his head, but this time she is certain the expression on his lips is another smile.

Evie's own expression darkens a little, despite her appreciating the gesture. "You've answered a lot of my questions, and I'm grateful. The one you seem to have avoided so far is why you did this. Why would you all risk your life to free me?"

"I didn't mean to keep anything from you," he says. "It just wasn't my place to explain. I am only a pair of hands."

"You don't give yourself enough credit," Evie insists. "But what do you mean? Whose place is it to explain?"

In response, Kray nods past her in the direction of the room's single doorway.

Evie turns her head and is surprised to find what at first she thinks is an old woman standing there.

Blinking, she sees the woman isn't elderly at all. She merely has shocking-white hair.

"Well now, the mission I gave you certainly took a turn, didn't it?" she asks Evie in a voice as familiar as Evie realizes the woman's face is.

Fire Star help me.

"Lexi," Evie barely breathes.

"Sparrow General," Kay says, "please meet our Ragged Matron."

Lexi smiles. "Both of us legends in our own time, it seems."

Evie is still stunned.

"We've met," is all she can manage.

SPILL YOUR GUTS

"YOU NEVER TRULY SAW BATTLE AS A SAVAGE LEGIONNAIRE, did you?" Brio asks Taru as he watches them secure the pieces of their leather armor to their body.

He rests his chin atop the shoulder notch of his crutch, seated on a tree stump inside the modest tent they share in the combined base camp of the rebellion and the Rok Islanders. It is where Brio will remain as the rest of them take the field against the Savages and the Skrain in just a few hours.

"No," Taru admits. "The only action I saw was when I snapped our wrangler over my knee before I escaped their sinking galleon. That was quite enough for my liking."

Brio breaks out in a wry grin.

"So then," he says cheekily, "that means I actually have more battle experience than you?"

Taru stops in the middle of strapping a shoulder pauldron to their breastplate, contemplating Brio's words.

"If you consider falling off a ladder during a failed siege and nearly being trampled to death 'experience,' I suppose."

Brio laughs. "One war story is more than enough for me. And you can't say I don't have the superior conversation piece."

He leans back slightly and raises the stump of his right leg.

Taru frowns sourly, looking from the appendage to his face, the disapproval clear in the retainer's eyes.

"Not quite ready to joke about that," Brio says softly. "I understand."

Taru finishes putting on their armor. The last act of personal preparation they perform is to examine the blades of their short sword and hook-end, an expertly forged version of the makeshift weapon common in the Bottoms, usually fashioned from the hooks used to secure unfinished ship hulls. The retainer inspects each inch of steel for any chips or cracks that might compromise the blade in the midst of the battle.

Satisfied, Taru sheathes their weapons, one at each hip.

"If our army falls today," they tell Brio, "scouts will ride back here to bring word as soon as possible."

"I know."

"If that happens," the retainer continues as if they did not hear him speak, "fall back immediately to the Tenth City."

"Taru," he repeats, "I know."

"You can make a final stand there if necessary, but hopefully you will be able to negotiate some peaceful surrender with them."

"I doubt they'll surrender to us," he muses.

"Brio!"

"Taru," he says, more sternly this time, "I know all of this. You can't worry about me now. Just go defeat them. That's all. Defeat them and let us negotiate *their* surrender."

Taru draws in a deep breath and nods.

"Whatever happens," Brio says, far more gently, "I am happy we got to see each other again. What you did to find me, and for the rebellion, is beyond any gratitude we can offer you. You are the finest warrior, the finest person I have ever known."

Taru swallows hard, not wanting emotion to overtake them in that moment.

Brio's words, however, mean more to them than any victory on a battlefield ever could.

He smiles softly on them. "I will see you after this thing is done, all right? We need not say goodbye or share an embrace, because we are not parting. Understood?"

Again, Taru nods, not trusting their voice enough to speak.

Brio says no more, and the retainer knows it is time to go. They bow their head to their De-Gen formally before turning and ducking out through the front of the tent.

The camp outside is bustling in final preparation for the army to depart. There was much debate over whether to march on the Skrain or wait for the Skrain to come to them. In the end, the Rok wanted to press on. They had every intention of fighting straight to the Capitol, they said, and they might as well make up some ground going to face the largest force of Skrain and Savage Legionnaires that Crache has yet mustered to face the rebellion.

The Rok and the rebels crossed the fork of the southern river two days before. The Islanders seemed happy just to lay eyes on water again, and Taru got the impression the Rok would prefer to fight their enemy on the riverfront. Sirach's shadow scouts reported that the Skrain and their puffed-up Savage Legion were massed twenty miles outside the Fifth City, preparing to meet the army their own scouts had since informed them was coming at them head-on.

Taru is surprised to find that Sirach has a fresh war mount waiting for them beside her own stead. She, Chimot, and Bam have already saddled up, each outfitted for a fight.

The retainer takes special note of Bam's impossibly large mallet. They doubt anyone besides the giant could successfully swing it.

"I was not certain where you wanted me in the formation," Taru says to Sirach as they climb up into the saddle beside her.

"You're the reason we're all here," Sirach reminds them. "For better or for worse. Besides, I've heard a rumor you're a fair hand in a scrap. Maybe you can keep me alive through this thing. Beginning to question how heavily I can rely on *this* one." Sirach nods at Chimot. "She's getting awful lippy lately."

Her lieutenant refers to Sirach by a name under her breath that Taru doesn't catch, but it can hardly be flattering.

A Rok chariot is pulled up in front of them, and Captain Staz sticks her shell-helmeted head above the rim of the basket.

"The children of Rok are ready," the old woman announces. "I hope your people's blood is pumping with the same fire."

"Fire, wine," Sirach muses. "Whatever gets the job done."

Staz ignores the jest, turning her attention instead to Taru.

"Fight well, my friend. Try not to let the ants take you. You are far too fine to fall to such trash."

"I will see you for celebratory soup," Taru promises the diminutive sea warrior.

Staz offers the retainer a smile before she motions to her driver to move the chariot along.

"Shall we go to war, then?" Sirach asks.

"Why not?" Taru says. "We are dressed for it, after all."

"A joke!" Sirach proclaims in delighted shock. "That cinches it. Today we're unbeatable!"

The rebels have waited for the Skrain to firmly establish their lines of battle before marching their own army to take up position on the field. That position has been carefully chosen: just far away enough to make charging impractical for the Skrain, as the Rok and the rebels do not want them unleashing the Savage Legionnaires before Brio's plan has time to reach its crescendo.

The Rok and the rebels arrange the chariot corps first, just as they were aligned during the last battle. Taru and the rest of the de facto officers on horseback wait behind the chariots with the main infantry, most of them on foot. The rebels have no archers, and the Islanders don't use bow and arrows, though each fighter is just as adept using their trident as a long-range weapon.

"You're sure they went through the wine?" Taru asks Sirach for what must be the tenth time.

"I served it to them myself, in full wench regalia," she reminds the retainer again.

"And you *just* spiked the barrels with our blood coin solution?"

"Yes. Although I would be lying if I said I wasn't tempted to slip a little something extra in those barrels and end this whole thing at their revel."

"That wouldn't have ended it. We would still be facing the Skrain."

"Only because they guard their wine supply much more fiercely than the swill they give the Legionnaires. Believe me, we've checked."

"This way will help us even more."

"It is certainly going to be unlike any battle I've ever witnessed, assuming we've timed things correctly."

Far away on the opposite side of their chosen battlefield, the Skrain ranks are almost totally obscured by the mass of Savage Legionnaires they have standing at the ready in the vanguard of their lines.

"I've never seen this many in one battle," Sirach marvels to Taru. "Not in all my years fighting them."

There are five thousand Savages if there are a hundred, composed of all manner of folk, from boys and girls barely out of childhood to the elderly who can scarcely hold the weapons they've been given. Still, despite their rusted secondhand weapons, despite their patchwork armor and broken shields, and despite the weakest links among their human chain, there are still plenty of able-bodied salts among the compelled ranks willing to fight with everything they have for what they believe will be their freedom. That remains the essence of the construct that is the Savage Legion.

The Sicclunan scouts have estimated there are far more conscripts than Skrain soldiers themselves, so depleted have the Skrain ranks become by fighting the rebellion. The Legion is their key to winning the field today and crushing both the Rok Island threat and the rebels once and for all.

That is one thing both armies have in common. Taru and the rebels are also banking on the Savage Legionnaires to fail.

In their own way, they are all betting this battle and the future of Crache itself on their ability to force the poorest members of their society into sacrificing themselves.

It doesn't sit well with Taru, but at least Brio's plan doesn't demand the lives of the conscripts.

The Skrain's battle plan is obvious. Tainting the Savage Legionnaire wine supply as the rebels have is far from an exact science, however. There is no real way of knowing when the effects will take hold, and the Rok and the rebels cannot make their charge until those effects are realized. Brio reckoned consuming the solution at the revel the night before would place the culmination of the solution's effect somewhere in the middle of the morning.

It is the middle of the morning.

Still, every conscript across the field is on their feet, more or less.

So, Taru and their friends wait.

The retainer is certain that the moment will come soon, at least at first. Then minutes become tens of minutes, and tens of minutes become an hour. Neither army makes a move. The Skrain are either puzzled by the rebel's posture or waiting on them to charge first or both. That first hour becomes two, and then three, and still both armies continue to wait for the battle to begin.

The fourth hour in, Sirach inexplicably begins laughing uncontrollably, her hysterics cutting through the relative silence and malaise like a blade.

"What strikes you as so funny?" Taru asks.

"This whole thing," she answers through ragged breaths. "Two armies staring at each other like a loveless married couple over their ten thousandth bland dinner."

"That is quite vivid," Taru remarks.

"Yes, in another life I might've been a poet," Sirach muses.

"I've composed several sonnets about different parts of Evie's body. She praised my lyricism."

Taru shakes their head. "You have a gift for answering questions no one asked, I will say that."

"What happens if they finally get restless enough to send their Savages anyway, distance be damned?" Chimot asks. "Before this plan of your one-legged friend plays out?"

Sirach shrugs. "Then hopefully they'll be too tired by the time they run all the way over here to fight."

"And what if the Skrain decide to break up and go home before this wonder tonic of yours kicks in, rather than attack or keep waiting on us?"

"If that happens," Taru answers her, "the solution we tainted their wine with will still take effect, and the Savage Legion will be unable to fight for at least a day. We will attack while they are incapacitated. Either way, this plan will give us our best chance."

"I suppose you've thought of everything, then," Chimot admits, somewhat begrudgingly.

Sirach leans away from her saddle to whisper to Taru, "*Had* we thought of all that before?"

"No," Taru says truthfully. "I was certain the solution would have taken effect by now. But everything we told her is still true."

Sirach nods slowly. "All right then. Good enough."

The fifth hour comes and goes, the afternoon sun hanging high above them. Taru, as patient and stoic as they are, is ready to burst out of their armor. They think if one more full minute passes, they may find themselves screaming their frustration in Sirach's face.

Fortunately, that final minute is enough.

Much of the Skrain line is one indistinguishable mass from their vantage, but Taru becomes certain they see a sudden commotion arising at several points along the thick rows of Savage Legionnaires.

"Something is happening," they say, their heart beginning to race faster in anticipation.

"I think they *have* decided to leave," Chimot observes ruefully.

"No, my most favored and deadly pupil," Sirach says with a new smile forming on her face. "That is not a recall. That is the beginning of an epidemic."

Sirach is referring to the sight of several dozen conscripts at the forefront of the vanguard clearly and abruptly doubling over and falling onto the sun-warmed ground.

It becomes more and more clear to the onlookers that Savage Legionnaires are now dropping to their knees by the dozen, each of them vomiting everything short of their stomach lining out onto the grass below. One by one, the blood coins forced down their gullets by the Legion wranglers are expelled from their bodies in torrents of liquid waste.

Sirach begins laughing anew, even louder and more hysterically than before.

Taru cannot find the same pleasure as the Sicclunan warrior takes in what they are witnessing. The retainer feels nothing but sympathy for the people from each Crachian city's poorest quarters being forced to live through this misery, even if it is to save themselves and the rebellion.

"When do we go?" Chimot demands.

"Not yet!" Taru snaps at the young warrior.

They are waiting for more of the first line of Skrain soldiers to be revealed. More and more Savage Legionnaires fall out, and it is clear the panic is reaching the Skrain officers in charge of the field. Mounted riders in resplendent armor are bounding up and down the line.

The Skrain cavalry and infantry remain more or less fixed in place, however.

That is military discipline for you, Taru thinks ruefully.

"It is time," the retainer says. "Roll the Rok chariots! Infantry to follow!"

Chimot nods, kicking her heels into the flanks of her mount to launch the horse into a gallop. She rides to where the Rok cavalry is lined up out front of the rest of their army, waving a frantic signal to Staz.

A replacement conch horn (Taru even begins to question what Staz said about the conch they broke being a centuries-old sacred relic) blares across the field. The drivers of Islander chariot corps snap their mounts into action.

Watching a full fleet of Rok chariots thunder across the field as one, as intended, is a sight to behold. It is a far cry from the broken, scattered half charge Taru triggered in order to save the rebels. The menacing war rigs and their powerful mounts look an absolute terror, a wave of spiked menace and mayhem fit to wash over the Crachian army.

The Skrain have no choice. Their own horseback-mounted cavalry is forced to ride forward over the prone and useless forms of their conscripts in order to meet the charge themselves. They have twice as many horses as the Rok Islanders have fielded chariots, their armored riders bearing forth lances a head and a half taller than the soldier wielding it.

Meanwhile, Skrain archers are primed and nocked behind the infantry line. The Rok are closing distance at an alarming, almost impossible speed in their turtle shell baskets. In seconds the chariots are within range of the Skrain's bows, and their archers are ordered to let fly.

Taru watches as a hailstorm of arrows is launched from the other side of the field, blotting out the sun briefly as they arc high in the air before falling lethally back to earth.

In the basket of each chariot, driver and the Island fighters they are ferrying raise what look like vastly smaller versions of the shells in which they sit. They must be harvested from the young versions of the gargantuan beasts. The shells the Rok are using as shields are marked with bumps that have yet to become the long and jagged spikes of their mature counterparts.

The chariots are barreling forward so fast that most miss the arrows at the forefront of the volley. The Islanders' improvised shields deflect the ones that do strike within the baskets. The arrows don't even stick when they hit the shells, but ricochet harmlessly off the incredibly hard surfaces.

"This is going to be ugly!" Sirach yells beside the retainer.

"For who?" Taru shouts back.

As if in answer to their question, the Rok chariots collide with the Skrain's cavalry only seconds later.

The chariots aren't even slightly slowed.

It is a bloodbath of horseflesh and armored Skrain bodies that are tossed so high into the air that the sight of them is almost comical. The Rok fighters do not attempt to strike from the chariots as the two forces meet. The basket-riders merely duck low and defend overhead with their shields again, allowing the chariots to do the rest.

The spikes of the turtle shell baskets pierce the flanks and sever the legs of most of the Skrain's mounts. The same spikes either skewer the riders who are taken down with their horses, or their armor is crushed into their flesh by the chariots' wheels.

When the Rok horde has quite literally rolled over and through the cavalry charge, the fighters in the baskets reappear. They take aim and fire tridents from the backs of the chariots, expertly lancing from a distance any Skrain cavalry soldier who is still moving or remains astride a horse.

"It's our turn!" Taru announces after a deep breath.

Sirach waves a sword high above her head to signal the rebel infantry to march. At the same time, every fish scale–armored, trident-wielding Islander in bare feet is already bounding across the field to join their compatriots. They aren't holding back, running at full speed, whooping and hollering battle cries at the top of their lungs as they go.

"They don't believe in taking their time, do they?" Sirach asks as she snaps the reins of her mount.

The de facto officers lead their rebels across the field after the Rok, double-timing their efforts, but Taru refuses to burn them out as quickly as the Islanders appear willing to risk.

Meanwhile, the Skrain infantry, watching their cavalry break like the Crachian navy has broken many times upon the reefs of Rok Island, are forced to march to meet their longtime enemies.

Carrying pike and shield, they brace themselves as the wave of spiked chariots crashes into them first, barreling through their ranks, creating massive holes in their advance.

Thundering past the Skrain lines, the chariots that are still upright break from the center of their formation, one side turning left and the other turning right, riding to once again flank their enemies.

The Rok fighters on foot have their turn. Taru finally bears witness to the hand-to-hand combat abilities of the Islanders, and if anything, their expectations are not only met but far exceeded. Though Skrain armor is far heavier and thicker than the petrified fish scales the Islanders wear, it doesn't seem to matter. The powerful thrusts of their barbed tridents pierce breastplate and shield. Their lighter armor allows them to move with more mobility and speed and grace than any Skrain, and the Rok have long trained on targeting the most vulnerable point in a Crachian soldier's armor.

Taru remembers Staz saying her fighters would take five enemies for every one of theirs, and from the retainer's vantage, they seem to be dead set on meeting that quota.

"See you on the other side," Sirach hollers at Taru as their mounts break into a heavy charge to join the fray. "One way or the other!"

Taru urges their mount to match Sirach's speed, drawing their short sword from its scabbard.

Taru, Sirach, Chimot, and Bam inevitably break apart and ride into the thick of the fighting. The retainer quickly loses sight of them all, concentrating on splitting the skull of every enemy within reach of their saddle. Their horse quickly gets bogged down in the dense sea of bodies, and soon it doesn't matter how hard Taru snaps the reins or digs their heels into the beast's hindquarters, the horse is either unable or unwilling to move any farther.

Feeling like a sitting duck atop their saddle, Taru makes the decision to abandon horseback to fight on foot. They swing their right leg up over the saddle and launch their large body from their mount's side, barreling over a pair of Skrain soldiers and a Rok Islander fighter on the way down.

Once their boots hit the ground, Taru fills their free hand with the handle of their wickedly curved hook-end. They use it to parry, deflect, and envelop any enemy blade that flashes near, Taru's short sword delivering counterstrikes and death blows, piercing and opening more than a half a dozen throats within the first few minutes of joining the battle.

Soon, conscious thought abandons them entirely. As Brio pointed out, Taru has never been in the thick of a full-scale war between armies before. They have killed in single combat, even excelled against multiple opponents, but melee fighting is another world altogether. They quickly find they have a finely honed facility for it. Taru becomes a mechanical death-dealing machine, sensing threats from every direction and pivoting effortlessly to meet them. They scarcely feel the burning of their exhausted muscles after a while, or the fire in their depleted lungs.

At some point, however, even the combat automaton that Taru has become cannot deny that the fighting has thinned immeasurably. Soon the foes stop running at them, and Taru finds themselves standing alone, ankle-deep in carnage.

They survey the field around them.

Far more of the Rok and rebel fighters are still standing than the Skrain.

I cannot believe it, they marvel, and even then, another voice is screaming at them to focus and not drop their guard just yet.

To illustrate the point, a Skrain sword appears in Taru's field of vision a hair of a second before its edge threatens to cleave the retainer's head from their shoulders.

Taru ducks, their topknot receiving a shearing from the enemy blade's razor edge. The retainer blocks a second blow with their blade. At the same time, they step in and ram the uppermost part of their forehead into the face of the soldier attacking them. While he's stunned, Taru slashes him deeply across the belly just beneath his breastplate. The Skrain drops his sword and falls to the ground on his back.

Taru takes him in for the first time and notices he is wearing an officer's insignia; he's a captain.

The retainer is surprised to see him this far up on the field. The Skrain really must have been spread thin.

Something about ending an already downed opponent though disturbs Taru, but this is warfare, and the man is already severely injured.

As they raise their arm to deliver the fatal blow, a shockingly strong hand grabs their wrist.

Taru instinctively shifts their weight and poises their opposite arm to deliver a palm heel blow to whoever has seized them.

Fortunately they recognize Sirach before they strike.

Her face, neck, and armor are spattered with the blood of her kills. Yet she does not even appear to be breathing heavily.

"If you don't mind," Sirach says with an eerie calm, "I am going to have to insist on having the honors where this one is concerned."

Taru doesn't understand, but dealing the death blow is neither particularly appealing nor important to them.

The retainer nods, stepping aside.

They watch as Sirach crouches down low beside the fallen Skrain officer.

Sirach flashes an utterly terrifying smile unlike any expression Taru has yet seen on her face.

"Captain Feng Silvar," she says to the prone and wounded man. "Do you remember me?"

The man says nothing.

"Think hard," Sirach bids him.

Silvar stares up at her, fear and pain scrawled all over his bloody face.

"I remember," he admits, as if confessing a wrongdoing.

"Good," Sirach says.

She jams a dagger into his side, circumventing his breastplate. The blade pierces between the man's ribs and finds his heart.

Taru cannot recall ever taking as much pleasure in anything as Sirach clearly takes in watching this man die.

Sirach removes her dagger and carefully cleans the blade on the cloth protruding from beneath Captain Silvar's armor.

The blaring of horns breaks Taru's morbid focus. They look up from the woman and whatever vengeance they just witnessed her take.

"Are those ours?" Sirach casually inquires.

"No," Taru says with certainty. "That is the Skrain. They are calling for a retreat."

Sirach nods, sounding bizarrely detached as she says, "Then I guess we've won."

Taru can see the Skrain soldiers left fighting on the field attempting to turn and flee. As the retainer looks on, several of them receive tridents in their backs.

The Rok Islanders have no intention of leaving any of the Skrain alive, Taru realizes. All of the Island fighters are charging forward from the newly abandoned battlefield, chasing down enemy soldiers who are scrambling to return to what remains of their line.

"The Rok will not let the Skrain retreat," Taru tells Sirach in alarm.

"Are they killing the Savage Legionnaires?"

"I . . . no, I do not believe so."

"Then why do you care?"

Taru looks down at her, eyes flaring.

"We are not butchers!"

Sirach shrugs. "We may not be butchers. Apparently the Islanders feel differently."

Taru doesn't know what to say to that.

"I wish Evie was here," Sirach says a moment later.

"Is this . . . is this you grieving?" Taru asks her. "What a frightening sight."

Sirach grins.

"I never thought I'd say this, but I don't want to fight any more battles. Let the Rok finish off as many Skrain as they can.

No more regrouping. No more mustering more forces to meet us. This ends here and now. I'm tired. I want to go find Evie. I want to spend whatever time I have left screwing her into oblivion and not skulking through the dark slitting throats and being responsible for the survival of an entire people. If that makes me a bad person, so be it."

Those sentiments, at the very least, Taru can sympathize with.

PART THREE

REUNITED

ASHORE

DYEAWAN'S FINGERTIPS BARELY BRUSH THE TOP OF THE ICY blue waters. She moves her hand slowly and gracefully back and forth above the tides lapping against the side of the rowboat. Her bloodstained cheek rests against the lacquered wood railing, her eyes mostly remaining closed, except to glance down now and then at the small ripples she creates in the surface of the Crachian seas.

Blinking, she watches as several drops of blood fall from the delicate point of her chin and splash below the water, one after the other.

Dyeawan isn't certain whether the blood is hers or someone else's.

Although outwardly she is calm and silent, much like the waves upon which their little boat sits, inside she is a frantic, broken litany of images and sounds and other random sense memories from the past few hours. Mostly she sees a cavalcade of faces.

There is Mister Quan's lifeless face before Dyeawan closed his eyes forever.

There is the face of Agent Strinnix, awash in surprise and outrage, as Dyeawan plunged a knife into her thigh.

Nia's face when Dyeawan told her she would have to choose, for good and for all, a choice she could never take back, whether to flee the Planning Cadre with her sister or remain there and never see Dyeawan again.

Riko. Her friend's face, smiling, eyes full of light and love and ideas for new toys.

Those same eyes staring blankly at the sky, filled with the storm clouds of encroaching eternity.

"Dyeawan?" Nia calls to her gently, especially for how stern her sister's tone usually is.

Nia sits in the center of the boat, crewing the two oars tethered to its sides. She has been rowing them silently ashore for what feels like an eternity, especially in the silence both inside and outside their vessel.

"Dyeawan? You're starting to worry me. Are you all right?"

Nothing is all right, Dyeawan thinks but does not speak aloud. *Things will never be all right again.*

"Yes," she says without moving or looking back at her sister.

Dyeawan had found Nia easily enough within the Planning Cadre after rolling clandestinely in that direction from her bedchambers. Nia was not surprised when her sister explained the situation, informing her that the coup had begun, that if they were going to survive it together, they would have to leave immediately. Nia was surprisingly calm in that moment. There was a look of certainty, even inevitability, on her face.

It was a moment of triumph and relief and joy amid the terror for Dyeawan when Nia simply said, "We must be quick, then."

The moments that followed are a blur for Dyeawan now. She

only remembers they tried to move with purpose and stealth, despite how palpably scared they both were. Had they packed clothing and supplies next? Or had the bags already been prepared for such an emergency? For some reason Dyeawan can't recall these details.

What is clear in Dyeawan's mind is the ghostly and emotionless face of Strinnix. The Protectorate Ministry agent cut them off in the corridor, the hilt of her dagger clutched in one dark-gloved hand. Dyeawan recalls not breathing as she pulled the lever on her tender's bolt launcher. The needle-thin, impossibly sharp and strong metal arrow flew almost right between the Ministry agent's legs, tearing open the inseam of her pitch-black trousers and slashing the woman's thigh without embedding itself.

Dyeawan can still feel the breath she exhaled after, the disappointment and panic and dread when she realized the shot had failed.

Strinnix and Nia then tussled in the corridor. Dyeawan remembers their bodies tangled into one, both of them making animalistic noises. She can't remember if Strinnix went for Nia first, or if Nia actually threw herself between the agent and Dyeawan's tender. In either case, Nia wrested control of the dagger with a ferocity Dyeawan did not know dwelled within her sister. Unskilled at combat though she was, her fury clearly surprised Strinnix.

Dyeawan then pulled out the knife that killed Mister Quan. She can still feel the weight of it fill her hand. She'd never stabbed anyone before. She'd bashed with bludgeons and slashed with pieces of broken glass at those who'd attempted to assault her or take what little food she had when she'd lived in the streets, but Dyeawan had never before plunged a blade straight into another person's body.

The resistance surprised her. That's what she remembers most clearly about stabbing Strinnix in the hip. But Dyeawan's arms are the strongest part of her body, honed from years of pulling herself around before she had her tender, and the hilt was the only thing that stopped the blade's descent into the agent's body.

Did other agents follow? Were they chased after that? Dyeawan remembers the mad dash to the kitchen doors on the ground floor of the keep, but she doesn't remember if they were pursued. They might just have been panicked by their encounter with Strinnix, afraid the agent would get up and limp after them for revenge.

In either case, breathing the fresh outside air had felt like a victory, if only a small one. They finally had to abandon Dyeawan's tender when they reached the rocky grounds between the keep and the island's modest dock. It pained Dyeawan, like she was leaving behind a limb. She knew the chances were slim she would ever sit upon the magnificent conveyance that had become as much a part of her as her heart or lungs or hands for these years, that had enabled her to navigate and experience the world in a way she never thought possible.

Nia carried her. The power of her sister shocked Dyeawan, although the older girl's determination shouldn't have.

They only had to make it to the dock. Perhaps that was a thought of Dyeawan's, or perhaps Nia spoke the words aloud. Again, those moments are hazy now in Dyeawan's mind.

The next part is the hardest on which to focus, the most difficult to replay in her mind. The entire scene seems to want to shake itself loose of her consciousness, fraying and curling and burning at the edges as if each image is consuming itself.

"Where's Riko?"

Dyeawan's voice asking the question. It echoes between her ears as she plunges her hand into the cold water below. Her jaw clenches against the railing of the rowboat, teeth grinding until pain shoots up to her temples.

Ministry agents were not guarding the dock, as Dyeawan had feared.

They had already been there.

Dyeawan and Nia found Riko's body at the bottom of one of the other rowboats tied to the dock. She looked as though she was sleeping until they turned her over. Her eyes were open, but her features were not contorted in horror like Mister Quan's had been. Riko looked peaceful.

They'd cut her throat. The blood was pooled half an inch around her body in the boat's bottom.

We should have taken her with us, Dyeawan thinks, wanting to scream. *We should have taken her. She'll end up at the bottom of the bay like all of Edger's other victims.*

Rationally, she knows it does not matter. Her friend is gone. The shell that was left behind was not Riko. Dyeawan could see that, as clearly as she sees her hand beneath the crystal waters now.

She recalls insisting the people Edger cast to the depths of the bay be brought up and buried. Dyeawan sees what a useless, pompous gesture that was now, much more about exercising her newfound authority than honoring husks whose owners were unable to appreciate further mercy or grace from the world they'd departed.

Of course they'd had to leave Riko behind. They had to leave. There was no time.

"I still don't see anyone," Nia says a while later, for perhaps the tenth time since she shoved them off the shore of the island.

If their boat is not being followed, it must be because they are still searching the keep for her and Nia, Dyeawan reasons absently. But Strinnix may not believe they are still running scared within the walls of the Planning Cadre. They'll find the missing rowboat eventually, of course, at which point they will no doubt broaden their search.

They needn't bother in either case, Dyeawan decides. It doesn't matter if she's dead or alive. She wants none of it anymore. Let the Protectorate Ministry have the Planning Cadre. Let them have Crache. Let them deal with the invaders from Rok Island and what is left of the rebellion. Let them play their shadow games with the Ignobles for control of the Crachian machine. Dyeawan would rather return to pulling herself along the alleys of the Bottoms on a pig-greased tin sheet, digging in ash cans for food, than return to that cursed hidden island ever again.

So you're giving up, yeah?

This voice isn't hers.

It belongs to Riko.

I'm not, Dyeawan insists. *I've been defeated.*

She knows what Riko would tell her, what Edger would have told her. They would point out, each in their own way, how Dyeawan's standards for defeat have changed so vastly in her time at the Planning Cadre. When she was starving in alleys as a child, cold and alone and powerless, she never once considered herself defeated. Every day was its own challenge to overcome, and she had. Her mind had overcome all of it, without the benefit of anyone to instruct or inform or encourage it. Even and especially after her legs were crushed under those wagon wheels and unable to aid her ever again, Dyeawan never once thought of giving up. It simply was not an option. Pressing forward, surviving, was her natural state.

Yet now, possessing knowledge that child never could have dreamed of attaining, with true family of her own concerned for her well-being and here, ready to aid her, Dyeawan is finally prepared to concede her first loss.

A new feeling pierces her immense grief, permeating throughout her and curdling her blood.

It is shame. Dyeawan feels guilty and selfish, like she has become the petulant child Trowel and the others among the old guard of the planners always presumed her to be.

She is still alive. She is alive, while Mister Quan and Riko are not. She has been warm and fed and educated, where the other children she grew up alongside in the Bottoms never were. Dyeawan had once vowed to change that and has yet to have the chance to make good on that vow. She owes it to all of them to place her grief in its proper place—not to stuff it down and bury it, but to own it and *feel* it and let it become part of what moves her forward.

Dyeawan rises from the rowboat's railing, wiping away the tears and blood staining her cheeks.

"What is our course?" she asks Nia.

Her sister is clearly still concerned about her, but she answers all the same, "I am taking us to the bay of the Capitol."

Dyeawan shakes her head. "No, we can't use the docks. We would be spotted, if not by the Ministry, then by Aegins, which could be just as bad."

"What do you want to do, then?"

"Row to the east," Dyeawan instructs her. "We'll come ashore away from the city and make our way to the woods beyond the Capitol. I've never been there, but I always heard stories about it and often read about it in the Planning Cadre. The trees are tall and ancient and feel like an endless maze. It's a good place to get lost. And we need to be lost from sight right now."

The prospect of living out of doors obviously does not appeal to Nia.

"What do we do when we get there?" she asks dubiously.

"Well. Find a wheelbarrow for me, first of all," Dyeawan answers. "And then we will devise a way to get back what they have taken."

"Just the two of us?"

Dyeawan looks at her with hard, determined eyes.

"That is far more than I started with," Dyeawan says.

THE RAGGED MATRON

"YOU LOOK DIFFERENT," EVIE SAYS OF LEXI AFTER SITTING for a time with the undeniable fact it truly is the same woman.

Lexi smiles, and there are phantoms of sadness there. She gathers her long, pure-white hair in one hand and runs it slowly through her closed fist.

"I expect I do," she agrees.

Evie shakes her head. "I don't mean your hair. You . . . everything about you seems . . . changed. You don't look like the head of a venerable Crachian Gen anymore, or even a Gen member at all." Evie quickly adds, "I don't mean that as an insult, Te-Gen. Please don't take it as such."

"I don't," Lexi says with a kind smile. "I understand what you mean. And you're right."

The two of them are sitting on the edge of opposite mattresses in the cellar safe house, facing each other as they sip from chipped cups of acrid tea. They shared what food they had with Evie, which amounted to little more than a few stale steamed buns and a half cup of rice. She remains grateful, however.

Lexi asked her about Brio, first and foremost, relieved to learn he is safe, especially from the disastrous battle against the Skrain outside the Tenth City.

Still, Evie thinks she detects some distance when Lexi speaks of her husband, a removed air. It is possible she has resigned herself to never seeing him again.

Evie isn't sure what to tell her on that score. It is indeed highly possible neither of them will ever reunite with the people they left behind in the Tenth City.

Lexi is quiet for several moments before she whispers to Evie, "I think I died?"

She seems as though she isn't quite certain herself.

"That's how it started, anyway," she explains. "I don't have any insights or otherworldly knowledge to impart, though, so don't bother asking. But that's not what changed me. It's being here, among these people. Getting to know them and their world, so unfathomably different from ours, despite it being only a few miles from here that we all laid our heads. Caring for them and about them, and seeing Crache as they see it . . . even as their pleader, *especially* as their pleader, I simply didn't understand. I was too shielded from the truth."

Evie watches her. Lexi seems so tortured by whatever it is she has been through, yet it has not made her hard. Evie sees the resolve in her, and something that is striving to remain kind and generous and trusting, to remain human.

The woman Evie knew is gone, but this Lexi may be finer for it.

"I belong here now," Lexi concludes, and while there is sorrow there, regret that is more like mourning someone who has passed away, there is also hope and joy and undeniable pride.

"I don't think I can ever go back, Ashana—oh, I'm sorry. Evie, yes?"

Evie smiles. "We've both changed more than we'd like to think, I suppose."

"You've done great things," Lexi praises her. "Beyond anything I could have imagined possible. I'm sorry you were thrust into all of it. I know it wasn't your choice, at least not at first. But I am amazed by the woman sitting in front of me."

Evie doesn't know how to respond to this. She was never comfortable being elevated *before* she led her army to defeat and herself to capture and failure.

"And the Ragged Matron?"

Lexi bursts out laughing, and soon Evie has joined her.

"Not a name of my choosing," Lexi admits. "I think that *was* my hair. But I hardly need to explain the complexities of the way others might see you, Sparrow General."

"That wasn't my idea, either," Evie says. "It was a nickname, and before I knew it those damn red birds were painted *everywhere*—on armor, shields, on standards. It was horrifying. Still is."

Lexi tells her of the Ignobles, the descendants of pre-Crachian nobility, and their mission to eradicate the bureaucracy of Crache in order to bring back the rule of noble bloodlines. She tells her how these Ignobles have spent decades, possibly centuries, infiltrating the machinery of the nation by leveraging themselves and each other into key roles. She tells Evie how they tried to use her to rally the people of the Bottoms against the Capitol and start a riot that they could stoke into a cleansing fire that would sweep the city, allowing them to set into the chaos as saviors to the people of Crache.

"When I defied them before the whole of the Bottoms, the Aegin that belongs to their leader ran me through. I knew it would happen; I had accepted it. I just . . . never expected to wake up again."

Lexi looks over at Kray, who has hovered silently in the corner the whole time, watching them with a curious expression on his scarred young face.

"It was Kray," she says with great affection. "He salvaged me from the crowd, took me to what passes for a healer in the Bottoms. They were able to bring me back from the brink. Whatever potion they used to salve my wound turned my hair white. A small price to pay, I suppose. Actually, I've begun to think it suits me."

Kray reminds Evie very much of Bam in that moment, though the giant and the slight young man could not be more dissimilar on the surface.

Lexi's expression turns dark and serious.

"The Ignobles are still hunting me. Any Aegin could be one of their assassins. There is no way to know. The Protectorate Ministry doesn't care about Lexi Xia, but their agents are keenly interested in finding the Ragged Matron, if she exists. Either way, I find myself caught in the secret war between them for control of the Capitol, and by proxy Crache itself. If not for Kray and the others, I would have been found and finished off long ago."

"So you've been in hiding since that night?"

Lexi shakes her head. "Not just hiding. We've been organizing down here. I suppose you could say we've been fomenting our own rebellion from within. Kray began recruiting and training fighters. I taught those who were suited to the task how to infiltrate Gens and the Spectrum as servants and laborers, where they could gather and bring back information to us. Crache citizens are so practiced at ignoring the people from the Bottoms, there is little they don't feel free to speak around them as if they weren't there."

She falls silent, contemplative. Then she begins again, her expression disturbed.

"I am not even certain what our goal was, but for a time it was working. We were able to stay out of the eye of the Ministry and the Ignobles. We were able to . . . acquire more resources, distribute more food and water to the people. But our efforts were deeply damaged by the Ministry when they ordered the Aegins to sweep the streets of the Bottoms clear. So many of our people were taken. So many families broken apart."

Evie can see the toll this has taken on her. Her whole body is wracked with pain by what has happened here.

"Anyway." Lexi blinks rapidly, as if to banish the troubling thoughts. "We still have our informants. When we learned you, the Sparrow General, were going to be paraded through the streets, I knew it was worth the risk to free you."

"I owe you everything."

"You owe me *nothing*. You were in that cage *because* of me. If anything, I owe you—"

"You only asked me to complete a mission," Evie reminds her. "I'm the one who chose this path. You have no reason to apologize. You've walked through hellfire since I've been gone. I can see it."

Evie reaches out and takes Lexi's hands, holding them gingerly.

Lexi smiles weakly as she squeezes Evie's fingers with her own.

"Now that I'm here, what can we—" Evie begins to ask.

A thunderous clatter coming from somewhere beyond the door leading up to the first floor of the building interrupts her.

Kray immediately steps out of the corner, his hands disappearing behind his back and reemerging with lightning speed holding two mismatched, clearly homemade knives. Both their handles are wrapped in hemp. One blade is long and thin and slightly curved, while the other is wider, like a butcher's knife. The flats of both blades are dull and tarnished, but their edges appear sharp as a Skrain sword.

The door to the cellar is flung open, and with knives at the ready, Kray leaps over two of the straw mattresses in the middle of the room to meet whoever or whatever comes through.

At first there is nothing, only the darkened and empty open doorway.

Then, slowly, a figure staggers into the cellar. It is one of the street druids who helped Evie escape from the Skrain and led her back here to safety with Kray. There is an Aegin's dagger sticking out of her chest. Blood pools in the corners of her mouth and dribbles from one of her nostrils.

The young woman manages a few more steps before collapsing onto the cellar floor.

There is more commotion and what sounds like the clashing of steel against steel through the doorway from above.

"They've found us," Evie hears Lexi whisper under her breath.

Kray's head snaps back to face them, his eyes wild and filled with fire.

"The stairs to the alley!" he implores them both. "Go! Now!"

Evie is already standing, helping Lexi to her feet. Despite her nearly mortal injury, Gen Stalbraid's last daughter moves with speed and vigor.

Evie snatches up a three-foot wooden club from where its owner left it upon one of the mattresses and leads Lexi up the rickety staircase to the double doors separating the cellar from the outside.

Once they've emerged into the alley, Evie looks frantically up and down its narrow length.

"There!" she immediately hears a gruff voice shout before spotting the three Aegins, daggers drawn, charging at them from the direction of the street.

"Stay behind me," Evie calmly instructs Lexi. She hefts the crude but lethally heavy bludgeon in her hand, preparing to face down the first opponent to reach her. Thankfully they are staggered far apart as they run at varying speeds, and the narrowness of the alley prevents all three from rushing her at once.

The first Aegin to arrive within striking distance is a head taller than Evie and outweighs her by at least a hundred pounds. She allows him to swipe at her first, ducking under his arm and bashing his hip with her club, swinging the bludgeon with both hands.

The Aegin shrieks in pain, but it only seems to enrage him further. He backhands her with the fist clutched around his dagger, its pommel striking Evie in the temple.

The blow causes an explosion of light in her vision. She momentarily loses control of her limbs, dropping to one knee, though she somehow maintains a grip on the end of her club. She shakes her head to clear it of fog, and Evie blinks away just enough of it in time to see the Aegin, his grip reversed on the handle of his dagger, raising his arm to stab down at her.

Evie brings her club up just in time to intercept the dagger's blade. It sinks three inches deep into the body of her bludgeon, and she finds herself struggling with the Aegin for control of both their weapons.

The larger man brings up his knee and smashes her in the chest. Evie flies against the alley wall, hands losing their grip on her club.

When Evie looks up, she expects to see a death blow descending to finish her and instead watches as Kray's sinewy form leaps overhead and bashes into the Aegin who was looming above her.

The man is sent stumbling backwards but manages to stay on his feet and maintain hold of his dagger.

Kray charges at him, but in the last moment feints to the right and leaps at the alley wall, leaving the Aegin swinging their dagger at empty air. Evie's wiry ally uses one foot to spring off the side of the building and launches himself at the Aegin from a different angle before the man can adjust. Kray shoots his right knife hand out as if he is throwing a punch, his blade swiping *through* the Aegin's throat and taking a knuckle-sized chunk of flesh and blood from his neck at its most vulnerable point.

By the time Kray has landed back on both feet, the Aegin is spilling the rest of his life's blood across the alley floor. The second Aegin rushes him with a thrust of his dagger, Kray sidestepping and skewering the man underneath his chin, the blade piercing his soft palate and eventually finding his brain.

He uses his secondary knife hand to parry a thrust from the final Aegin's dagger, still attempting to wrest his other blade from the second man's skull.

Thankfully Evie has recovered and retrieved her club. As the third Aegin is hacking and slashing at the defending Kray, she comes up on his unseeing side and quickly caves in the man's head.

The Aegin slumps against the alley wall, and Kray is finally able to free his weapon from the one he lanced through the brain.

"Your boy has spirit, Lexi!" a friendly voice shouts at them from the other end of the alley.

It belongs to a graying Aegin with an easy manner who looks more like a friendly shopkeeper than an enforcer of Crache. He stands alone at the mouth of the alley opening onto the street. He does not advance towards them. It looks as though he's alone, at least for the moment.

Evie glances at Lexi, seeing a look of dark recognition on her face.

She knows this Aegin.

"Kamen Lim," Lexi says quietly. "He's the one who stabbed me."

Evie hears a pounding of several heavy objects against wood and looks over to see someone, probably Kray, has secured the cellar doors with what looks like a broken broom handle. There are at least a few very determined people on the other side trying to break through.

"We need to go," Evie says to Lexi.

"The other way," Kray bids them. "We can lose them between the buildings."

"Come back to us, Lexi!" Kamen Lim cheerfully calls to her. "All will be forgiven! We can still do great things together! Lady Burr will welcome you."

The sight of him has clearly rattled her, enough that Evie has to grab Lexi's arm and shake her back to the moment.

"Lexi!" she hisses. "Let's go!"

Lexi nods, the color drained from her face. She gathers her robes and follows Kray deeper into the alleyways, Evie covering their rear.

"If they found us here, the Bottoms are no longer safe," Lexi reasons as they run. "We must leave the Capitol."

"I've got an idea," Evie says, almost before she is certain she actually does. "For now, just keep moving."

STRANGE BREW

THE INESCAPABLE TRUTH OF THE EVENING THUS FAR IS that Taru does not feel like celebrating.

They should. The rebellion's defeat of the Skrain was more decisive than any of its leaders could ever have imagined before the day of the battle. The soldiers who did escape the prongs of Rok tridents or the wheels of their chariots have scattered to the winds; rebel scouts report that only a small number of the Skrain who survived returned to the Fifth City. Whether the others are seeking safety elsewhere or have outright deserted is unclear, but in either case it weakens their ability to regroup that much more.

The massive force of Savage Legionnaires that Crache conscripted and fielded to defeat the combined might of the Rok Islanders and the rebels has been disbanded. Many have fled, hoping to somehow return to the homes or streets from which they were snatched. Many others, including those unable to travel on their own, have remained with the rebellion. Their ability to feed and care for everyone was a concern, but in the short term at least, taking the Skrain army's mostly abandoned base camp and ransacking their larders and supplies has solved the problem.

There is, finally, no more Savage Legion, or at least if there will ever be one again it will have to be rebuilt from scratch, and the Skrain's capacity to do such a thing has been deeply hindered.

For all intents and purposes, one of Crache's ugliest and most destructive creations has been abolished.

More cause for celebration should not be required. Still, something feels unsettled to the retainer.

Perhaps it is the dead, the fallen rebels and Islanders who are not there to join in the revelry. The rebels, whose ranks had already been diminished during the disaster of the penultimate battle, lost three fighters to every one of the Islanders claimed by the Rok. What is left of the rebellion is a shadow of how tall it stood at its height. Counted among them must be Evie, who, even if she is still alive, remains in Crachian custody and is not here to witness the culmination of that which she created.

Perhaps it's the memory of how comfortably and even easily Taru took to mowing down enemies on the battlefield. Being a capable fighter has always been important to them, even integral to their identity, but they have never truly contemplated the "war" aspect of being a warrior until now. What felt natural, even satisfying at the time, now feels disturbing to Taru, possibly because of the undeniable *pleasure* the melee brought them.

When they were conscripted into the Legion, Taru resented the word "savage," seeing it for what it actually was; Crache's attempt to take the humanity and personhood away from those they oppressed and used as weapons.

But that is how Taru feels now, thinking about their acts on the battlefield. Those acts were brutal; they *were* savage. Taru has lived up to the moniker imposed upon them by a nation that truly exemplified the word.

That is the worst feeling, they realize. That is the thing that keeps their heart from accepting the triumph being celebrated by those around them.

If Taru is happy about anything, it is that the war appears to be reaching its conclusion.

Whether or not they are a willing participant, the party is in full swing at the camp. It is alive with music and singing and laughter and half-drunken recounting of the day's glory. Taru has yet to see the rebels and the Islanders mixing as freely and friendly as they do now, all of them having cut their teeth as a single army, bound by the blood they have spilled together.

Taru sits with Sirach, who may be the one person at the revel as sullen as the retainer. Bam looms quietly near them, sipping from an absolutely giant mug of rice wine, but silence is his usual state of being.

Brio is off somewhere, probably attempting to speak with Captain Staz about what comes next for the rebellion and its push towards the Capitol.

The retainer is still stricken by their Sicclunan counterpart's speech before and after she gutted Captain Silvar.

"How many battles does today mark for you?" Taru asks Sirach.

"I never kept count. At this point, asking how many battles I've been in would probably be like asking how many breaths I've drawn. That's what being a Sicclunan means. Your bureaucracy tells you we're some vast enemy nation, so you all picture us doing the things you do that aren't war. Keeping shops, ferrying our brats to school, building taverns. But we have no cities. You took them all from us. We can only fight, survive, defend the next mile of land you need to claim to feed your little piece of paradise."

Taru nods thoughtfully, absorbing this.

"So," they say tentatively, "a lot of battles, then?"

Sirach side-eyes the retainer, taken aback at first. Then, slowly, she begins to laugh.

Taru doesn't quite join her, but the retainer does crack a smile.

"That's two jokes in one war," Sirach says. "You'd better watch yourself."

A while later, Chimot, who was dispatched along with a rebel contingent to the Fifth City to "negotiate" with the lumber Gens, joins them.

"Good to see you made it back," Sirach greets her.

"There wasn't much left to stop us one way or the other," Chimot informs them. "I didn't see a single Skrain. All that's left are Aegins and retainers. The Gens that really run the city seem to think that will be enough, though. They won't open the gates to the rebellion."

"Did you explain to them it wasn't really a choice you were offering?" Sirach inquires.

Chimot shrugs, pouring herself a mug of wine. "They're rich old men and women. They have high walls and they still think they rule the world. What else can I say?"

"One more breath to draw, then," Sirach says pointedly to Taru.

The retainer is even less enthusiastic with the idea of laying siege to the Fifth City than they would've been before the hollowness from the day's battle struck.

"Do we have to sack the city?" Taru asks.

"Well," Sirach begins weightily, "it's going to be *real* hard to keep feeding our army if we don't, unless you want to settle here and start planting crops. By the way, can you also grow horses and steel from the ground? We'll probably need some more of those, too."

"You have made your point," Taru assures her dryly.

"We've won a major victory," Sirach says, more seriously this time, "but we will need the Fifth City as a launching point—its resources, its people, its geography—if we're going to take the Capitol."

"I thought you said you were done with fighting."

"Did she just kill someone?" Chimot asks. "She always says funny things right after a kill. It's kind of like that hour after eating a big meal where you feel like you don't ever want to eat again."

Bam grunts loudly in apparent agreement with that statement, surprising the other three and obliterating all their concentration for a moment.

The rebels and Islanders throughout the rest of the camp begin cheering loudly. Taru stares through the throng of constantly shifting bodies, and as they all begin parting to permit the passage of whoever or whatever they are approbating, the retainer spots Staz. The Rok elder has traded her shell helmet and fish scale armor for the familiar puffy sea coat that swallows all of her except her impossibly tiny head.

Staz leads a procession of her crewmembers, pairs of them lifting giant steaming cauldrons, the aroma of which announces them as tonight's supper. The wine has flowed freely for hours, but food has yet to be served to the army and its new acolytes. Everyone is starving, and the appearance of the large pots of famous Rok soup has whipped them into an understandable frenzy of delight and anticipation.

Taru can't help but smile at the small woman in her ridiculous coat. She has led an entire island nation across the sea for the first time in their history to decimate the greatest army the world has ever known, and they have succeeded, yet she still took the time to prepare a no doubt elaborate soup.

Captain Staz addresses the assemblage: "I have prepared a special soup for tonight. It is not a recipe I use often. Takes three days simmering to get it just so. I began these batches in hopes we would celebrate victory this evening. And neither the children of Rok nor our new friends have disappointed me. You have all *earned* this meal!"

The gratitude and approval of the crowd are deafening.

The *Black Turtle*'s crew sets up the soup cauldrons alongside one another and brings forth stacks of bowls and baskets of spoons to accompany them. Several long, fevered lines begin to form, their occupants ranging from eager to raucously impatient. Both Islanders and rebels have to be checked by their fellows more than once for instigating trouble as they wait for their turn to eat.

After a fair portion of the lines have been fed, Staz and her first mate serve Taru's table themselves, bringing over several tantalizing bowls of soup for the retainer, Sirach, Chimot, and Bam.

"May we join you?" she asks.

"Of course," Taru offers, more warmly than they usually address anyone.

Staz settles beside the retainer. She does not appear to have brought a bowl for herself.

"You're not eating?" Taru asks.

Staz shakes her head, causing the heavy collar of her coat to rustle unpleasantly.

"I am given to a sour stomach after battles. It is a strange quirk, but we all have one of our own, I imagine."

Taru nods, spooning a first piping-hot bite of the rich broth past their lips. They have to breathe heavily around the mouthful to cool it to a bearable temperature, but it is undeniably delicious.

"How is it?"

"Everything I would expect," Taru answers after swallowing the soup, their eyes watering.

"Where's Brio?" Sirach asks through her own half-consumed mouthful of soup.

"We spoke for a while. He decided to retire early. I believe his leg was bothering him."

"What did you speak of?" Taru inquires.

The captain is quiet for a moment before answering.

"The future," she says.

Sirach arches a brow. "Oh? Do let me know what you decided on that score. Sounds like you included all necessary parties in the conversation."

"Sirach—" Taru begins sternly.

"I am only asking what they talked about," she insists.

"Eat your soup," Staz bids them. "You all look thin. The future will keep to itself for the night, I expect."

Taru is surprised this answer seems to placate the Sicclunan warrior, but they also suspect Sirach is just hungry.

Oddly, after just a few more spoonfuls, Taru finds their own appetite diminish to nothing. Perhaps, like Staz, their stomach is sour after the battle and all the complicated thoughts and feelings it has inspired in the retainer. In either case, they push the bowl away and contend themselves with sipping water from a mug.

They speak with Staz of small things, talking about what the elder woman misses most about Rok Island, what the retainer misses most about the Capitol, and how they both hope to return to the place and the people they know. The conversation helps Taru's heart to feel a little lighter, their shoulders a little less weighted down with all the problems of the world and their own mind.

Later into the evening, a sound like the teeth of a saw blade biting into the hardest tree bark draws their attention. Bam, arms folded across his mountainous chest and head slumped forward, has fallen asleep and is snoring loudly.

Taru grins slightly, shaking their head in affectionate amusement.

"We should wake him and send him to his bed," the retainer says to Sirach and Chimot, though they only continue to watch the slumbering giant.

"Sirach?" Taru persists when they receive no answer, looking back at the usually gregarious Sicclunan.

The retainer finds the woman's cheek pressed against the tabletop beside her soup bowl, her eyes closed and her breathing loud and steady.

What's more, Chimot is slumped over her commander's back, face buried against Sirach's spine. Her lieutenant too is sleeping like a babe.

"What . . . ?" Taru begins to speak, but is seized by a sudden bout of dizziness.

Their head spins, and the world looks and feels as though it is tilting on its side. Taru looks away from the table and gazes out across the camp; they have to strain to keep their eyelids open.

Everywhere they look, bodies are sprawled on the ground, slumped against one another around fires, or passed out in their chairs. The music and singing and laughter and chatter have all ceased. The silence, or rather Taru finally taking note of it, is eerie and fills their already-upset stomach with a sudden dread.

It is then a part of Taru's mind, even as it recedes into some murky void, takes notice of the fact that all those who've gone unconscious are either rebels or liberated conscripts from the day's battle.

Every Rok Islander is still wide awake and surveying their incapacitated fellows with blank, emotionless faces.

Taru attempts to stand up from the table and finds their legs lack the strength to even support their weight. The retainer immediately falls to the ground in front of Staz's chair. Taru notes idly that the Rok elder's feet don't quite reach the ground.

Their every limb feels as though it has been filled with heavy stones. Taru can barely lift their head off the ground to stare glassily up at the captain, who looks down at them with a calm, slightly sorrowful expression.

"I will ask your forgiveness for this," Staz laments to Taru. "For polluting you like this—it is not our way to poison our enemies. Not like you, though you did give me the idea."

You've poisoned us?

Taru thinks they've spoken the question aloud at first, but a moment later they realize neither their lips nor tongue are answering Taru's commands.

"But that is just it, you see," Staz continues. "You are not our enemies. We know that. I do not want to kill you. I have come to be as fond of you as if you were one of my own children. And I could not harm my little Brio. But neither can we allow any of you to gain the ants' power and continue this monstrosity they have created, however pure your intentions."

Taru shakes their head heavily and lethargically in protest, desperately straining to form words.

None are forthcoming.

It is all Taru can do to remain conscious.

"Oh, I know," she assures Taru, correctly interpreting their feelings on the matter, "you think you have set out to destroy the machinery of their empire. I am sure you believe that, my friend. But you will merely take over the helm of that machine, you or your Sicclunan comrades or some other. Even my darling Brio, as good as his heart is, even he I would not trust to rule. Crache is the real poison. It taints and corrodes everything it touches. It will do so to whoever takes it into their embrace and tries to steer it. That is why we cannot simply part ways as friends now that our shared fight is at an end."

Staz glances over at Sirach, snuggling cozily with her fellow warrior.

"We will always be seen as a threat by whoever takes the place of the ant. Your comrades here, these Sicclunan nomads, they have fought too long. They have no home to which to return. They would become the thing they have finally defeated, I promise you that. No, we cannot allow anyone to take the seat of the ant. We must smash that seat into a million pieces and make sure no one can ever sit there again."

Taru wants their sword more than anything. They want to run it through the woman's ridiculously puffed-up coat for this betrayal. But they cannot even feel their hands.

"We won't be pressing on over land," Staz explains. "We see no reason to contend with your corrupt Gens, or attempt to lay siege to every Crachian city. We will return to the northern shore, where our fleet is still anchored. From there we sail to the bay of the Capitol. We could have taken it easily to begin with, I have no doubt, but then we would have been defending its walls from Skrain siege, and cowering behind city walls is not our way, either.

"We have crushed the ants on the field. We have taken their mandibles. The Skrain with their so-called savages have always been Crache's only true hammer. That is over now. Their leaders are politicians with no teeth of their own. I expect they will give the Capitol over easily."

Taru's head falls back against the cold ground. They can no longer summon the strength even to hold it up.

Their eyelids slip beyond their control, and the darkness that descends over their gaze is seductively welcoming.

"No more grand empires," Staz vows. "No more nations the breadth and length of the seas themselves. We will sweep the Capitol of the ant into the sea brick by brick, and then we will let the rest of your cities know they are on their own. We expect, without the standard of the ant to cower behind, that rather than come together, your Gens will tear each other apart. They will fight one another to control their cities. They will fight other cities to control what meager resources they have left. It will be bloody, but in the end, it will be better. The politicians will be whittled away. The fighters will have dominion, and the strongest among them will lead their own crews, as the Rok do. As it should be."

Staz leans down over Taru, small, withered hands clasped before them as if in prayer.

"You understand the children of Rok better than I once credited you," she tells them. "We act as the situation dictates. We know we cannot change the path of the wave, we can only ride upon it. There is no malice in that. You were right when you said this situation called for an alliance. That alliance won the day on the field of battle. But that day is over, and just as the tides shift, the situation has now changed. I hope you understand that, as well."

Perhaps she keeps speaking, or has she fallen silent? In either case, Taru finally lets go, and the unnatural sleep wrought by Rok potion takes them far away from the troubles of this world.

INTO THE WOODS

EVIE REMEMBERS HER LAST CAMPING TRIP IN THE GREAT forest outside the Capitol. She was accompanying the first children for whom she was retained as bodyguard after being put out of Gen Stalbraid. Evie was still young enough herself to be excited about exploring the ancient forest, which has stood since before the Renewal, which formed what became the nation of Crache. She remembers the impossibly tall trees, seeming to stretch all the way into the clouds. The canopy was so thick, they walked in shadow most of the day. The sounds of a hundred different animals the likes of which she'd never heard flew at them from every direction.

That was ten years ago, and the forest through which they stalk now is a twisted wraith of what Evie remembers.

The Crachian machine has cannibalized the centuries-old trees. Entire acres are graveyards of nothing but clear-cut stumps. Some deforested areas extend for miles, all the way to the edge of the woodland itself. The trees that are still standing are clustered in lonely groups of a dozen or more. They look like huddled masses of tragic mourners bearing witness to the devastation of their once-mighty kingdom. The remnant of the great forest is almost totally silent, only adding to the already disturbing mood of the place.

"The cost of paradise," Lexi offers as they survey the desolation around them. "Also the reason the warfront never ceases expanding, according to Brio. Our cities are too bloated and eat through resources too quickly. Not that you'd ever hear such a thing spoken aloud in the Spectrum or anywhere outside the Bottoms."

"I remember how easy it was to get lost here," Evie marvels. "That's why I thought we'd be safe, at least for a time. But there is . . . significantly less cover now."

"On the plus side," Lexi reasons, "very few people come out here anymore, as I understand it. It holds nothing for them."

They weren't able to escape the city with much in the way of supplies. Evie was counting on the great forest to provide water, vegetation, and game. She hopes, at the very least, Crache hasn't depleted all its streams.

She was desperately hoping for a bath.

They trek for more than an hour after reaching the edge of the ravaged woodland, hoping to find a spot to camp with good concealment and fresh water.

"Do you have any idea where you want to go from here?" Lexi asks her.

Evie takes several deep breaths before answering. The question has been weighing heavily on her.

"You want to go back to the rebellion," Lexi surmises.

"I want to find out if my friends are still alive," Evie says. "And yes, if there is anything left to salvage, I owe it to everyone who rallied behind me to continue the fight, whether it is against Crache or the Rok or both."

"Why do you hesitate, then?"

"Because I have the feeling you won't want to come with me."

It is Lexi's turn to contemplate in silence.

"I want to see Brio again," she says. "Truly, I do. But I cannot abandon those who remain in the Bottoms. My fight is still there, however hard they have tried to break us."

"Even if you can hide from the Ministry, it seems as though the Ignobles won't let you rest, and they have more ears to the street."

"I know."

Ahead of the two of them, Kray abruptly stops moving. Evie can almost feel his whole body tense as much as she sees it before her. Lexi's protector then holds up a warning hand to them to halt, which they obey.

When the crunching of leaf and stick under their feet ceases, all of them can make out the faint but steadily rising, terrified screams of what sounds like more than one young girl.

Without further warning, Kray breaks into a run, bounding with surprising speed in the direction of pleading cries.

"Stay here," Evie urges Lexi.

She takes off after the street soldier, braining club clutched in her right hand.

Together, they race around another lonely cluster of tall forest trees, the high-pitched shrieks growing louder and louder.

After the past few days, Evie expects Skrain soldiers or Protectorate Ministry agents or perhaps even Aegins acting as assassins for the Ignobles.

What she happens upon instead is a dozen sawdust-covered woodcutters tormenting and toying with two young women.

There is an overturned wheelbarrow, and attempting to crawl away from the woodcutters several yards in front of it is a dark-haired teenager whose legs do not appear to work. Evie thinks at first she has been injured by them, but then she wonders if the girl didn't arrive in the woods in the wheelbarrow.

A second, slightly older-looking girl with her hair pulled back into a stern bun is being held on her knees, that bun clinched in the fist of a toothless woodcutter wearing a straw hat.

"Come on then!" a burly man with a dark and wild beard and an ax draped over one shoulder taunts the girl crawling across the ground. "You can make it!"

"Stop this!" Evie barks at the lot, loudly and with the thunder of rage in her voice.

The scattered laughter and jeering stops, and for the first time, all heads turn towards her and Kray, who stands at the ready beside her.

The younger girl stops crawling, looking back at the source of the command with faint hope in her eyes.

For a moment they each look concerned, this woodcutter contingent, as if worried they've been caught by some authority figure, or at least a high-ranking citizen of a Gen who could cause them no end of problems if they decided to take an interest.

When the woodcutters finally take in the sight of the pair, however—Evie's and Kray's shabby clothing and generally disheveled appearance—the smiles slowly return to their faces.

"Oh piss off, will you?" the bearded one shouts back at them. "This doesn't concern you. Unless these strays belong to you?"

"They belong somewhere," Evie insists.

The woodcutter chuckles.

"Not that they've said! Won't even tell us their names. A couple of runaways or thieves or both, is my guess."

"What are you going to do with them?" Kray asks in a quiet tone only Evie seems to recognize as lethally dangerous.

The smile fades from the bearded one's face again, replaced by a look of irritation and impatience.

"Whatever we please! So unless you want to be part of our afternoon's amusements, why don't the pair of you fuck off and don't cross my eye again."

"This is all very boring," Evie says, because it is, not to mention woefully predictable. "In the next minute, all of you will be walking away back to whatever work you were doing, having left these girls in peace."

The woodcutters, even the bearded spokesman, seem a bit caught off guard by the confidence and command in Evie's tone.

None of them are aware they are speaking to a general, of course.

They don't say anything right away, but neither do they move to comply with her.

Evie sighs wearily.

"This is the part where you ask me, 'or what?'" she informs them.

"All right," the bearded one says, shifting the ax handle from his shoulders and hefting the menacing-looking tool in his hands. "What if we don't walk away, then?"

"In that case—" Evie begins, preparing to explain how all of them will end up losing their life's blood on this desolate ground.

Kray, it seems, would prefer to illustrate the same point with action. He springs forward, the dull blades of his unmatching knives flaring dimly in the afternoon sun.

The woodcutter nearest him raises a two-handed saw blade to defend himself, but Kray thrusts one knife through the opening created by the saw's wide handle, ramming the knife home into the man's midsection. At the same time, he reverses his grip on the handle of his second knife, bringing the blade down into the crook between the man's neck and shoulder.

When Kray removes the weapon, blood shoots five feet into the air above their heads.

"All right then," Evie says, striding forward with her club at the ready.

Kray has cut down two more woodcutters before Evie even reaches the fracas. She watches out of the corner of her eye as the boy's shockingly strong arms heft the entire body of one of the woodcutters into the air like a hay bale he's skewered with hooks, slamming it to the cold, hard ground.

For Evie, who has spent the last year fighting hand-to-hand against the most highly trained warriors in the nation, the woodcutters appear to be moving at half speed at best. Their footwork is sloppy and lethargic, their "weapons" handling inefficient and unskilled, and their sense of coordination generally quite poor.

She easily ducks and feints blows from the men's and women's tree-chopping and shearing tools, cracking skulls and kneecaps with her club.

All the while, their bearded mouthpiece is backing up, away from the battle, clutching the ax handle in his hands so tightly his knuckles are white as ghosts.

Moments later, he finds he is the last woodcutter standing.

Evie approaches him cautiously, knowing even a cornered housecat is dangerous. She is breathing heavily from swinging the club, the thick of which is stained with blood, hair, and at least two teeth.

"Tell me what you were going to do with them," she demands, blood still rushing from the heat of battle. "Say it out loud."

"Just . . . just fooling about . . ."

"Liar!" Evie thunders at him.

In response, the final woodcutter raises his ax defensively.

Evie begins to take another step forward. As she does, Kray appears, a blur in the corner of her vision. Before Evie can truly say she sees him move into view, one of his knives is plunged into the side of the woodcutter's skull.

The ax-wielding brute never sees him coming, either. The expression frozen on his face in death is one of utter and horrific surprise.

After a moment, Kray withdraws his blade, mostly to allow the woodcutter to fall forward onto his shocked face.

"Lexi is fortunate I respect her so much," Evie tells him. "Otherwise I'd try to poach you for *my* army."

Kray grins a bit at that, but he doesn't say anything in reply.

The older girl the woodcutters had been restraining by her hair is still resting on her hands and knees. She chokes back the tears and snot she's been shedding and gathers herself up, smoothing dirty hands over the front of her gray tunic and slowly rising to her feet.

"We . . . we owe you our gratitude. I thank you for intervening."

She addresses Evie very formally, almost importantly, despite her current circumstances. Her manner, even as shaken as she is, speaks to Evie of high breeding and station, or at least the self-perception of it.

"You're all right now," Evie assures her. "I'm sorry you had to witness this, but I promise we won't hurt you."

Evie walks past the overturned wheelbarrow to where the other girl is now sitting on the ground. She has taken the time to fold her unresponsive legs beneath her and is looking up at Evie with a disarmingly calm and warm expression on her face.

That face is familiar, Evie realizes, though she cannot immediately place it.

"I know you."

The girl nods. "I never expected to see you again," she says. "We met in a dungeon in the Capitol."

Evie's breath catches in her throat as her mind re-creates the scene.

"Little Slider," she breathes in disbelief.

"Dyeawan. My name is Dyeawan. You were gone when I awoke. They'd already taken you."

Evie nods. "And you?"

"They took me too, but they brought me somewhere much different from where they brought you."

Dyeawan's companion makes a noise, drawing both their gazes. She is staring at Dyeawan with alarmed eyes, clearly not wanting her to say any more on the subject.

"It's all right, Nia," Dyeawan assures her. "We can trust Evie and her friend."

"His name is Kray," Evie tells her. A look of sudden recall comes to her face.

"Kray!" she says. "Go find Lexi, make sure she's all right."

The boy nods, hustling back the way the two of them came.

"I recognize him, as well," Dyeawan says.

Evie looks back at her, confused.

"You do?"

"You do?" Nia repeats, equally surprised.

"Yes. We grew up together on the streets in the Bottoms, though I doubt he remembers me. His scars are hard to forget, even for someone whose memory is not as sharp as mine tends to be. They are unique. I also remember reading about them in a Ministry intelligence report, one of the last I was privy to before we . . . elected to leave the Planning Cadre."

"The Planning Cadre?" Evie asks, the words feeling foreign in her mouth.

"I read that, as well," Nia recalls. "It was part of the only description we have of one of the robed street people who attacked the prison caravan . . . carrying the Sparrow General through the city."

Nia's gaze begins to drift to Evie as she finishes her thought.

Dyeawan is staring intently at the woman as well.

"You?" Nia asks in disbelief. "You're the Sparrow General?"

Evie grins slowly.

"It sounds like we both have some secrets we have to be careful about sharing," Evie says. "Maybe you'll fill me in on yours, as well."

PENT-UP

THE ROK HAVE NO PRISON WAGONS, SO THEY'VE COMMANDEERED a caravan of cage-covered buckboards from the Skrain army the Islanders have either killed or sent fleeing to the four corners of Crache. There are a dozen dungeons on wheels, stuffed to their iron gills with the remnants of the Sparrow General's once-mighty army. The Rok did not imprison everyone, however. They allowed the most recently freed Legionnaires to go their own way, provided none of them caused problems. A few salty stragglers aside, the majority of the former conscripts were happy to remain passively behind.

The seasoned rebels they offered a simple choice: walk away from the rebellion and its leaders. Go off where you will, but offer no more allegiance or service to the absentee Sparrow General's army.

Taru watched that process from behind bars, for the Rok were taking no such chances with the officers by offering them the same choice. It panged the retainer to see more than half of what was left of the people who had just fought alongside them readily renounce their comrades and leave the camp. The retainer understands, of course. Most of them were conscripts themselves. They never asked to fight. But fight they did, and Taru knew they've all done far more than should ever have been asked of them.

If they have people and homes to which they hope to return, who can fault them for walking away?

Perhaps Taru should be more surprised by those who remained behind, knowing all that awaited them was a cage beside those they'd trusted to lead and protect them. But such can be the bonds of war, or at least mythologizing one's own place in the world by way of the commanders they serve.

At some point the retainer allowed themself to fall asleep from sheer exhaustion. The Rok had broken camp and their caravan was already on its way to the coast when Taru regained consciousness. They awoke in the back of the same caged wagon as Sirach, Chimot, Bam, and Brio, the people who had quickly become the retainer's family, if only by default. They'd all been relieved of their weapons, though Brio was allowed to retain his crutch.

"She said she was sorry," Brio had told his retainer, "she" being Captain Staz. "She wanted me to go with them, but she knew I would never go along with any of this."

Taru could see how deeply it wounded their cherished De-Gen. The Rok captain had been like a beloved aunt to him.

Taru is forced to admit the prison wagons are well built. The bars are solid iron. The frame is secured to the thick wood of the buckboard with flat-headed spikes that cannot be pried or jimmied loose. The lock on the cage door takes two special, separate keys to open, and each keyhole is shrouded to make it heavily resistant to tampering and lock picks.

It is the middle of a cool evening. The breeze from the ocean wafts mercifully through the bars. They reached the coastline that morning, at which point the Islanders began setting up camp, preparing to enjoy one more night on land before retaking command of their ships and setting sail for the Capitol.

They lined up the prison wagons just outside their camp and detached each one's horse team. The beach and the Rok fleet beyond are within sight of where the prisoners all sit inside their cages.

"How long have we been here?" Sirach asks the rest of them. "Two days? Three?"

Brio cocks his head at her. "Do you mean how long have we been conscious inside this cage, or how long ago did they throw us in here, unconscious?"

"Conscious."

"It is at least a three-day ride from the Fifth City to the northern shore," Brio posits. "So three days."

Sirach nods. "Good. I figured I'd wait at least this long before saying I told you so. I didn't want to be accused of being an opportunist."

"Saying it now is no more constructive than it would have been then," Brio points out.

"But it's still true!"

"What choice did we have?" Brio asks.

"The *right* one," Sirach insists. "The *exact opposite* of the one we made, which was to forget they tried to see us slaughtered and choose to fight alongside them as allies!"

Brio tries to remain calm. "It was agreed upon by everyone in this wagon."

"I just wanted to get Evie back! If she were here, she never would have—"

"She's *not* here!" Brio finally erupts. "*You* couldn't deliver her to us."

It is clear he knows it's wrong as soon as he says it, but he has already broken the threshold in their heated argument.

Taru has been quiet more or less since they awoke in the group's current captivity. They remember every single word Staz said to them before they finally succumbed to the darkness brought on by her "special" soup. The retainer has been replaying the whole scene in their head ever since.

"It doesn't matter," the retainer says, breaking their silence to rebuke Sirach.

"What do you mean, it *doesn't matter*?" she demands, clearly incensed.

"How this has developed, the Rok's betrayal, us ending up here, it is all irrelevant. We could not have chosen differently. This alliance had to be made to defeat the Skrain."

Taru isn't even certain what the Rok have done to them can be considered a "betrayal," at least not by their standards, but that piece of perspective the retainer holds back.

"We could have done what the Islanders did," Sirach insists. "We could have let them and the ants destroy each other and then swept in to pick the bones."

"They would have lost," Taru states matter-of-factly. "The Rok would have drowned in the Savage Legion, and the Skrain would have finished them. And the Skrain would not have been weakened enough for us to defeat on our own."

"You don't know any of that!"

"Yes, I do, and so do you."

It isn't clear whether that actually strikes a chord within Sirach, or whether the Sicclunan warrior becomes just too weary to argue further.

Either way, she falls silent.

"I believe I had learned how to think like them," Taru says, speaking aloud what has been spooling through their mind the past days. "The Rok. But I could not, until now, fully set aside thinking as myself at the same time. Measuring and judging and anticipating the Island folk by the standards I applied to them. With the Rok, there is only what is necessary, and that changes as readily as the tides."

"Well, you've certainly mastered their irritating use of sea analogies," Sirach comments.

"There is no malice of thought in how they view what is necessary," Taru continues unabated. "To us, to me, that lack of malicious intent made me believe their actions would always be peaceful. When you or I make an allegiance, that allegiance is sacrosanct. To break it is dishonorable. But the Rok never agreed to be held to those standards. I cannot hate them, even now. But I think I finally understand them."

"Fascinating," Sirach says dryly. "And where does all of that insight leave us, except still in this cage?"

"It leaves us with what is necessary," Taru concludes. "What is necessary for us here and now is to stop the Rok from destroying the Capitol and hurling the entire nation into chaos."

"And how do you propose we do that, retainer?" Sirach asks, illustrating her point by pounding her forearm against the bars behind her hard enough to cause the entire cage to vibrate.

"That is precisely what I have spent our time in this wagon contemplating. Perhaps I already knew, but it was not until I smelled the salt and laid eyes on the shore this morning that I think I was able to . . . accept it."

"Your calm is beginning to disturb me a little," Sirach says, watching them with more caution than anger now.

"What is it, my friend?" Brio asks.

"We cannot fight them," Taru reasons. "Even if we managed to free every one of our people they have imprisoned, we would never overcome them in combat."

Sirach grins sourly. "That's the first thing you've said today that I agree with."

"The Rok are indeed fierce fighters, but their power is in their fleet. It always has been."

"And so?" Brio asks, almost as if he is afraid to hear the answer.

"We are going to escape this cage. Sirach and Chimot will lead us stealthily to the beach. Once there, we will burn the Rok fleet. We will burn as many of their ships at anchor as we can before they kill us. And they *will* kill us all. There will be no way to escape if we commit to what I propose."

"You really know how to motivate people," Sirach says.

"Burning their ships won't stop them from fighting," Chimot points out.

"No, but it will strand them here. It will wipe out their excess supplies. They will be forced to try and lay siege to the nearest city if they wish to survive, let alone continue their campaign. They will not be able to sack the Capitol, in any case."

"Their ships are sacred to them," Brio reminds his retainer.

"The Rok. They are passed down through generations. Their whole history is bound up in those hulls, Taru."

"We are beyond politeness and consideration at this point, De-Gen. Far beyond."

"Fine, you've sold me," Sirach relents, "but you painted over exactly how we get out of here in the first place."

Rather than responding to that, Taru rises from their seat and walks to the door of the wagon's cage, encircling their hands around the bars.

There are only two Rok fighters armed with tridents guarding the rear of the prison wagon caravan several yards away from the officers' cage. The Rok seem to be trusting Crachian engineering to keep their captives secure.

"You!" the retainer hisses at the nearest Islander. "Come over here!"

"Subtle," they hear Sirach mutter under her breath.

The Rok fighter looks over at the wagon, but only briefly. They quickly return to talking to their fellow guard, ignoring the retainer.

"Shame," Sirach laments. "It was a good plan."

The retainer ignores her.

"Hey, ugly!" Taru taunts the Islander. "Your mother's soup tastes of horse piss!"

That draws the guard's attention for longer than a fleeting glance, and he frowns deeply at the retainer.

Staz had said Taru understood the Rok better than the captain had credited them.

His friend in tow, the Rok fighter tromps over to the door of the wagon's cage.

"Say that again about my ty-ty's soup," he dares the retainer, extending his trident to jab them through the bars.

Taru reaches out with frightening speed and grips the haft of the weapon, yanking it forward with equally frightening power.

The Islander is caught completely off guard, stumbling forward within arm's reach of the retainer. Taru grabs the back of his head, holding him by the scruff like an ornery puppy, and rams the bridge of his nose against the bars. When his body is close enough, the retainer reaches through and pulls the dagger sheathed at his belt from its scabbard, rearing back and hurling the knife at the other Rok sentry.

The blade pierces the man's throat just to the left of the lump there. The dagger is embedded several inches deep. Rather than words or alarmed cries issuing from his mouth, all that spews forth is a torrent of blood.

A moment after Taru lets the dagger fly, they reach up and again grip the scruff of the bloody-nosed Islander pressed against the cage. Their other hand grasps his chin and jaw tightly. Taru snaps his neck in one fierce jerk.

Before letting his body fall to the ground, the retainer reaches down and relieves him of the keys also dangling from his belt.

Taru draws their arms back inside the cage, turning away from the door and holding the large key ring up in front of Sirach's face.

"All right," she admits. "I'm taking this whole plan of yours a *little* more seriously now."

EVERYTHING THEY WANT

"SO," EVIE BEGINS, STRUGGLING TO FULLY COMPREHEND and accept the tale spun by Dyeawan, "you have basically been the unseen empress of Crache for a year?"

"It does not work quite like that," the girl corrects her with the same kind smile a teacher might offer a pupil who simply can't seem to grasp their arithmetic.

"The Planning Cadre is not unlike the Crachian bureaucracy you know. Even sitting at the head of the planners, the Cadre's most powerful group, I was blocked and vetoed and stonewalled at almost every turn by the rest of them, by the Protectorate Ministry. I could not accomplish a tenth of what I wished to do for our people."

"Also, we *share* leadership of the planners," Nia interjects. "My sister and I co-chair the planners. Or rather, we did . . ."

"I meant no offense," Evie says to the girl.

They buried the bodies of the woodcutters she and Kray had killed, purely out of caution. Dyeawan and Nia insisted on helping even after Evie told them there was no need. The sisters, for that's what they revealed they were, clearly had a lot of grit despite how Evie's party had come upon them.

Once the vile men and women were in the ground, the quintet sought out a collection of trees with enough shade for them all to share and collectively made the decision to rest. Kray left them to find and collect water, allowing Evie and Lexi a chance to question the unexpected young women.

"I remember you as such a lost little babe," Evie recalls with equal amounts of wonder and confusion. "It was clear you were far smarter and sharper than anyone would give you credit for being, but you were just a girl."

"I still am," Dyeawan reminds her, reclining in her reclaimed wheelbarrow.

"Yes, but you know what I mean."

"You were kind to me when you had no reason to be," Dyeawan says to Evie. "Sleeping beside you in that dungeon, I felt safe. I want you to know I was grateful to you for that. Even if you did reek of cheap wine."

Evie laughs. "I was playing a role! Besides, cheap wine is standard in the Bottoms."

"Yet you went from a conscript to lead the only successful rebellion in Crache's history, known or hidden."

"This is all very interesting and emotionally resonant," Nia assures them impatiently, "but we have far more pressing matters to discuss."

"While I don't mean to be as curt as my sister," Dyeawan begins, adding when she catches a flash of the girl's resentment at that statement, "I have to agree."

Lexi, having no personal connection to Dyeawan, is more fixated on her explanation of where they came from.

"I just can't believe this Planning Cadre could be as powerful as you describe *and* remain concealed from the rest of the bureaucracy and the Gens. It's not that I don't believe you; I simply can't imagine how it's possible."

"How have the Ignobles amassed the power and influence you've described to me while remaining hidden?" Evie asks pointedly.

That seems to resonate deeply with Lexi, who falls silent.

"Crache was created to obfuscate truth and power," Dyeawan says. "That is among the most important lessons I learned in my time there. This nation was made for people like the planners and the Ignobles to hide."

"If the Rok continue to gain ground, especially if the Crachian rebels regroup, the Protectorate Ministry will have its hands full," Lexi reasons. "The Ignobles will see that as their ultimate opportunity. They'll attempt to seize the Capitol again, and this time they might succeed. They won't negotiate with any hostile army. They're too arrogant. If they hold sway when the Rok or the rebellion or both come, they'll fight and force others to fight to the last person. It will be a bloodbath."

"The Protectorate Ministry isn't equipped to stop the rebellion either," Dyeawan affirms. "They're not military strategists or warriors. They're saboteurs and assassins."

"We can do nothing about any of this," Nia insists. "We can only attend to our own survival."

"Well now," Evie muses, "it does occur to me that might not be entirely true."

The heads of the three others turn towards her.

At that moment, Kray returns with fresh water for them and begins silently distributing them rations of it.

"It occurs to me," Evie begins thoughtfully, "that right here, we have almost everything the Ministry *and* the Ignobles want."

Lexi and Dyeawan turn and look at her expectantly.

Nia, on the other hand, seems as though she is ahead of the others in deciphering Evie's meaning.

"Us," Evie explains. "The Sparrow General, leader of the rebellion. The Ragged Matron, symbol of hope among the people of the Bottoms and all disenfranchised like them. And Slider, the deposed upstart who escaped assassination and still has supporters in this mysterious Planning Cadre that appears to secretly orchestrate our lives."

"Yes, but how would we leverage all of you to our advantage?" Nia presses on. "We have no power, no position, and no support. We are alone, running scared for our lives."

"First, we stop running," Evie says firmly. "Second, I believe we have just enough leverage to do what the Rok Islanders attempted to do with the rebels and the Skrain: watch our enemies destroy one another."

They all stare at her in confusion except for Dyeawan.

She sees it, the plan that Evie is suggesting. Evie can tell by the look on the younger woman's face, the way Dyeawan's eyes are already searching unseen quarters for further steps and possible pitfalls.

"There is risk," Dyeawan reminds Evie, as if they have already discussed the details.

"There is," Evie agrees. "For all of us. But your sister and Kray will have to decide to offer themselves up first if this is going to work."

"What are we discussing here?" Nia demands, clearly frustrated with them speaking about and around her.

"I believe," Lexi interjects, seemingly catching on as well, "we are discussing emissaries. Yes?"

Evie nods.

"Emissaries?"

Dyeawan turns to Nia. "I need to ask something of you that will seem . . . unwise at first, even quite mad."

Her sister frowns. "I get the sense it is not to braid your hair again."

"No," Dyeawan laments. "I need you to return to the Planning Cadre."

Whatever Nia might have been expecting to hear, those words defy all logic and explanation to her.

"*Back?* That is not mad, that is suicide! You are asking me to commit suicide. For what *possible* reason?"

"I am not, I promise you. You are going to go back and you are going to tell them you have reconsidered. That hiding in the streets with me changed your mind about our relationship and our future together. You wish to return to the planners. In exchange for their amnesty, you will offer me up to them."

"They won't believe me."

"They *will*," she insists. "The planners will. You're like an estranged daughter to them. You were Edger's chosen. They desperately wanted to sway you. Let them believe they have, and they will convince the Protectorate Ministry of your sincerity."

"And then what?" Nia asks, still obviously unconvinced.

Dyeawan looks briefly over at Lexi, then up at Evie.

Evie nods, silently encouraging her to go on.

"You tell them where they can find me, in the Bottoms. You tell them I am with a new movement of rebels gathering there. For this reason, the Ministry must come in force. Tell them they cannot trust Aegins or even the Skrain, as the Ignobles have their hooks in most of the ones left in the Capitol. They must send their own agents—in full force. We want as many to be there as possible. The whole of the Ministry, if we can manage it."

"At the same time," Lexi follows on the heel of Dyeawan's words, "Kray, you'll find Kamen Lim. Turn yourself in to the Aegins in the Bottoms if necessary. You're going to tell him that I have had enough. The Ministry wants my life. Our people are starving and hounded in the streets. My only option is to come back to the Ignobles."

There is no hesitation or even questioning from Kray. He listens intently, his eyes saying he is ready to do whatever the Ragged Matron asks of him.

Again, Evie thinks of Bam. She also remembers the faces of countless people who joined the rebellion because they believed in the "Sparrow General" with that kind of unquestioning faith. Many of them are dead now, perhaps even most of them.

It gives Evie unpleasant chills.

"But," Lexi adds, "I will only come back to them as an equal. I wish to meet with Lady Burr and the other descendants of nobility I've yet to see. I want to know they exist, and it's not just her on her own. I need to know she really does have the power to protect me. That part is important."

Kray nods. "I understand. I'll convince them, I promise."

Lexi smiles gently, reaching out to squeeze his thin wrist with her hand. "I know you will. I'm just sorry to ask you to do something so dangerous."

"Are you going to apologize to me?" Nia asks her sister pointedly.

"You can always refuse," Dyeawan reminds her.

It is clear the intention of their plan has come into focus for Nia. She seems calmer, if nothing else.

"You really believe we can maneuver them both like this? And even if we can, will the result be what you expect?"

"You have seen how the Ministry prefers to solve any threat presented to them with their daggers," Dyeawan reminds her. "We both have."

"And I can vouch for how bloodthirsty the Ignobles are," Lexi adds. "Killing and cruelty are like nostalgia for them, a thing they miss being able to inflict at their will."

"As I see it," Evie says, "the Rok aren't going anywhere. Hopefully the rebellion isn't gone, either. We need Dyeawan and you, Nia, back in control of this Planning Cadre, and we need to remove this threat of the Ignobles from the Capitol if we have any hope of keeping the entire nation from falling to total chaos, or in even worse hands than the ones we've been attempting to lop off at the wrist."

Evie becomes aware Dyeawan is not merely listening to her as she speaks; she is studying Evie with a strange smile.

"What is it?" Evie asks.

"I see now why so many people have followed you to war. This is very much the conversation I'd hoped we might have before you were taken from us. I just never thought we would have it under circumstances like this."

"Better late than never, Little Slider," Evie says with a grin, and then corrects herself. "Forgive me. Dyeawan."

"Not to dampen the mood," Nia offers, "but we have not solved anything yet. This is only a plan, and quite a desperate one, if you ask me."

"Desperation is our business, Nia," Lexi informs the stodgy young woman.

Desperation is our business.

"Yes," Evie agrees. "Indeed it is."

EVERY SHIP'S DECK IS AN UNLIT FUNERAL PYRE

IT HAS NEVER OCCURRED TO TARU UNTIL JUST NOW, AS they prepare to torch the hull of every single one to which they can lay hands, just how beautiful Rok-built sailing vessels truly are.

Long, sleek, and slender to the point of being narrow, they are designed for speed and to practically slice through the hull of enemy vessels. The Rok began by building simple canoes, and their full-scale ships call back to those early vessels, with hulls constructed of hollowed tree trunks and bamboo sealed together through some arcane process to which Taru has not been privy. The bows and sterns, however, are constructed from bone, large polished pieces from what must be fish larger than the retainer has ever seen. Many of the sails have been upgraded to cloth through trading with Crache, but many still utilize the massive leaves of the burry fruit trees woven together.

A Rok ship is as much art as function. There is nothing else like them, and Taru is going to reduce an entire fleet of the remarkable vessels to piles of smoking ash upon the tides or die in their attempt.

The Rok fleet is anchored a hundred yards offshore. They

chose a landing point with no docks, because a harbor would mean people, a community with which the invaders would have to contend. Dozens upon dozens of longboats line the beach in a seemingly endless row, as well as large square floats fashioned to be towed by the longboats, which the Rok use to transport their chariots, native mounts, and other heavy weapons, equipment, and supplies back and forth from the main ships of the fleet.

The Rok army is enjoying a typically boisterous evening in their camp, perhaps a hundred yards inland. From what Taru recalls, the Islanders left just enough crew aboard each vessel to maintain and watch over them when the rest of the force went ashore.

Taru and the others liberated just as many rebels as the retainer and Sirach agreed it would take to get the job done, about a dozen men and women in all. Taru hid the bodies of the guards they killed under the wagon, and the rebel officers even moved new prisoners to the cage they left behind, padding the space around Brio so it would not appear empty. They needed their escape to go unnoticed for as long as possible. Taru knew eventually, inevitably, alarms would be raised, and they wanted to at least be in the water by then.

The rebels took what weapons they could from the guards. Chimot and Bam collected pieces of clothing from the fighters they left behind, planning to use them to fashion torches for their end goal. Taru takes it for granted they will find a good source of fire along the way or strike one from the rocks on the ground if necessary.

Sirach and Chimot led the sabotage party to the beach and concealment behind a large dune overlooking the Rok landing point, and then the two Sicclunans disappeared.

Taru surveys the sand below and waits with the rest for the shadow scouts to return. There are a few long, burning torches staked into the damp sand, but the scene is mostly lit only by moonlight. They think they spy a few tall shadows moving among the surf, but it is difficult to make them out.

The retainer hears the sand shifting on the other side of the dune, and in the next moment Sirach and her lieutenant are slithering back up to the rebels' position.

"The Islanders haven't thought to post many sentries with the landing boats," Chimot relays. "We only spotted a few walking up and down the beach. One of them is fishing off the shore in a chair."

"Can you take down the sentries without one or more of them running back to camp to raise the alarm?" Taru asks.

"I am going to ignore that question and the deep offense it calls for," Sirach whispers back. "Just watch for our signal and be ready to move fast and quietly when it comes."

The retainer nods, seeing no reason to belabor the discussion.

The pair disappears anew, and though Taru attempts to track the two's progress, they quickly lose sight of the Sicclunans.

They are *good*. There is no denying it.

The wait is torment, so eager is the retainer to charge down the dune.

Taru watches as one of the Rok sentries approaches the nearest end of the long line of landing vessels, spinning his trident above his head obliviously.

He has just strolled past the last one when Sirach appears from the bottom of the boat. Taru never even saw her take up position inside the thing.

No sooner has she broken cover than Sirach leaps onto the Islander's back, a stolen dagger flashing in her hand for only a moment before the two of them hit the sand below.

Sirach recovers from the tumble.

The sentry does not, remaining motionless on the beach at her feet.

The Sicclunan warrior quickly gathers enough sand around the body to conceal it from sight. Once that is done, she waves her arm at Taru and the others watching from atop the dune.

The retainer can only guess that farther down the line of longboats, Chimot has seen to the other sentries.

"Stay low and follow me," Taru instructs the others. "Single column. Keep yourselves tight and watch our flank."

They lead the others down the face of the dune. As the company races along the incoming tide, Taru begins pulling the sparsely arranged Rok torches from where they are buried in the sand. Reaching the nearest longboat, Taru begins distributing them among their force. They also wrap the tridents they've collected from the Rok guards in spare cloth and begin setting those ablaze as well.

"Two to a boat," they instruct the rebels. "Each pair takes a torch. Light the hulls above the waterline in as many places as will catch fire. Once the thing is ablaze, move on to the next ship. Does everyone understand?"

No one raises a voice to say they do not, which the retainer takes as assent.

"Sirach, will you ride with me?"

"Thank you for not making it an order," she says to Taru. "It will be my pleasure. Chimot, go with our stoic friend here."

Her lieutenant moves towards Bam, and the rest pair off around the torches that have been handed out, racing to push the nearest available boat across the sand and into the water.

"And keep your torches covered as best you can until you reach one of those ships!" Sirach hisses. "They'll see them a mile off if they're looking."

She joins Taru in dragging one of the longboats into the rolling tide of the evening. When they are both knee-deep in the ocean, they pull their bodies over opposite sides of the vessel, Taru carefully lifting and balancing the torch so the water splashing about does not touch its flame.

Sirach finds long-handled paddles at the bottom of the boat and hands one to the retainer.

Taru carefully props the torch between the slats upon which they and Sirach sit, securing the torch's long pole between their knees. With their hands freed, they dip the head of the paddle into the dark water and begin rowing.

The small fleet of landing vessels slowly disperses from the shore, paddling in different directions to cover as much of the waiting fleet as possible.

Taru works the paddle powerfully and furiously, forcing Sirach to increase her own rowing just to keep up. Before long Taru can hear the Sicclunan warrior breathing hard and fast from the effort, but they do not and cannot slow down.

The entire time, Taru expects to see and hear commotion from the decks of the increasingly-tall-and-large-in-their-vision Rok sailing fleet. They are sure the small boarding party will be spotted right away, but no such warning cries come.

With Sirach straining to keep pace with the retainer, the pair reaches the edge of the fleet before any of the other rebels.

The commandeered longboat drifts slowly alongside the closest Rok vessel to shore. When they are close enough, Sirach deftly extends the haft of the paddle in her hands and uses the end to brace against the hull, halting the longboat in the water within arm's reach of the long ship's sleek body.

As she does, Taru pulls their makeshift torch up from the bottom of the boat and begins inching towards the side, being careful not to tip it with their weight too much. They wave the flaming head near the hull, extending it upward until the well-traveled wood begins to look the least damp.

Taru hesitates. They feel that deep sense of unsettlement again, as they did back near the Fifth City reflecting on the battle with the Skrain before the Rok drugged them all. They can't help thinking this will be another day of violence and destruction with which they will have to live, even if they don't have to do it for long once the Islanders see their beloved vessels burning.

They were so certain about this course of action only moments ago. It had solidified in their mind over the past few days inside the prison wagon. They had accepted who they believed the Rok to be, no longer regarding them as friends even if they could not hate the Rok for being who they are. The retainer knew beyond doubt *this* was now necessary.

Now, however, Taru simply isn't sure.

"What are you *waiting* for?" Sirach hisses. "The wind to carry the flame for you?"

"What will this accomplish?" Taru asks aloud, though the question is not entirely meant for Sirach.

The Sicclunan warrior is livid. "Are you *kidding* me right now?"

Taru turns their head towards her. "I am serious."

"This was *your* plan, you ass!"

"*Listen* to me! This will stop them from sacking the Capitol, but it will only beget more fighting between us all. It could even lead to their extermination, if the Gens muster enough of a force to defend the cities against them."

"*We, my* people, have already *been* exterminated, in case you hadn't noticed. By these soup-slurping, double-talking bastards!"

"We haven't," Taru insists. "We are all still alive. They did not kill us. They did not even harm us. They have done nothing to us we can't fix. The rebellion can be re-formed, rebuilt."

Sirach shakes her head fiercely in utter disbelief. "What are you *saying* to me?"

"This is not the answer. I was wrong. This will only worsen matters beyond repair. It may end up costing us everything, in the end. This is what the Skrain would do."

Sirach looks as though Taru just struck her with their fist somewhere tender.

"You have *some* stones saying that," she whispers dangerously to the retainer. "To *me*."

"The Rok only needed convincing once," Taru practically

pleads with her. “They can be convinced again. They saw in us what they see in Crache. We merely have to correct that perception. It will change the situation, I know it.”

“Taru,” Sirach begins carefully, her entire being crackling with menace, “burn the damn ship. *Now*. Or give me the torch and I’ll do it.”

Again, Taru hesitates. But then the retainer abruptly dips the torch over the side of the boat and into the water, extinguishing its flaming head in a hiss of white smoke. They never take their eyes off Sirach.

Her eyes wide and pale as the moon above, she tenses visibly, her spine stretching like a feline predator before the killing strike.

Taru is certain the Sicclunan warrior is going to attack them, but in the next moment all the air seems to leave Sirach like a deflated wineskin. She falls back into the stern of the longboat, sprawling out against its wooden slats and staring up at the night sky hopelessly.

“You are the most exhausting person I have ever met in my entire fucking life,” Sirach opines. “I am so exhausted, I can’t even summon the energy to murder you right now.”

“I do not wish to fight you.”

Sirach only grunts.

“How do you intend to stop the others from torching the rest of the fleet?” she asks.

Taru sighs.

“You are . . . decidedly *not* going to enjoy this part,” the retainer warns her.

“Oh yes. As opposed to the previous parts of this evening, which were delightful. What are you—”

"Hello on deck!" Taru shouts up at the railing of the Rok sailing vessel, gloved hands cupped around their mouth to amplify their voice. "Escaped prisoners down here who wish to surrender! Your fleet is in danger! You must raise the alarm for the rest of the ships!"

Both of Sirach's eyebrows are reaching for her scalp as she stares at Taru in awe.

"Well, at least I won't have to murder you," she says. "The others will certainly beat you to death with their boots."

A DIFFERENT KIND OF FEAST SCENE

AS THE THREE OF THEM—EVIE, LEXI, AND DYEAWAN—survey the scene they have set, Evie can't help thinking of how far each woman has come from where they began their separate journeys, and the unexpected turns their courses have taken. Yet they have all found themselves here, together once more, after coming up against mortal trials and seemingly impossible odds. Evie also can't help wondering if there is some reason for it, hoping their reunion was fated for what is about to happen next.

Although it is entirely possible that, like so much in the world, it is merely a coincidence, a random result of the unyielding chaos.

It is not without a sense of poetry or irony that they chose the same back-alley square, in front of the same unfinished building, where Lexi became the Ragged Matron. It was here that Kamen Lim attempted to murder her, handing her wounded body to the masses that loved her. Tonight, it will also be where they will attempt to bring about an end to two of the most insidious forces in Crache.

Their emissaries were successful. Nia did not return to them, which was expected, but Kray did, conveying Lady Burr's "excitement" at the prospect of having Lexi back in the fold of the Ignobles.

They would not know the outcome of Nia's gambit until the evening.

Evie, Lexi, and Dyeawan watch from the concealment of a darkened room and a window overlooking the small square, which is walled in by a dozen shabby buildings.

The Ignobles arrive first, or rather their security does: dozens of armed, cloaked bravos and a fair number of men and women in Aegin uniforms.

Kamen Lim is among them, issuing orders in his terrifyingly perpetually cheerful way.

When they feel they have secured the square, the Ignobles themselves filter in from the concealment of the alleys leading into the square. Burr is the first among them. Lexi points her out to Evie. She has chosen to wear the elaborate and colorful frock of her noble ancestors rather than the drab Gen Franchise Council tunic she is usually seen donning in public.

Joining her are perhaps twenty of what Evie and the others can only hope are the highest-ranking Ignobles in their secret fraternity. Some of them the women recognize. Some are the leaders of prominent Gens from the Capitol and other cities. Some wear the tunic and insignia of various departments of the Crachian bureaucracy. None of the others have chosen to be as bold as "Lady" Burr in their manner of dress that evening.

Evie watches Burr pull Kamen Lim close at the center of the Ignoble assemblage, whispering to him. They cannot hear the words, but Evie thinks her manner looks curious. She is probably wondering where Lexi and her people are.

"How long will they wait?" Evie asks her.

"Hopefully the Ministry is punctual," is all Lexi offers in answer.

Evie begins to feel truly anxious. If the Ignobles grow impatient or suspicious and vacate the square before the Ministry arrived, their plan amounts to nothing. They do not even possess the force to battle what the Ignobles have brought with them.

It is not until Evie spies the first Protectorate Ministry agent stalk into the square that her heart truly begins to race. The agent is young yet pale, and white-haired to the point Evie assumes she was born that way.

"That's Strinnix," Lexi whispers. "Burr's man killed her sister. As far as I can tell, she is the highest-ranking agent among them now."

Three-dozen fellow agents join Strinnix. Neither Lexi nor Dyeawan have ever seen that many Protectorate Ministry capes gathered in one place at the same time before. They cannot know for sure, but once again their hope is that the Ministry has brought the bulk of their hierarchy with them tonight.

The Ignobles' security quickly springs into action, forming a line in front of their charges with weapons drawn.

The Ministry agents respond in kind, daggers pulled from sheaths in a chorus of steel and leather whispers.

"*What* is this?" Burr demands, shouting her outrage and having it echo throughout the tops of the old buildings.

"So many faces I recognize from our reports," Strinnix observes calmly. "A few I am surprised to see among the others, I will admit, but this is a very illuminating assemblage. Thank you for arranging to get together like this for us."

Dyeawan is holding a small, jagged shard of mirrored glass. Evie nods to her, and Dyeawan angles the reflective piece to catch the firelight, signaling the others Lexi has arranged throughout the buildings overlooking the square.

In the next moment, a thunderous booming fills the space as heavy fishing nets weighted by barrels they have filled with rocks fall between the buildings into the alleys leading from the square. Every open doorway looking out into the space is slammed closed and bolted from within. Every possible way to exit the square is cut off in a span of seconds.

"This is a trap!" Strinnix hisses. "An ambush! We must all—"

"Now!" Evie commands.

Again Dyeawan uses the small, broken piece of mirror to reflect the torchlight from the square outside.

This signal is intended for Kray, stationed in the shadows on the other side of the sudden congregation of Ministry agents and Ignobles.

They all debated the first target fiercely, each woman having their own idea about who it should be and why. Their biases shone through and were called out by the others. Dyeawan argued it should be Strinnix, painfully recounting the people for whose death she was responsible. Evie, still the general, argued for Kamen Lim, the strongest soldier among them.

In the end, they collectively decided if they could only kill one villain in that square, it must be Burr. The Protectorate Ministry is more like one malicious creature made of many limbs. From what Lexi had witnessed, the maliciousness and cruelty of Burr was what shaped the Ignobles and the sychophants they commanded.

Kray's spear spirals through the air. It is a powerful throw, and it appears to come from out of nowhere. Kray remains totally unseen.

"My Lady!" Kamen Lim cries in utter horror, spotting the projectile in flight.

It is the first time Lexi has seen the psychotically jovial Ignoble enforcer succumb to the dark emotions she knows truly drive the bizarre creature.

There is something satisfying about finally seeing it, unsettling as it is.

Unfortunately, that emotion drives Kamen Lim to act with uncanny speed. He grabs the nearest hired thug by the neck and arm and thrusts the man's body in front of Burr's small pear-shaped form. Kray's spear pierces him cleanly a split second later. The weapon's jagged and rusted point emerges from the base of the human shield's spine.

Time in the square seems to slow to a crawl, or at least it seems so as everyone ceases to move or react for several long seconds. All eyes turn to watch the impaled man fall to his knees, hands grasping the half of the spear protruding from his torso.

No expression is more affronted or horrified than Burr's, upon whom it is clearly dawning that the spear was meant for her.

"Kill . . . kill them! Kill them *all*!"

Agent Strinnix is shaking her head, the full weight of what is happening crushing them to earth.

"Wait—"

That is all the woman is able to get out before Kamen Lim strides forward in a rage and drives his dagger through the guts of the nearest Protectorate Ministry agent to the weapon's hilt.

When the first Protectorate Ministry body hits the stained ground of the square, however, it is as if someone has dropped the flag to signal the start of a race. The blade of every weapon carried by both sides flash in the light of the torches, and the Ministry agents and Ignobles and their minions go for one another like scalded dogs fighting over a chicken carcass.

Many of the Ignobles themselves, in the grand tradition of their forbearers, attempt to flee the violence they have wrought and leave their underlings to contend with the fallout. Some of them fall to Ministry daggers before they can make it out of the square. The rest are caught in the nets blocking the alleys, on the other side of which, in the shadows, await Kray's people.

Of all the places these privileged descendants of an outdated royal court thought they would die, Evie is certain a stinking alley in the Bottoms never made the list.

The three of them watch Crache's would-be rulers cut one another down. The Protectorate Ministry and the Ignobles' force were matched in numbers when the battle began, but it quickly becomes clear the Ministry agents lack melee skills. The Ignobles recruited Aegins and retainers, men and women trained and experienced in fighting in the streets of Crachian cities. Two black capes are soon splayed on the pavement for every one Ignoble soldier who falls.

"I cannot see Strinnix anymore," Dyeawan comments beside Evie. "Where is she?"

Evie only shakes her head. There is too much chaos and too many figures swarming one another for her to keep track.

As the fighting reaches its thickest point, doors are unbolted, and Kray and dozens of his robed street druids emerge from the buildings surrounding the battle. They focus their attention—and their weapons—on the Aegins and Ignoble bravos outmatching the black cloaks. Kray's people have better melee sense than the Protectorate Ministry. They attack each Ignoble fighter in pairs, sometimes trios, using the numbers to mitigate and overcome each enemy fighter's impressive skill.

Through the bloody tangle of bodies, Evie spies Kamen Lim spiriting Burr, blood spattering her elaborate frock, away from the fighting. He leads her to the mouth of one of the adjoining alleys covered by a fishnet, where he uses his Crache-issued Aegin's dagger to cut a hole in the netting just big enough for Burr to squeeze herself through, which she does with haste.

Before he can slice a larger hole that would allow him to follow, however, Kamen Lim is forced to turn to meet the charge of a wild-eyed and bloody-faced Ministry agent who rushes him.

"Burr's getting away," Lexi says with a sudden desperation underpinned by clear and present rage. "That side street opens up onto the docks."

"You two stay here," Evie orders them, turning briefly to look in turn at each woman.

Dyeawan, however, is nowhere to be seen in their little place of hiding and surveillance.

Evie is confused and alarmed, but there is no time to puzzle over the girl's abrupt and stealthy departure.

"Fine, *you* stay here," she says to Lexi firmly.

The Ragged Matron of the Bottoms doesn't answer, but the defiant look she flashes Evie, along with the obvious hate she harbors for Burr, makes Evie dubious.

She draws a lengthy blade given to her by Kray and leaps from the window that has provided their view of their plan's bloody fruition. Evie lands firmly and deftly on the cobbles below, several yards from where the fighting continues. She does her best to circumvent the heart of the battle, tracing the edge of the square to the slashed fishnet where the Ignoble made her escape.

Halfway there, one of the Ignobles' hired killers wielding an ax comes at her, swinging high for her neck. Evie ducks the honed edge of the ax's blade, staying low as she thrusts her long knife through the center of the man's abdomen, piercing the large portal vein there. She removes her blade just as quickly and cleanly, leaping back to avoid the several wild swings the man takes as his life's blood pours from the wound and he begins to lose consciousness.

The brief and brutal encounter delays her reaching her destination, and by the time she does, Kamen Lim is nowhere to be seen. The Ministry agent who went for him is laid out on the cobbles with their throat cut.

Evie feels a rough hand touch her shoulder. Surprised and cursing herself for not hearing anyone approach her flank, she immediately turns at the hip and swipes with her knife hand to decapitate whoever it is.

The same rough hand intercepts her wrist, forcefully blocking the blow, and Evie finds herself looking into Kray's scarred eyes.

Evie relaxes the lethal tension in her arm.

"Burr went through the net," she tells him between hotly elevated breaths.

"I saw her man climb over one of our blockades there," he

says, pointing a long knife sheathed in viscous red at the barricaded entrance to an adjacent alley. "We go after him first."

There is a trail of bodies leading up to the spot he's indicating. Evie can only guess Kamen Lim was pushed back there by the fighting and had no choice but to flee down a different alley than the one he sent Burr.

"What about the Ignoble?"

"If she's on her own," Kray says with unemotional certainty, "then the Bottoms will take her. We go after her man."

He doesn't wait for Evie to agree with him before setting off towards the barricade over which he said Kamen Lim escaped.

Evie is far less convinced than he seems to be about Burr, but her instincts tell her not to let him go off alone.

Cursing under her breath, she hefts the handle of the blade in her hand and runs after him.

DRY DOCK

THE WATER OF THE BAY IS BLACK AS COAL OIL, OR AT LEAST it appears so under the starless night sky. Almost every berth along the wharf is empty. The docks have always been one of the Capitol's most bustling centers of commerce and humanity, making it one of the most bustling in all of Crache, but that was before the streets of the Bottoms were swept by a locust plague of Aegins and Protectorate Ministry strong-arms. They not only cleared the streets and hovels and alleyways of the Bottoms, but raided the entire wharf. The market hasn't seen a single crustacean shucked or sold in weeks. The rows of deserted wooden stalls with their well-used butchering blocks stink of dried, rotting fish guts that haven't been cleaned in weeks. Every resident of the docks from the beggars to the fishmongers have either been taken into custody or sent into hiding.

Rok trading ships stopped coming into port long before the Bottoms were cleared. Now there are no ships whatsoever, Crachian or otherwise. All seabound traffic and trade, as well as permission for any foreigner to disembark, has been suspended. A skeleton fleet of Skrain naval vessels patrols the waters a mile offshore, on high alert for any Rok Islanders that come calling.

It has become a ghost port, and as such is perhaps the perfect place to lay vengeful spirits to rest.

Burr clearly refuses to run, even though haste would surely serve her best at this moment. In fact, Lexi never loses sight of the Ignoble once she spots Burr heading from the edge of the city towards the water. Lexi is able to track and follow at a leisurely pace, though she feels anything but leisurely in that moment. She can't know how the battle far behind her now is unfolding, if indeed it is still being fought. The Ignobles and the Protectorate Ministry both train and outfit their soldiers well, far better than anything the Ragged Matron's meager resistance has to offer. Lexi only knows the force she has fostered in the Bottoms is a fierce one, all of them burning with the same fire that fills young men like Kray. She has to trust that she, Evie, and Dyeawan have afforded them enough of an advantage to prevail.

Lexi also knows that no matter the outcome of their collective gambit, the most important move she can make now is to remove Burr from the board, permanently.

Besides, she owes the woman so very much.

She cannot know what Burr's plan was, if indeed the older woman had one to begin with. It is entirely possible Burr simply ran in the direction from which she fled their trap in the alley corner. Perhaps she thought if she reached the bay she might escape by boat, whether by commandeering, commanding, or bribing one into her service.

Whatever the case, Lexi can see, even from afar, that the Ignoble was unprepared for the scarce conditions of the waterfront. Lexi watches Burr abandon her brisk pace and stop walking for the first time when she fully takes in the abandoned state of the wharf. There is no crowd in which to lose herself. There are no ships to ferry her away. There is no one for her to bully or buy as she is accustomed to doing in order to achieve her goals. Lexi imagines that for someone who puts so much stock in the complete servitude of others and her own natural, blood-born right to rule them, finding herself alone and self-reliant is Burr's worst nightmare.

Lexi stops walking when she sees Burr halt her step. The two of them cannot be more than fifty feet apart now. Lexi waits, allowing Burr to soak in the scene she has helped create. The rebellion in the west may have upturned life in the Capitol, but Burr and her Ignobles only escalated matters further by using that chaos in their attempt to wrest control of the people and thus the city from the hands of the Planning Cadre and the Protectorate Ministry. They are as responsible for what's become of the Bottoms as the Aegins and Protectorate Ministry agents who laid siege to the streets and the people here.

Not to mention she tried to have Lexi killed.

For the first time, Burr casts a glance over her shoulder and spots her, white-clad and white-haired and stark against the night, seeming to almost float behind Burr.

Even at a distance, Lexi can see the sagging flesh of the Ignoble's face drain until it is the same color as Lexi's clothing and hair.

Lexi stares through the thin, illusory veil of fog wafting throughout the docks. She offers Burr nothing with her expression, only watching and waiting and observing Burr like something caught and displayed under glass, very much the way Burr looked at Lexi when Lexi was in her captivity, being half swallowed by a manipulated carnivorous pod plant on the Ignoble's hidden estate.

Now Burr begins running, or at least jogging. The Ignoble makes her way onto the nearest dock and travels all the way down its length until she is forced by its warped wooden edge to accept she has quite literally run out of road.

There she waits, staring out over water that is almost indistinguishable from the sky above, her back to Lexi as the Ragged Matron of the Bottoms steps out on the dock.

"Good evening, My Lady," Lexi says, addressing the Ignoble in the same ancient and long-antiquated fashion as Burr insists her underlings do, feeding her illusions of resurrected nobility.

She can see Burr's shoulders stiffen, then slowly relax as if the woman is forcing a steely calm over her body.

When the Ignoble turns around to meet her, Burr is wearing a smile that might seem entirely authentic and casual to the untrained observer, but Lexi knows it is as frail and artificial as a paper mask.

"And what a fine evening it is," Burr rejoins. "I never knew it was so . . . peaceful here by the bay."

"It's only been so lately," Lexi reminds her.

Burr swallows, hard, and it looks as though maintaining that smile and her calm demeanor is becoming more of a struggle.

"It really is you, isn't it?" she asks, the undertone of disbelief the only genuine thing about how she is presenting herself. "Kamen Lim assured me you were dead."

"Not for a lack of trying, I promise. You know, I think he's a far better killer than Daian was? Not that I'm an expert on killers, but I've come to know a lot of them lately. Daian was more terrifying on the surface, but he was also like a child, pulling the wings off flies. And he liked to hear himself talk. Kamen Lim had no words for me when he stabbed me. I don't think he took any pleasure in it, either. He had the look of a man cleaning up a floor because someone spilled soup on it. I was just . . . a necessary task to him. Because he was acting on your orders."

Burr's manufactured smile slowly begins to fade into a frown.

"It wasn't what I wanted. I wanted you to live. Not just live, but thrive and be a beacon to these . . . to the people here."

"But they're not here anymore, are they?"

Burr takes a determined step towards her.

"Because you failed to rally them properly!" she all but spits. "We could have seized control of the entire Capitol by now if you'd only *done as you were told*!"

Now, finally, it is Lexi's turn to smile.

"There is the woman I came to know so well when I was a guest in her little hidden kingdom," she says. "That's who I came to meet here tonight."

"I'm sorry," Burr corrects herself quickly. "I am. It is good that we find ourselves alone together. I had hoped we would have the chance to speak again."

"But we're not alone, My Lady," Lexi corrects her.

The Ignoble looks confused, cocking her head like a dog watching some sleight of hand.

Lexi raises her voice several octaves. "No one is alone down here. That is what I've learned, what I've tried to show the people you would've used as disposable tools, the same way Crache does, has always done. You all see those who dwell here as savages. Because you project onto them every ugly thing you conceal within yourselves."

Burr looks at a loss for words, but her expression is still one of confusion. The fear doesn't begin to overtake it until she hears the first rumblings under the boards beneath her feet.

The Bottoms are never truly empty, just as the walls of any home are never the barren space their owners imagine them to be. Those who were there before simply remain hidden, forced into the shadows and nooks and crannies by the polished people determined to maintain a clean and tidy veneer over what they perceive as *their* world. The reality is that there was always life thriving there before the new owners came, no less valid or vibrant or deserving despite being cast out and supplanted.

Now, all around Burr, the people banished and hounded and hunted into those nether spaces, out of sight and out of mind, begin to emerge again. They crawl from beneath the waterlogged wooden docks. They slip from under the upturned hulls of broken or half-built boats littering the shore. They part from the shadows as if born by them, encroaching onto the slender dock where Lexi and Burr stand face-to-face.

"Keep them away from me!" Burr all but shrieks at Lexi.

What enrages Lexi most is that the Ignoble's words still sound like an order.

"But you sent me here to rally them," Lexi reminds her. "Don't you remember? This is what you wanted. You wanted me to deliver you an army of the outcast and forgotten and trod upon by Crache to do your bidding against it. Well, here they are. Although I'm afraid they won't be as easy to command as you'd hoped."

Burr takes several desperate steps towards Lexi, speaking faster now, holding up her hands in front of her as if she's pleading, her fingers curled into clawlike things.

"All my plans can still come to fruition," Burr insists. "You've weakened the Protectorate Ministry. You have all these people practically worshipping you. Can you not see the precipice at which we stand? I can make you a queen."

To Lexi, the older woman might as well have been offering to turn her into a fairy princess.

"Do you remember Chivis?" she asks Burr, and it is immediately clear from the Ignoble's blank-faced silence that she does not.

"He tends your lantern garden," Lexi explains. "He has lived in captivity on your family's estate his entire life. He has no knowledge of the outside world. He doesn't know he is not bound to serve you by any law or requirement, that he should be free to leave anytime he wishes. He has no idea you've simply kept him prisoner since he was born, as you have done to who knows how many others. His whole existence is that garden. He will never know anything else, because of you."

"What has this got to do with *anything*?" Burr demands.

"I simply wanted you to think about him, about Chivis. I don't imagine you've ever once given him a moment of your time. I wanted him to be in your head right now. If possible, I want him to be the very last thing you think about."

Burr's begging and bargaining and scheming inevitably turns to frustration and rage, as Lexi knew it would.

"You simpering hag!" she all but spits in Lexi's face. "You thoroughly unremarkable peasant! I am the blood of ages! I am the *descendent* of God Kings! I am the *rightful* heiress to everything the light touches in this world!"

"You are a small woman in very silly clothes that went out of fashion centuries ago," Lexi tells her, deftly slipping a hand beneath her stained white tunic. "You belong to the past."

"There are others!" Burr insists, righteously and threateningly. "Those you call 'Ignoble' are legion! There are lost heirs and heiresses hidden in plain sight *everywhere*! This does not end with me! The blood of nobility *will* rule this land again!"

"We'll find them, too," Lexi calmly assures her.

Before Burr can muster more insults or threats, Lexi removes a weapon from beneath her clothes and stabs the descendant of noble blood in the neck.

Her weapon is not a knife; it is a hollow needle affixed to miniature bellows. Lexi squeezes the bellows' leather bladder, injecting Burr with the substance concealed there as the Ignoble watches her, wide-eyed and stunned, body locked in surprise.

"This is the same concoction you once had forced into my veins," Lexi enlightens the suddenly terrified woman. "Do you remember? I had ample time during my convalescence to learn about such things, and as it turns out, Aegins and the Protectorate Ministry use something similar when interrogating people from the Bottoms, though that is quite illegal, of course. Obtaining it was surprisingly easy. When I was under its influence, I saw such visions. They were so horrible, so vile, so false, yet seemed as true as anything I'd ever known at the time."

She yanks the needle from Burr's neck with very little care or tenderness.

Burr's small hand flies to cover the point of injection on her neck.

Even in the relative blackness, Lexi can see the dark parts of the Ignoble's eyes widen into vast pools. Burr's head falls back, and she seems to stare up at the starless night without really taking in any of it. The potion is causing her vision to invert, to turn inward.

"Everything I saw when you filled me with this poison," Lexi continues, "I saw because the fear of it lived deep inside me. What's waiting for you there, My Lady?"

Burr's head lolls to one side, then another. She blinks her dilated eyes at the ragged and hungry figures of the survivors of the Bottoms creeping in around her from all sides.

Lexi cannot know into what twisted monsters Burr's mind warps the strong and simple people around her, but the naked fear is evident on her face. All the color has drained from withered features contorted into an unnatural expression of terror. She begins to careen about as if trying to escape invisible hands grasping for her, though not a single soul has touched her. She screams into the night, spittle and curses flying as she attempts to ward off the clawing of the horde of lessers she is imagining in her head.

Burr spins wildly around, turning away from Lexi, and for a moment Lexi thinks the Ignoble is simply going to collapse in a tormented heap there upon the wooden planks of the dock.

Instead, with a shriek like some wraith calling for the blood of the living, Burr sprints the few steps between her and the dock's edge and plunges herself headlong into the blackened water of the bay.

For several moments Lexi does nothing, only stands unmoving there on the dock. She listens for the sounds of a small body thrashing in the water, for frightened shouts pleading for aid. When nothing breaks the relative silence, Lexi steps carefully to the dock's edge to peer down at the calm obsidian surface of the bay.

There is no evidence anywhere in sight that a person entered the water just a few moments before. The water is almost totally still.

Lexi waits for Burr to reemerge, but she knows if the Ignoble has not come up by now that she never will.

There are others, Burr promised her.

"Yes, but it's a start," Lexi says aloud to no one in particular before casting the bellows and syringe into the water.

SNARED

THE ROOFTOPS OF THE BOTTOMS ARE A WORLD UNTO THEMselves, a patchwork civilization stitched together over many decades by refugees fleeing the streets and alleys and docks below. These mud-colored plateaus often provided the closest thing to a haven in the Bottoms. Aegins rarely bothered to scale the many cracked and treacherous staircases or climb the ramshackle ladders leading up to the rooftops. Unless they were chasing a fugitive, and even then it would have to be someone who committed some grievous offense against the city's dagger-wielding enforcers. The people who carved out an existence atop these roofs could largely exist in peace, at least from the authorities.

However, even the rooftops have not escaped the recent purges that turned the streets into a barren landscape. The wind being blown in from the bay wafts through empty makeshift tents and lean-tos, over cold and disused hearths. It blows the broken pieces of dropped pots and mugs back and forth and over the ledges, littering the alleys below. There may be the stray soul who ventures onto a random roof to forage for what was left behind, but they skitter back into obscurity as quickly as they appear.

Strinnix tears through a ragged curtain hung in a lopsided doorway that separates the interior of the building from one such open roof. The senior Protectorate Ministry agent finds nothing but a deserted, uneven plateau awaiting them, empty and quiet save for the soft, somewhat eerie whispering of the sea breeze wafting in from the shore.

Strinnix clenches the handle of a blood-stained dagger in her gloved hand, halting what had been a flat-out charge up the inside of the building behind her. She continues to pant and heave from the exertion as she surveys what looks like a hastily abandoned campsite that stretches for miles in every direction.

The Protectorate Ministry agent co-authored the plan to sweep the Bottoms, both to fatten the ranks of the Savage Legion and to institute a swift and brutal lockdown of the Capitol's hidden underclass, but this is the first time she has seen the results of that order.

The unrelenting efficiency of it should probably please her, but seeing evidence of a victory only reminds her of the failure with which she was just involved below on the street.

"Idiots!" she hisses under her breath. "Insipid, predictable puppets! I *told* them all—"

Strinnix has only taken a few steps past the threshold of the doorway leading up to the rooftop. She doesn't hear the trap when its sprung. Strinnix doesn't even feel it until she is swept from her booted feet entirely. There is only a sudden and slight pressure around her right ankle, high where the bony appendage begins to thicken. That pressure quickly becomes a painful pinching. Strinnix feels the impossibly slender piece of wire that has sliced cleanly through the thick leather of her boot begin to dig into the meat of her calf muscle, but before she can scream in pain the wire yanks her foot out from under her and the impact of landing against the rooftop drives the breath from her body entirely. The dagger flies from her hand.

When the pain hits it is quite excruciating, and Strinnix feels blood begin to fill her boot. Moving would be difficult enough even if she weren't suddenly tethered by snare to the rooftop. She clenches her jaw shut tight to quell her own screams, trying to tamp the pain with it, and immediately begins scrabbling for her weapon, finding it just beyond reach a few feet away.

As her eyes seek out the lost dagger, they are drawn above it to the ledge of the roof. A wooden board has been leaned up against that ledge, almost like a ramp leading seemingly to nowhere.

For the first time, Strinnix becomes aware that every movement she makes against the trap, in addition to sending new waves of agony crashing up through her leg, also causes a series of bells to ring loudly, as if alerting the hunter their prey has been snared.

Beyond the ramp, several large wooden casks are strapped together, hanging off the side of the roof on the end of a thick strand of rope at the top of a very tenuous-looking pulley. The casks abruptly drop below the lip of the roof as if the line holding them has been cut. The wheels of the pulley spin and whir as the rope passes through them. A moment later, a small platform ascends above the roof's edge, raised by the opposite end of the same thick strand of rope and the counterweight of the bound and heavy casks.

Dyeawan has each hand wrapped around one of the support ropes securing the platform to the pulley's line. She is cradled inside what looks like a heavily modified wheelbarrow. In addition to the wheel at its front, another set has been added to the end, along with an axle. The rear wheels are large enough that they extend above the rim of the barrow itself, and each one has a series of short handles affixed to it that allow Dyeawan to control the contraption herself.

Strinnix watches in disbelief as Dyeawan steers the wheelbarrow from the platform, down the waiting ramp, and onto the rooftop.

"How are you here?" Strinnix demands in abject disbelief. "How could you possibly know I'd flee up to *this* rooftop."

"Because you didn't choose it at random," Dyeawan explains. "It's the tallest building in this part of the Bottoms. Anyone could see that at a glance from where we gathered you all. The tallest building would offer you the best escape route. It would give you the clearest view of the landscape, and easier access to other rooftops."

Dyeawan wheels herself alongside where Strinnix is laid out. She had wondered when she set the trap up here if an errant snare would perhaps sever the tendon in the back of Strinnix's leg. Perhaps the Protectorate Ministry agent would bleed out before the two of them had the opportunity to speak.

Strinnix is still alive, however.

The woman is panting for every breath now, her chest heaving violently. There is blood pouring from her nostrils and mouth after the brief but fiery battle below, and much more and darker blood spilling from her boot and pooling out over the surface of the roof.

"You have a strategic mind," Dyeawan observes, more clinically than anything else. "Much like me. I imagine it is common among agents of the Protectorate Ministry. You're taught to think in machinations and schemes. It is how you conspire to control things. But strategy is not imagination. You need both, I've found."

"And how did you *imagine* we'd end up here?"

"I thought you'd be suspicious enough to bring contingencies with you, but not suspicious enough to refuse the invitation."

The Protectorate Ministry agent makes a rueful sound that isn't quite laughter.

"I feel very cold."

Strinnix isn't really speaking to Dyeawan anymore. The pale agent is staring straight up, seeing whatever those close to the veil see towards the end.

"You feel cold because the blood is leaving your body so fast," she explains to the black-clad woman snared pathetically below her wheelbarrow. "From what I've read, that means you will die very soon."

Strinnix nods absently, staring at the pitch-black canvas that seems to stretch to eternity high above the rooftop.

"There will be chaos, you know," Strinnix assures her. "Without us. Crache will fall to abject ruin."

Dyeawan shrugs. "No one knew you ruled to begin with. No one will know your reign is over. Crache is a machine constructed so that its people never know or see who is at the controls. All we are doing is taking over those controls."

Strinnix either has no answer for that or can't summon the strength to voice it.

"You have it all figured out then, it seems," she finally manages.

"Is my sister alive?" Dyeawan asks her.

Strinnix nods, or at least she appears to. It is difficult to tell with how severely she is convulsing now.

"For . . . the record," the Ministry agent manages through the pain and the blood, "I knew . . . I knew this was . . . a trick. I . . . told . . . I *told* them, those decrepit . . . old fools! They . . . they never listen!"

"That is why you could never lead," Dyeawan says. "Despite all of your bluster, you still need someone to tell you what to do. That is why Crache will not fall into chaos. Everyone who wields the illusion of power is still waiting for the nameless authority above them to tell them what to do. They won't know the difference between our voice and yours. As for those 'old fools' back on their peaceful little island, my sister and I shouldn't have any problem bringing them in line once they know you're gone."

Strinnix stares up at her with unmasked loathing. She opens her mouth to rebuke Dyeawan one last time, but the words never come.

Dyeawan watches the woman's final few moments unfold, trying to decide how she feels about it.

In the end, there is no satisfaction for her. Mister Quan and Riko are still gone. And Dyeawan has only added many more bodies to the death toll for which she is directly responsible.

She stares down at the expression eternally sculpted onto Strinnix's face, a monument to the agent's last aggrieved moments of life.

For the first time, Dyeawan wishes her mind did not insist on storing the vivid recollection of everything she has ever seen.

THE DUELISTS

KRAY KNOWS THE BACK ALLEYS OF THE BOTTOMS ON A level that is steeped in the blood. It is far beyond what Evie remembers or was ever able to glean during her time posing as a drunken vagabond in these streets, committing acts of vandalism and violence in hopes of being arrested and conscripted into the Savage Legion. As such, she follows his lead through the winding maze of narrow passages, on the stalk for Kamen Lim. They both have their long knives drawn and held at the ready.

"He's one Aegin," Evie reminds Kray. "Is he worth running down like this? We should get back to Lexi and Dyeawan."

"He's the one who tried to kill our Matron," Kray says with a single-minded rage that catches Evie off guard. "He's the Ignoble's chief assassin. Without him she has no teeth. He has to die, just like the rest of them."

There is nothing in the street soldier's voice that suggests he'll brook further argument, so Evie refrains from offering any.

Still, she knows Kray trusts the men and women he has trained for Lexi's resistance army, but Evie can only hope they're continuing to hold their own against the Protectorate Ministry's reinforcements.

They round what must be their dozenth corner, coming upon a configuration of wine barrels stacked halfway up the length of the buildings walling in the alley. The barrel mountain is wide enough to block their path around it.

Kray halts mid-run, Evie stopping short alongside him.

"This shouldn't be here," he says quietly, seeming more confused than concerned.

"Your people didn't do it?" Evie asks. "You're sure?"

Kray nods silently. He certainly looks sure.

"Should we backtrack? Maybe—"

Evie feels what is incoming before she hears it, like some sixth sense she didn't even know she possessed. She is simply aware something is descending upon them, looking up just in time to see the barrel about to fall on both their heads.

"Look out!" she shouts at Kray while simultaneously shoving him from the barrel's path, throwing her own body to one side at the same time.

The large wooden drum sails through the suddenly empty space between them and smashes upon the cobbles below, splashing them with jets of wine and flooding the alley floor.

Evie covers her face with her arm to protect her eyes from the spray and splintery debris, turning away from the crash.

She is still catching her breath and just beginning to survey the scene again when what feels like the weight of a mountain collides with the left side of her skull. Evie isn't even aware of falling. The next sensation she actively experiences is landing in a shallow pool of wine and feeling the hard ground at the bottom of it. There is no pain, but her body feels impossibly light and far away and she can't seem to command it anymore.

Though her vision is hazy, it is still clear enough for her to look up and see Kamen Lim, the Ignoble's man. She isn't even certain where or from which direction he came. He's using all of his weight to wedge Kray's much more slender body between himself and the alley wall, immobilizing the younger man's arms, though Kray thrashes and struggles with every ounce of strength he's got. His wrist attempts to flick the knife in his hand, but the way the Aegin has trapped him has taken away all the necessary leverage.

Evie hears a violent, grotesquely wet sound and watches as Kray's body stiffens straight and taut between the wall and Kamen Lim. She never even saw the dagger fill the Aegin's hand, but now its blade is piercing Kray's stomach.

"It's all right, young man," Kamen Lim assures Kray, sounding wholly congenial and not at all as if he is currently ramming four inches of steel through the boy's guts. "You can let go now. You have acquitted yourself quite well. You're a credit to your people."

Kray seems unconvinced. He continues rocking from one side to another, as much as he's able, hissing at the Aegin through painfully gritted teeth.

Kamen Lim yanks the blade from Kray's body in one smooth, deft motion, displaying the grace of a practiced killer. Removing the dagger's tongue seems to be more devastating to its victim than the stabbing was, as Kray finally lets out a brief yelp before sliding down the wall onto his knees, rocking and thrashing no more.

Evie watches Kamen Lim coil his strong fingers around Kray's scalp, tilting the younger man's head back to expose the pulpy meat of his throat. The Aegin angles the edge of his already-bloody blade parallel to the pulsing vein raised in the skin of Kray's neck.

Evie summons every scrap of hate and will and anger within her, focusing it all into her arms and legs. The strain and determination draws a guttural scream up through her body, and when it explodes forth from her lips she springs from the stained cobbles like some coiled and feral cat.

Leaping across the cobbles, Evie swipes her knife arm and slashes Kamen Lim across the right shoulder blade. It's enough to stop him from cutting Kray's throat and draw his attention away from Lexi's lieutenant and protector.

Meanwhile, Evie's momentum carries her past the Aegin, and her body practically bounces off the alley wall. She is already backing up and attempting to regain her balance when he turns away from Kray to face her.

Despite a newly open wound and blood no doubt streaming down his back, Kamen Lim is wearing a terrifyingly convivial smile, as if he were perusing the offerings at the morning market and perhaps admiring the shape and color of a basket of plums.

"I watched them parade you through the streets outside the Spectrum," he says. "Before your brazen, and admittedly quite spectacular, escape. You didn't cut much of a figure inside that cage, if you'll pardon me saying so. But then, I imagine that was most of the point. Still, you aren't what I would've expected of a newly minted legend. A general, no less."

"It was always more of an honorary title," she manages between ragged breaths.

Her head is pounding where she was struck, and each pulse is its own torture. Every inch of her skin feels like it is on fire. She can feel herself blinking rapidly and uncontrollably, and it is all Evie can do to keep the knife gripped firmly in her hand and stay on her feet.

"In any case," Kamen Lim prattles on amiably, "I can't say I took you for much of a fighter, to be honest. And you seem in even less of a state for combat now. Are you sure you're up to what comes next here?"

As if for emphasis, Kamen Lim flips the dagger in his hand, plucking its twirling hilt from the air easily.

Evie stares at the crimson-soaked blade. She thinks back to Laython, the gargantuan wrangler of Savage Legionnaires who once commanded her, and then later tried to kill her on the battlefield. She remembers how he tried to crush her between his massive arms, and how she rammed a blade through the bottom of his chin and skewered his brain.

"I've fought and killed worse than you," she tells him.

"I imagine that's precisely why they lost," Kamen Lim muses. "Because they were worse than me." He laughs. It's a hollow sound. "Excuse me, I don't mean to joke. But you young people take things so terribly seriously."

"If you don't mind," Evie bids him, the irritation evident in her voice, "talking to you is beginning to feel worse than being stabbed. I'd also like to get to the fight before I pass out."

"Oh, of course!" Kamen Lim says with rancor. "Please forgive me. By all means, to 'the fight,' as you say."

Evie pushes herself away from the alley wall with her empty hand, moving to the center of the wine-stained cobbles.

Kamen Lim steps away from Kray's crumpled form to meet her there.

Evie is painfully aware that this isn't the melee fighting to which she has become accustomed during her time with the Savage Legion and afterward, leading the rebellion. This is a duel against a trained killer, which she is also aware she has never been in before.

"You weren't trained as a soldier, were you?" he asks as he begins circling Evie.

She moves to match him step for step, knife held defensively in front of her.

"As a retainer," she says.

Kamen Lim nods. "The Skrain would've taught you not to lead with your knife hand."

He reaches out with stunning speed, seizing Evie's extended wrist and yanking her forward and off-balance. As he pulls her past his own body, Kamen Lim slashes her across the shoulder.

"There!" he proclaims with glee. "Now we're even!"

Evie turns her body as soon as she regains any semblance of balance, slashing wildly to ward him off, though Kamen Lim doesn't pursue her.

Maintaining her distance and forcing herself to calm down and stop wasting motion and energy, Evie briefly examines her wound. It isn't deep, but it does sting.

"Thank you for the lesson," she says through clenched teeth.

Evie shifts her stance, cocking her knife hand at her side and holding her other hand out in a defensive posture, ready to swat away or block an attack.

Kamen Lim steps forward and takes a testing, almost playful swipe at her. Instead of meeting him, Evie jumps back out of range.

The Aegin laughs, looking terribly satisfied with himself.

The sight and sound of this makes Evie mad, even furious, but rather than let the anger fill her, she banishes it and forces herself to focus. She was always taught that the best place to be in a knife fight, or any other kind of fight, is behind your opponent. She lets that thought guide her feet as she advances on the Aegin, then sidesteps at the last possible second.

Unfortunately, every time Evie tries to feint and pass Kamen Lim's guard in order to get behind him, he makes her pay for it, biffing her with the hilt of his dagger or nicking a fresh cut into her flesh with the blade.

"Are you always this slow?" he asks her. "Or is that nasty bump on your head affecting you?"

In answer, Evie abandons any thought of flanking him and rushes straight at Kamen Lim, staying low and attempting to lance him clean through the middle with her long knife.

He is able to grab her wrist and stop the strike before her blade pierces him. Kamen Lim prepares to slash back at her, but before he can, Evie thrusts her empty hand up into his face, driving the heel of her palm into the man's septum and nostrils.

The blow stuns Kamen Lim, both halting his knife hand and causing his other hand to release its grip on her. Tears immediately fill his eyes and obscure his vision.

Evie tries to capitalize on the slim moment of opportunity, but the Aegin's instincts are strong. As soon as the pain hits his brain and the salty droplets fill his eyes, he bursts forth with a powerful front kick that lands directly between Evie's breasts.

The knife flies from her hand as her body goes sailing across the alley, smashing into the front of one of the stacked barrels hard enough to cave in several of its wooden ribs. The strength vanishes from Evie's legs, and she collapses onto the cobbles.

Between the pain and pressure in her chest and the throbbing of her head, Evie can't seem to scrape herself up off the ground this time. It is all simply too much. Her body has finally decided it will give no more.

She watches Kamen Lim cross the alley, in no particular rush, it seems. He stands over her, knife in hand, cocking his head and staring down pityingly at the mess she no doubt looks in that moment.

"I guess you were right," she says, barely more than a whisper.

Kamen Lim swipes the tip of a thumb against his nostrils, coming away with a good smear of his own blood, which he examines with mild amusement.

"You were better than I expected," he offers.

There is the streaking of metal against stone, and Evie's eyes are drawn to Kray's dagger. He had enough strength to slide it across the alley towards her.

Just beyond arm's length, unfortunately.

"Well, that *is* a shame," Kamen Lim remarks.

Evie sighs, but then one last desperate thought strikes her. The idea is so absurd she almost laughs in spite of her impending death, but instead she scrounges up the best performance she has within her.

"Kray, no!" she screeches, staring past Kamen Lim as if the leader of Lexi's street monk army is behind the Aegin. "He's mine!"

Kamen Lim hesitates just long enough to flick a glance over his shoulder, finding nothing there.

In the space of that half second, Evie rolls to her left and seizes the handle of Kray's knife, lifting it from the alley floor and plunging the blade between Kamen Lim's legs in one smooth motion, burying the steel to its hilt.

The Aegin immediately doubles over, his eyes going wide and vacant and his hands reflexively moving to his groin.

Evie quickly twists the knife before ripping it away as violently as her shoulder and arm will allow.

A good heaping of blood and entrails follows the blade's exit, and Kamen Lim topples over onto his side next to where Evie lays.

"That was a bit of a dirty trick," Kamen Lim manages through what looks like a painfully clenched jaw. "If you don't mind me saying so."

Still, despite everything, he forces a strained and twisted version of that fatherly smile across his lips.

"I feel terrible about it, I assure you," Evie says. "You're a deeply disturbed man. You know that, right?"

Kamen Lim tries to laugh and instead vomits half a pint of blood onto the already damp and stained cobbles.

When he's finished, he lifts his head and smiles at her again, baring teeth stained a sticky red.

"As I said, you young folk, you take things far too seriously."

Those prove to be his last words.

When she's certain he's dead, Evie leaves him there. She crawls across the alley floor on her hands and knees to where Kray is still slumped against the wall where Kamen Lim pinned him. He has jammed half a fist into his stomach wound.

"This is just another day in the Bottoms," he reminds Evie, adding to it after a labored breath, "General."

"I'm retired," she tells him.

Evie finds a renewed strength in her legs. It is not quite enough to go running fast and free, but it allows her to stand, and to support Kray's weight as she helps him up from the blood-and-wine-covered cobbles.

The trek back to where they began pursuing Kamen Lim is a long one for them both. When they left the scene it was loud and chaotic and filled with the clashing of steel.

What they return to is quiet but could in no way be called peaceful.

Bodies and blood obscure most of the ground. The majority of those bodies are Protectorate Ministry agents and the Ignobles' guards. Kray and Lexi's forces have prevailed. They sacrificed many of their own, from the look of it, but the only people left standing belong to the resistance born in the Bottoms.

Lexi and Dyeawan are standing right in the middle of it all, waiting for them.

"Kray!" Lexi calls across the concrete battlefield when she takes in the full measure of him. "Are you all right?"

"I will be," he assures her.

"He needs tending," Evie says. "And I mean right now."

Lexi quickly summons half a dozen of her people to take Kray into their embrace and begin ministering to his wound.

"Burr?" Evie asks Lexi after she has handed off her charge to the others.

"She escaped," Lexi answers. "To the bottom of the bay."

Evie only nods, satisfied with that.

"I would ask about Kamen Lim, but from the look of you two, you found him, and I don't imagine you'd be here if the results were unfavorable."

"'Unfavorable' is a good word," Evie agrees.

"Can anything good truly come from this?" Dyeawan asks Evie and Lexi, surprising them both. "What we do from here, if it is rooted in this . . ." She gazes at the horrific scene engulfing them, the bodies piled atop one another, slashed and hacked to pieces.

"Everything is rooted in this," Evie says. "Whether we like it or not doesn't matter. Everything people do ends up steeped in this. The reason these people were able to be so callous and cruel is that until tonight, they never had to stand knee-deep in the blood and the shit created by their orders. If nothing else, we've already done better than them in that way. We're here. We're wading through the result of our decisions right now. We know the weight of it."

"We *will* do better," Lexi promises Dyeawan. "We'll make our own mistakes. It may all fall to pieces in the end, but whatever we do, we will treat the people they saw as livestock, as raw material to feed their empire, like *people*. That, at least, I can assure you."

"We trust in you, Ragged Matron," Kray says to Lexi, devoutly, surprising them all.

She bows her head to the boy who has fought so hard at her side without asking for anything in return.

Lexi turns to look at Evie then, both of them sharing the same thought.

"Yeah," Evie says. "We really have to do something about the titles we've acquired."

WHAT FEAR NECESSITATES

"ARE YOU STILL ANGRY WITH ME?" TARU ASKS SIRACH, largely to break the unyielding silence of the past several minutes.

"You'd just better hope they kill us first," she says, still refusing to look at the retainer.

The two of them are kneeling on the forward deck of the *Black Turtle*, surrounded by Rok crewmembers pointing the barbed prongs of their tridents at the rebels. None of the other members of the sabotage party whose mission Taru aborted at the last moment have been brought aboard, and the retainer can only assume they are in similar captivity on other ships. At least, they hope that is the case. They hope the rest of them surrendered when the alarms were raised, or perhaps even reversed course and rowed back to shore.

They have been waiting for several hours. It took that long for the *Black Turtle*'s crew and the rest of the Islanders tending the fleet to fully comprehend and deal with the situation before sending people back to the Rok camp on the mainland to inform and retrieve their captain.

When Staz finally climbs back aboard the vessel she has commanded for decades, Taru thinks the Rok elder looks tired more than anything. They must have roused her from her bed after the evening celebrations.

Even on their knees, Taru is almost able to meet Staz's eyes. Such is the diminutive stature of the Rok elder. So much obvious power and authority and fierceness contained in such a small, seemingly frail body, Taru cannot help but marvel.

"You remain a puzzling young person," she says, regarding the retainer with cocked head and weary eyes. "Why would you escape only to surrender yourself?"

"I wished . . . to speak to you again."

"You could have just asked to see me. You've caused a lot of commotion and trouble for nothing."

"I did not want to speak to you with the bars of a cage separating us," Taru says. "I wanted to speak to you as equals."

Staz glances around them as if to indicate the retainer's current predicament, and how that predicament contradicts the idea that they are equals, at least at the moment.

Taru frowns, but they are undeterred.

"We set out to burn your fleet tonight. Every ship anchored here."

Staz nods. "I know. You owe Captain Florcha a new masthead for the *Razor Fin*. Fortunately, we were able to extinguish the flames before they reached the deck."

"It could have gone much differently. We could have set half your ships ablaze before any of you knew what was happening. We did not. I did not. Do you know why?"

"Because you appreciate our fine naval craftsmanship?" Staz posits.

Her crewmembers laugh heartily.

"This is already going well," Sirach mutters.

Taru ignores her, and the guffaws of the Islanders watching them.

"I realized I was behaving the way you have been behaving, and that doing so was only going to lead to more unnecessary bloodshed and misery among all of us."

Staz folds her hands in front of her, enveloping them inside the sleeves of her puffy coat.

"If you were behaving like one of us, you would have finished what you started," Staz chastises the retainer like a disappointed grandmother.

Taru sighs, having hoped the woman would be at least a little more receptive, but it is clear she isn't really listening to what the retainer is saying.

The Rok have not bound their wrists or ankles or otherwise restrained them, beyond putting the two rebels on their knees. Yet another entirely Islander quirk, Taru remembers thinking when they were first taken aboard. It is rare they take prisoners, as evidenced by their lack of ability to deal with incarcerating the rebel leaders they drugged.

As Staz just said, the Rok believe in finishing what they start.

Taru moves fast, twisting their waist and reaching out to seize the nearest trident just beyond its triple prongs. They pull the Islander holding it forward and drive the heel of their palm hard and deep into the man's crotch. As he doubles over from the blow, Taru deftly slips the dagger sheathed at his belt from its scabbard and springs to their feet.

Almost as quickly as they made their move, Sirach also reacted, rolling beneath the nearest trident pointed at her head and sweeping the legs of its wielder out from under them. She has taken the fallen crewmember's weapon, twirling it about her body expertly, the flourishes confusing the other Rok guards and forcing them to take a step back to avoid the whirling ends of the trident.

Having prevented them from rushing her, Sirach extends the weapon out and jabs the nearest Rok fighter in the gut with the blunt end of the trident, following it up by smashing him in the temple.

Taru leaps over the bent form of the Islander whose weapon the retainer has borrowed.

Staz still stands directly in front of Taru. The *Black Turtle*'s captain has not stirred a foot to stop them or run from the retainer.

Taru once again kneels down, but this time it is to press the edge of the blade in their hand to the soft, dangling, wrinkled flesh of Staz's throat.

Behind them, Sirach is still taking on all comers, and from the sound of it dealing out punishment to the crewmembers who come for her.

They made no plan beforehand. The Sicclunan warrior is merely going on instinct, Taru knows.

"Sirach!" Taru barks at her. "Hold!"

Sirach backs off from her current opponent, glancing back hotly at the retainer.

"The rest of you keep your feet planted where they are!" Taru instructs the Islanders.

Everything stops. The crew of the *Black Turtle* only sees the fine edge poised and ready to spill their captain's lifeblood onto the deck.

None of them relinquish their weapons or take even a single step back, but neither do they close in further around Taru.

"I could kill you right now," Taru says to the Rok elder on the other side of their blade. "Do you agree?"

"Yes," Staz says calmly, probably not wanting to risk nodding just now.

"And do you believe I would?" Taru asks her. "Do you believe I will open your throat, knowing full well your crew will end me here on this deck immediately thereafter?"

"Yes," Staz says again, though the old woman has begun to sound confused.

Taru's expression begins to melt from hard-bitten and determined to almost desperate.

"I do not want your life," Taru practically pleads with the Rok elder. "Just as you did not want mine. I do not want to destroy that which the Rok hold sacred. *All* of this must stop, Staz. I am not your enemy. My friends are not the enemy of the Rok. The *people* of Crache are not your enemy. I have been trying to show you this since you came ashore, and you refuse to see it."

Staz takes a slow, careful breath against the blade at their throat. "I can only see what is in front of me. Right now that is you, holding a knife."

Taru quickly removes the edge from her neck and drops the dagger. It clatters nosily on the deck below.

Several crewmembers make a move towards the retainer, but Staz raises a head to halt them.

She waits, staring intently at Taru.

"I only wanted to prove a point," they say. "That even if we have a blade we can hold to your throats, we will not use it. We do not want to."

"You do not speak for the other ants, my friend."

"But I am no different from them! We are no different from you, either! We all want the same thing. To be free of the yoke of Crache, to live without the fear of conscription or domination as we watch the very land around us consumed and stripped to feed and keep in comfort only those this nation deems worthy. We do not want *more*, endlessly more than we have, as Crache demands from everything and everyone. We only want to live freely.

"You say the Rok act out of necessity," Taru reminds her bitterly. "I say you act out of *fear*. It took such courage to join this fight, to launch yourselves across the sea and risk the future of the island and the people you've fought so hard to keep and protect in the past. You have risked so much that you are determined to do anything to win this fight, but what you *fear* is everything that comes *after*."

Staz is quiet, but only for a moment.

"You call it fear," she says. "We call it preparation."

"Preparation for *what*? A future in which you have destroyed anyone who is not you? You see no end to your enemies! You look at those who have allied with you and fought with you and died beside you and you see betrayal that *has not even happened yet*. You feel like you have to destroy everything and everyone, not only those who threaten you, but all that which could possibly threaten you in the future. That is not the Rok way. That is the way of the ants. You say the Sicclunans will become that which they have fought for so long. I say you have already become that which you've fought against."

There is angry murmuring and scattered cursing all around them, as there is no bigger offense the retainer can offer the Rok.

Taru cannot decide whether Staz, for her part, is angry or disturbed by the idea the Rok Islanders are the ones letting themselves be molded by the enemy they are battling.

"These are words," Staz says. "And even if there is wisdom in them, even if there is truth, they are still only words. They cannot shape the future."

"We can and *we* will," Taru vows. "Together. One way or the other. Either we shape it by destroying one another or by living together. We wish to live *with* you, Staz, and the Rok. You are a good and honorable people. You have simply been pushed too far too long to the brink, and you are tired. You want that threat to end. We all do. But when you see threat in everything, there is no end. We are not a threat to you."

They look to Sirach, the retainer's eyes asking for their help.

Sirach responds by casting the commandeered trident in their hands to the deck.

"My people have only ever wanted to live," Sirach speaks earnestly to Staz. "We just want a few patches of land no one will take from us where we can live again, build something again. Become ourselves again, whoever that is and whatever that looks like. It's been so long, even we don't know anymore. But we don't want more than that. We don't want what you have. We would *never* take a people's home, the place that bore them. That is what was done to us. To me."

"You do not need to destroy everything and everyone in Crache to be safe, Staz," Taru says. "You need to help us turn Crache into something better. Please."

"What is it you are asking of us, exactly?"

"Do not sail for the Capitol. Do not sack the city. Do not plunge what is left into chaos. Let us, together, the Rok and the rebellion, as we began this, *negotiate* with those in power, now that they cannot use the Skrain to insulate them anymore. Let us see if we can find a path that ends the war."

Staz frowns, clearly finding the idea of "negotiation" distasteful.

Taru is not surprised. Diplomacy is also not the Rok way.

"And if the ants do not wish to be reasoned with, even now?" she asks the retainer.

"Then we continue the fight," Taru agrees readily. "But we do it together. And you give me your word that you will not break our alliance the moment you feel the situation has changed."

"You would trust my word?"

"You have never lied to me. It was always I who made the assumption. I assumed when you agreed to fight Crache, to fight with us, that meant our alliance was guaranteed until the end, regardless of what came. I understand now that is not the Rok way. But I know if you agree to see this through with us to the end, you will do so."

Staz smiles. She reaches out and pats Taru's taut cheek with her tiny, wrinkled hand.

"You finally understand the whole of being Rok," she commends Taru.

The retainer waits, knowing that is not an answer to their question.

Staz draws in a deep breath, exhaling thoughtfully as she regards the pair of rebels.

"We are *not* the ants," she declares to her crew. "Are we?"

The Islanders of the *Black Turtle* decry the idea violently and loudly.

"You have my word," Staz promises Taru. "I will get the other captains to agree. We will see this thing through together, your way, and then ours if necessary. In either case, we will . . . have faith in you to do right by the children of Rok. You have earned that much, I think."

Taru feels like slumping forward onto the deck, so powerful is the feeling of relief and how much tension has been lifted from their being.

Instead, they stand slowly to their feet, offering the Rok elder their hand.

Staz takes it, cupping the retainer's gauntleted fist in both of her small palms.

Taru looks back at Sirach, who is watching them with arms folded across her chest and a half grin on her face.

"I'm still going to murder you," she assures the retainer.

Taru has no laughter in them at the moment, but they appreciate what is unspoken between them and the Sicclunan.

"Well then," Staz proclaims. "That's settled. We should eat."

"Yes, I know, I look thin," Taru says with mock exasperation.

"No," Staz muses, appraising the retainer from head to toe. "No, I think we're finally fattening you up properly, my friend. Yes. You have come far."

Despite every ugly thing that has passed between them and the Rok, this piece of praise means something to Taru.

They have all come far, the retainer realizes.

Taru only hopes they will all finally arrive at their destination.

HOMECOMING

EVIE HAD NEVER REALLY BEFORE CONSIDERED WHAT HER last act as the leader of the rebellion would be. When she has imagined any kind of ending, it usually involved a picture in her head of her own broken and bloody body littering some battlefield. Even when the Skrain locked her inside a giant birdcage and marched her as a spoil of war through the streets of the Capitol, it did not occur to Evie this was the end of her time as the Sparrow General. When you are a rebel, it becomes necessary to live perpetually in the moment, she has found. Existing on the cusp of defeat and annihilation at all times doesn't leave room for thoughts of the future.

She only began thinking about an ending to all this, or at least an end to the myth and legend of the Sparrow General, when they received word from Taru that there would be no assault on the Capitol from the Rok Islanders. Coupled with the fact there was no longer a Protectorate Ministry to orchestrate a campaign against what remained of the rebellion, effectively the war was over. Evie's services, at least as a military leader, would no longer be required.

As much as it lifted a weight from her shoulders, the news also provided its own burden. Fighting a war was one thing, but rebuilding after a war was an entirely different beast.

Evie consoled herself by remembering that at least she wouldn't have to do it on her own. Dyeawan, Nia, Lexi, Brio, Taru, Sirach—they were all there and alive and would take the next crucial, heavy steps with her.

There are some things about the dissolution of the rebellion she must face alone, however.

In the end, there is no question for Evie what her final official act as the Sparrow General should be. She began the war as a conscript, a Savage Legionnaire, branded in her flesh and forced to become living artillery, fodder for the Crachian war machine. She fought alongside so many others who'd endured the same, and was fostered and taught by many of them, like Mother Manai, who Evie still mourns every day.

She has chosen to end her military career by returning to its beginnings. Every Savage Legionnaire is told if they survive one hundred battles, they will be rewarded with their freedom. It is a fantasy and a fallacy invented to placate them, to imbue them with enough false hope to keep charging the enemy's front line and sacrificing their bodies and their lives for as long as luck and their own will preserves them. So many among the Legionnaire ranks have died chasing that ridiculous dream.

Evie has officially, and with Dyeawan's and Nia's blessings and assistance, disbanded the Savage Legion. More than that, however, Evie sees it as her duty to ensure every surviving conscript, regardless of whether they defected and fought for the rebellion or were forced to fight against the rebels, returns to whatever home they once knew safely and with hope for a future.

It is far from an easy task, but Evie won't consider herself rid of the mantle of Sparrow General until she has seen it through to the best of her ability.

Still, one case in particular is significant for her, and far more a pleasure than a chore.

She sits atop the buckboard of a tiny wagon being pulled by a single enthusiastic horse. Towering beside her is Bam, Evie's self-appointed protector throughout most of the rebellion. She doubts there has ever been a fiercer or more loyal warrior with a gentler heart than this colossus of a man with his giant flattened nose and long stringy curls ever hidden beneath the hood of a cloak.

"Don't wanna do this," the usually stoic giant grouses for perhaps the dozenth time on their journey.

Evie's voice is gentle and filled with care, but she remains firm. "You don't want to do it because you're afraid no one will be there, or because you're afraid they *will* still be there?"

"All of it," he confirms.

Evie reaches up and squeezes as much of his massive shoulder as her hand can manage.

"If they're not there, you need to know," she insists. "If they are, they're going to be so happy to see you."

Bam doesn't say anything else for a while, but she can tell it's only because he is trying to articulate his thoughts.

"What if they aren't happy to see me?" he finally asks.

Evie sighs heavily. "Then they're fools, and you'll always have a home with me."

That seems to lighten his spirts, if only by small measures.

The Second City sits below a large mountainous range. Within those mountains, long have people like those in the Bottoms of the Capitol, the poor and the forgotten and the infirm, carved out an existence with little to no aid from the Crachian machine. With few resources in those mountains, Crache considers worth harvesting, Skrain soldiers and dagger-wielding Aegins are a rare sight. Mountain dwellers are left to their own devices, foraging from slim trails, uncovering hidden aquifers, and attempting to herd the wily and unpredictable goats that naturally populate the ranges.

Evie was surprised to learn Bam came from those mountains, largely because she was surprised to learn Bam came from anywhere. He seemed so elemental to her, as if he'd grown naturally among the ranks of the Savage Legion itself.

Their wagon, though small, thoroughly tests the limits of the winding goat trails that snake through the base of the mountain range. It takes them half a day once they reach the foothills to navigate their one-horse team to the place Bam recalls as his point of origin.

"Why did you leave?" Evie asks him, having put off the question until now for reasons she can't name.

"Too many mouths," he explains simply. "Mine was the biggest. Heard they had prizefighting in the city. Thought I could bring something back."

"What happened?"

Bam shrugs his mighty shoulders.

"First pack of Aegins I ran across, they all laughed at me."

Evie nods, entirely unsurprised.

"How many of them did you kill?"

Bam turns his head and blinks down at her from under his favorite hood.

"Right," Evie says wryly. "All of them."

Many of the dwellings deep in the mountain range are carved from the rock itself. The residents seem to take over natural caves and build a ramshackle veneer of walls and windows and doors over the mouths of such depressions.

After a time and Bam's tenuous direction, they come upon one such place with a voluminous goat hide the color of dried tree bark covering the entrance.

"Is this the one?"

Bam nods, but he seems unsure.

"I think so."

Evie climbs down from the buckboard first, looking back up at Bam to find him hesitating like a child who doesn't want to attend his first day of schooling.

"Come on," she bids him. "You're not alone. Whatever we find, we'll find it together."

With a sigh like distant thunder, Bam gathers the folds of his billowy cloak and lumbers down from the buckboard.

Evie pats him proudly on the back.

"You're doing great," she says. "And even if it's not what you remember—"

She falls silent as, several yards ahead of them, that lush goat hide is slowly drawn aside by small, withered hands.

Evie waits, watching as a wrinkled woman barely half Evie's height emerges from within the mountain dwelling. She's wrapped in the same treated pelt that serves as her front door.

"I killed those goats," Bam says quietly, surprising Evie. "There were two of 'em. I took them both down, one in each arm."

Witnessing him reconnect with the memory of this place and realizing they have indeed come to the right cave, causes an expansion inside Evie's chest that aches and comforts her at the same time.

The tiny, elderly woman is clearly stricken by the sight of Bam, as most people are when they see him. But her reaction is not awe or fear. There is clearly recognition. And a deep sorrow and something else beneath, perhaps a glimmer of hope?

"Son?" the impossibly small woman ventures, seeming as though she is afraid to believe her own eyes. "My son?"

Evie looks up at Bam, craning her neck to peer into the shadows of his hood. She finds his wide, sad eyes there.

They're filled with tears.

A fist-sized lump filling her throat, Evie practically has to shove Bam forward with both hands to get him moving towards the woman who somehow, despite her stature, is clearly his mother.

He clomps the few steps it takes him to close the gap, and when he reaches her, Bam immediately drops to both knees in front of the old woman.

He is still a head taller than her.

With her withered hands shaking, she reaches up and carefully peels back the hood covering his head and obscuring his face.

For the first time, she smiles.

"I came home, Mama," Evie hears Bam whisper to her.

His mother nods gratefully, and in the next moment she is practically buried in his chest as Bam engulfs her in an embrace.

Evie looks on, a hand cupping her mouth as tears begin streaming from her own eyes.

She thinks of all those she knew who will not be able to return home to their loved ones, and marvels at how she can be so deeply grateful and grieve so profoundly all at once.

Bam and his mother hold each other for a long time, and for Evie the scene still does not last nearly long enough.

LASTLY

THREE SIDES OF A FLIPPED COIN

DYEAWAN

"NO, NOT LIKE *THAT*!" NIA SHOUTS AT THE WORKERS TRANSporting the gargantuan stone sculpture across the cavernous room. "I told you, we're not arranging by classification right now, we're arranging by the *era* each piece is labeled as originating in!"

Dyeawan watches her sister do what Nia does best, order people around and stringently organize things.

They are in the relics vault Edger first brought Dyeawan to long ago, when she was no more than a messenger and errand girl at the Planning Cadre. This space warehouses countless items representing the myth, folklore, religion, history, and culture of the civilizations that were consumed to form Crache. Edger and those before him had spent centuries stripping all of that identity from the people of the cities, until it and any individual histories ceased to exist and one homogenous nation remained.

Edger believed there was nothing more dangerous than stories.

Dyeawan agrees with him.

Reintroducing the relics and the history and stories they represent is one of several new initiatives being undertaken by the Planning Cadre. The relics will gradually be "discovered" by mining and construction crews throughout Crache. Studies will be undertaken, with revelations and lost facts fed to scholars by the Cadre. Slowly, each city will be reawakened to its origins, its myth, its stolen gods, heroes, and founders.

The goal is that this will inevitably lead to each Crachian city re-forming its identity as an individual realm and reclaiming that status. This will, Dyeawan and the others hope, pave the way for the reintegration of the displaced Sicclunans and B'ors whose lands were taken from their ancestors by Crache.

If they can guide it correctly, the end result will be a country of cooperative of independently governed cities that coexist rather than submit to one banner, one bureaucracy, one endlessly consuming machine.

In the meantime, Dyeawan has also spearheaded another initiative to replant and revitalize Crache's forests and other natural resources that have been decimated. In order to do that, those lands will be entrusted to the care of Sicclunan refugees, who will also live and form their own communities there.

It is a stopgap measure, of course. It is not handing what was taken from them back to Sirach's people, but there is no way to do that without restarting the war.

Dyeawan discussed openly dismantling the Crachian government with the rebel leaders. After all they'd each endured under the banner of the ant, it was tempting simply to tear the whole thing down and tell the people every ugly truth that had been kept from them.

It wasn't a practical solution, of course. Even devising a way to disseminate all that "truth" to the people would be a logistically impossible nightmare. The Gens would all revolt, unwilling to relinquish their control of cities, lands, and resources. It would invariably lead to a civil war.

No, they decided. Bureaucracy created the Gens, and bureaucracy would be used to gradually phase them out. It would seem the effect of smaller policy changes, not of political or social uprising.

They would dismantle Crache the same way it was built: step-by-step.

Even the Rok agreed to this in the end, although Dyeawan suspected that was largely so they could return home as quickly as possible after learning most of the mechanisms behind the repeated historical invasion of Rok had been wiped out, and the one the rebel leaders were willing to vouch for remained, namely Dyeawan.

It was also surprisingly easy to convince Trowel and the old guard of the planners to once again embrace Dyeawan and accept her ideas about moving forward in the wake of what had ended up becoming several successful rebellions throughout Crache. The old guard had always had the Ministry and its agents to protect them and carry out their dirty work, either through their own means or by using the Skrain. With both the military and the Ministry in shambles, Trowel and the rest found themselves completely unprotected, with no enforcers to enact their will.

Conversely, Dyeawan had a rebel army waiting in the wings. It made Trowel vastly more susceptible to reason.

Dyeawan runs her fingers over the smooth wood of her tender's right paddle, still grateful to be seated upon her trusted conveyance once again. From the litter in front of her folded legs, she picks up the last invention Riko completed, the little mechanical toy horse that gallops with the same gait and grace as the real thing.

Sliding forward to lay flat atop the litter, Dyeawan lowers the toy over the front edge, placing it on the floor of the relics room and winding up its gears.

All work ceases, and heads turn as the metal stead begins clattering loudly across the floor.

Even Nia is speechless.

Dyeawan watches the remarkable creation gallop for several yards, then stop when the gears run out of momentum.

The toy teeters precariously as its legs stop moving, and it finally collapses onto one side with a loud, hollow bang.

Nia looks from the mechanical horse to her sister, her expression deeply puzzled.

Dyeawan merely waves at her amiably in response.

Nia sighs heavily, shaking her head, as Dyeawan has to visibly hold back her laughter.

Dyeawan thinks she detects a grin tugging at the corner of Nia's mouth, however.

"Back to work, everyone!" Nia instructs the others.

Dyeawan stares at the fallen toy on the floor for a long time after.

"That's okay, Riko," she whispers to herself with a small smile. "We can fix it."

LEXI

"WE ARE AN ATTRACTIVE PAIR, AREN'T WE?" BRIO ASKS HER as he and Lexi sit atop a row of fishmonger crates, staring at their reflection in a dirty storefront window.

Lexi laughs, studying the illusory image of them, she with her shocking-white hair, swathed in her humble robes, and he less half a leg since she last saw him, several scars marring the once unblemished flesh of his face. They are both much thinner and gaunter than they once were, neither having enjoyed access to the well-stocked larders of the Gen Circus for a long time.

"We are far from the portrait of our wedding day," she admits.

"I actually quite like your hair like that," Brio says.

"Thank you. I do too."

His voice turns earnest, even trembling a bit with emotion. "You are every bit as beautiful as the last time I laid eyes on you."

Lexi closes her eyes to stem the tears she knows are coming, hanging her head.

"I'm sorry," he says quickly, encircling an arm around her shoulders and holding her close.

Lexi presses her head into his slight chest and lets the tears flow for a while.

As she does, she begins to feel a few stray drops of moisture on her cheek and temple, and Lexi realizes he is crying with her.

When they're done weeping, she remains there, quietly listening to his heart and just enjoying the *feeling* of his presence, of him simply being there.

Lexi very gently runs her hand over the rounded stump of his leg.

"Does it still hurt?"

Brio shakes his head. "It itched terribly for a long time. Now I just get phantom pangs, as if the rest of my leg is still there."

She smiles, reaching up and tracing her fingertips over the long-healed scars on his face.

"My battle-forged warrior," she whispers.

They both laugh at that.

"I know," he says. "Who would have ever thought?"

She presses her lips to his, and what begins as a gentle kiss becomes deeper, prolonged and more desperate, for both of them. They lose themselves in each other for the first time in what feels to Lexi like ages, as if their marriage happened in another lifetime.

Their foreheads are still pressed together when their lips finally part.

"I worried you'd let me go," Brio whispers. "Not that I would have blamed you."

Lexi smiles. "You're a stupid man. I toppled an empire to get you back."

Brio slowly leans away from Lexi, looking at her with pride and love in his eyes.

"You did, didn't you?"

"Well," she confesses, "I had a little help."

"May I ask, why did you want to meet *here*? After all this time, and all that's happened, I thought we'd reunite in our home."

A little bit of the joy of the occasion leaves Lexi then.

"Brio, I . . . I can't go back to the Gen Circus. *This* is my home now. With these people. Dyeawan is going to assure that we finally get the resources the Bottoms needs, not only to feed and clothe everyone, but to build, to grow it into a community as vital as the rest of the Capitol for the people here. I want to be part of that. I need to be. They look to me now—they rely on me."

"Yes," Brio says, looking to Kray, who stands sentinel-like a respectable distance from them.

The boy refuses to let Lexi out of his sight. He seems neither jealous nor resentful of Brio, but neither does he trust him alone with his Ragged Matron, at least not yet.

"Think of him like a much smaller Taru," Lexi suggests.

"He's clearly devoted to you in a way that I . . . you really *have* become precious to the people here."

"I hope you can understand. It has nothing to do with you, or how I feel about you. But the idea of returning to Gen life . . ."

Brio nods, a pensive expression on his face.

"I'm not much of a builder, but maybe we can take over one of the places that is already built down here."

Lexi stares up at him in surprise.

"You're talking about living here in the Bottoms?"

"It's where you are, isn't it?"

"I thought . . . you would be more upset about the towers—"

"They're brick and wood," he reminds her. "The Gen Circus is a place. It doesn't matter. My home is wherever you are. *That's* what I've come back to, if you'll have me."

Lexi grasps his cheeks and kisses him with renewed fire.

"You're still their pleader," she says. "You still lead Gen Stalbraid. We need you."

"And you?" he asks, grinning.

"I can think of a few things I have *definitely* been needing from you," Lexi says, nodding most assuredly.

She clearly catches Brio off guard, because his sudden burst of laughter actually causes him to choke a bit, and he begins coughing.

"Save your strength," she advises, patting him gently on the back.

"Okay," he relents, as if it will be a mighty chore. "Your new friend will have to wait outside, however."

"Afraid to perform in front of an audience?"

"Well, I am somewhat rusty," he says with mock gravity.

They nettle at each other and flirt for a long time, their hands finding one and another atop the fishmonger crates, their fingers lacing as they continue to take in their reflections, finding peace in these new versions of themselves coming together.

EVIE

SIRACH'S NAKED BODY IS WRAPPED AROUND HERS LIKE A blanket, as it has been for most of the night. The sweaty, wonderfully torturous part of that has been over for some time now, and they merely sit upon the grass together and stare up at the pale light of the moon.

Evie is enjoying staring at it anyway.

Sirach's gaze keeps darting around to take in what's left of the great forest, cast in the moon's glow.

"This place really is a shithole," she says for perhaps the twentieth time since they arrived at the first of many reclamation sites created to funnel Sicclunans back into Crache and give them their own fertile land to resettle.

Sirach was chosen to lead the largest of those settlements, in the oldest Crachian forest, just outside the Capitol. This will also allow Evie easy access to the city when she is needed for matters of state.

"It will be what we make it," Evie reminds her again. "And I'm not going to listen to you whine the entire time we're here, either."

She punctuates the statement by poking Sirach repeatedly in the ribs with her forefingers.

"How *dare* you!" Sirach protests, squirming wildly.

She snatches Evie's wrists in her hands to restrain them, and in the next moment they are rolling around in the patchy grass again, laughing. When they settle, Sirach is atop her.

"If you didn't want to hear it, you could have gone with Taru," she reminds Evie, kissing her way down Evie's abdomen. "You could be breaking more Skrain skulls."

"It sounds like *you* wish you could have gone with them," Evie observes, lightly gripping both sides of Sirach's head. "Besides, I'm retired."

There was much debate about what to do with the Crachian military. The old Skrain have been scattered, but hardly eradicated. Besides which, Dyeawan's incremental restructuring of the nation would require the sense of security a strong military instills in its citizens.

It was decided that the rebel leadership would take the reins. Not openly, but like everything else they were attempting to do, under the veneer of Crachian authority. Evie was the natural choice, everyone felt, but she refused. Her official reason was that she might be recognized as the Sparrow General, especially after her starring role in that parade through the streets of the Capitol.

Unofficially, she just didn't want to.

In the end, they all chose Taru, who was at first even more reluctant than Evie. The now former retainer did not want to abandon Brio and Lexi, both of whom gave their blessing and assured Taru they were well taken care of in the Bottoms by Lexi's devoted followers.

Taru further protested by reminding them all that many soldiers would not accept an Undeclared as their commander.

Dyeawan told them that was good. It would help immediately weed out anyone who wouldn't serve the new military as needed.

Taru was given a commission as General Supreme, and the gleaming armor and helmet to go with it. They became the first Undeclared to join the ranks of the Skrain, let alone lead the army.

To provide them with the support they'd need, an entire regiment of former rebel fighters was formed, among them Bam, whom Evie had gently and lovingly asked to act as Taru's second-in-command.

She likes to picture them both out there right now, looking resplendent and absolutely ridiculous (at least to their friends, who knew them as tattered rebel grunts) in their shining Skrain armor. Evie imagines Taru, Bam, and their regiment will be quite busy for a long time rounding up what's left of the original Skrain and rooting out those who can be folded into the new army from the ones who can't be trusted.

She trusts she will see them again, though, in time.

"You really think we can manage this?" Evie asks Sirach. "Two fighters trying to live as farmers. Especially you. I worry about you being able to vent your frustrations with no enemies around to kill."

"That's what I have you for," Sirach reminds her, kissing around the inner curve of her right thigh.

Evie laces her fingers through Sirach's hair and gently tilts her face up so she can look into her eyes.

"Seriously," she says.

Sirach sighs wearily, resting her chin against Evie's stomach.

"Seriously? There will *always* be enemies to fight, no matter where we settle or how many trees we plant. In the meantime, I am looking forward to an extended holiday from war. I think we've both earned it. I *know* I have. Is that fair enough, Sparrow General?"

"Fair enough," Evie relents, feeling a bit better on the subject. "Just stop calling me that."

"Yes, General," Sirach mocks her, burying her face between Evie's legs.

Evie giggles madly, and soon that giggling rolls into moaning. Not long after that, the moans become ecstatic screams.

There is no one around to hear them except the trees.

ACKNOWLEDGMENTS

I'd like to thank all of the readers who made the effort to discover this series, and who have taken the ride with me to the very end. I'd especially like to thank those readers who took the time to reach out to me in whatever form that took to let me know they cared about this story and these characters and were excited and even desperate to know what happens next. You kept me writing during some of my darkest periods, when I very much wanted to give up on these books. This entire trilogy is for you.

And thank you to Alexandre Su, Kathryn Kenney-Peterson, Chloe Gray, Caroline Pallotta, Emily Arzeno, Lisa Litwack, and Jéla Lewter for shepherding this manuscript through its many stages of production and design at Saga Press. And of course, to Chris McGrath for yet another wonderful cover. You've really captured the heart of the Savage Rebellion.